Potions *and* Pastries

A Magical Bakery Mystery

Bailey Cates

BERKLEY PRIME CRIME
New York

BERKLEY PRIME CRIME
Published by Berkley
An imprint of Penguin Random House LLC
375 Hudson Street, New York, New York 10014

ISBN: 9780399586996

First Edition: November 2017

Printed in the United States of America
1 3 5 7 9 10 8 6 4 2

Cover art by Monica Roe
Cover design by Katie Anderson

PRAISE FOR THE *NEW YORK TIMES* BESTSELLING MAGICAL BAKERY MYSTERIES

"Katie is a charming amateur sleuth. . . . With an intriguing plot and an amusing cast of characters, *Brownies and Broomsticks* is an attention-grabbing read that I couldn't put down."

—*New York Times* bestselling author Jenn McKinlay

"Cates is a smooth, accomplished writer who combines a compelling plot with a cast of interesting characters."

—*Kirkus Reviews*

"[The] sixth of the Magical Bakery Mystery series remains as entertaining as the first, with a mythology that is as developed as Katie's newfound talent and life within the Savannah magical community."

—Kings River Life Magazine

"If you enjoy . . . Ellery Adams's Charmed Pie Shoppe Mystery series, and Heather Blake's Wishcraft Mystery series, you are destined to enjoy the Magical Bakery Mystery series."

—MyShelf.com

"With a top-notch whodunit, a dark magic investigator working undercover, and a simmering romance in the early stages, fans will relish this tale."

—Gumshoe

"As a fan of magic and witches in my cozies, Cates's series remains a favorite."

—Fresh Fiction

"Ms. Cates has most assuredly found the right ingredients . . . a series that is a finely sifted blend of drama, suspense, romance, and otherworldly elements."

—Once Upon a Romance

ALSO AVAILABLE BY BAILEY CATES

THE MAGICAL BAKERY MYSTERIES

Brownies and Broomsticks
Bewitched, Bothered, and Biscotti
Charms and Chocolate Chips
Some Enchanted Éclair
Magic and Macaroons
Spells and Scones

Acknowledgments

Many thanks to my agent, Kim Lionetti, and to the terrific team at Berkley Prime Crime: Miranda Hill, Jessica Wade, Roxanne Jones, Michele Alpern, and all the others who helped this book come into being. Also, a shout-out to my critique partners: Laura Pritchett, Laura Resau, Mark Figlozzi, and Bob Trott. Patrick Jasper Lee's fascinating book *We Borrow the Earth* provided the initial impetus for the idea of introducing Irish travelers as part of the story line, and I blatantly borrowed (with permission) Laura Resau's whimsical take on a writing prompt to provide a twist to the mystery plot. And, as always, Kevin Brookfield provided encouragement, support, and the occasional kick in the pants.

Chapter 1

The bleat of a boat horn drifted from the river to mingle with the sounds of the Savannah waterfront. Tourists and locals strolled along the brick and tabby sidewalks. A pack of kids ran by, their laughter sparkling through the air. The intense aromas of she-crab soup, garlic, and onions drifted from Huey's Southern Café. Moments later, the sugary fragrance of custom-made candies outside River Street Sweets filled my nose. If I hadn't just finished off our celebratory meal at Vic's with an indulgent serving of sweet potato crème brûlée, I might have dragged my companions inside for a piece of salted fudge.

"I can't believe it's already been two years," Aunt Lucy said. She and Uncle Ben were walking ahead of Declan and me, their arms twined around each other's waists.

Ben smiled and drew her closer. "The time certainly has flown by."

She laid her head against his shoulder, and a long tendril of gray-blond hair escaped from its messy bun to curl against the back of her neck. Hand in hand, Declan and I followed at a leisurely pace.

We passed a man strumming a guitar and crooning "Mr. Tambourine Man," occasionally blowing into the harmonica suspended by a metal bracket in front of his face. A bearded gentleman dropped a few dollars into the guitar case at his feet, and they exchanged nods. A toddler in shorts and a chocolate-stained T-shirt ran by at an impressive speed, his harassed-looking mother barreling after him, half bent over with her arms spread wide to sweep him up. Streaks of color pinked the western sky as the sun dipped toward the horizon.

A dragonfly flitted in front of us. Declan squeezed my fingers as the iridescent beauty dodged the watchful gaze of a gull on a nearby light post and zoomed toward the Savannah River. Our steps slowed as we both took note of its path.

"Is that one of yours?" he murmured.

I shrugged. "There's just the one. Probably on the hunt for supper."

"Seems a bit late in the day," he answered with mild skepticism.

"Mm. More mosquitoes out now, though."

Aunt Lucy noticed the mosquito hawk as well and shot me a conspiratorial look over her shoulder. She and Declan both knew dragonflies were my witch's totem, a kind of metaphysical tap on the shoulder that told me to pay attention to whatever was going on.

But I was feeling happy and lazy, my skin caressed by the soft April air, my belly full of good food, and the evening blessed with the company of some of my favorite people in the world. At the moment, I wasn't interested in taps on the shoulder—metaphysical or otherwise—calling me to action. Still, I couldn't help a quick glance around, intuitively probing our surroundings. Nothing along Rousakis Plaza appeared amiss, and I dismissed the winged visitor as a coincidence.

The four of us were taking our time returning from a thoroughly decadent supper at Vic's on the River. We'd been celebrating the second anniversary of the grand opening of the Honeybee Bakery, as well as the success our enterprise had enjoyed during the past two years. There had been a few low points, of course. Heck, before we'd even managed to open the doors to the public, Uncle Ben had been the main suspect in the murder of crotchety old Mavis Templeton. Nevertheless, I would be forever grateful that he and my aunt had talked me into quitting my boring, poorly paid position as an assistant bakery manager in downtown Akron to move to Georgia. Ben had just retired as Savannah's fire chief, and their brainstorm of teaming up with me to start the Honeybee had saved my sanity. Plus, getting far away from the guy who had dumped me mere days before our wedding had seriously saved my pride.

Of course, I'd learned Lucy had another reason for luring me south. Out of the blue, she'd sprung the news that she and I were both hedgewitches. *Magic in the kitchen,* she'd said. *A natural green thumb.* Some call those of us with a gift for cooking and garden spells "green witches." Whatever moniker you choose, our kind has been helping and healing for centuries by tapping into the natural magic inherent in herbs, spices, and food.

It had taken a little convincing, though. Imagine having someone you love suddenly dump *that* bombshell on you one afternoon over a cup of tea. Lucy had assured me hedgewitchery was a family heritage my mother had long hidden from me. At first, I'd scoffed and rolled my eyes at my hemp-wearing hippie aunt's airy-fairy notion. I mean, who wouldn't? However, I'd eventually realized that it explained an awful lot about my childhood—and my adulthood, for that matter—and came to accept my magical gifts.

I brought my thoughts back to the present. Near the Anchor Monument, an elderly couple held hands and gazed out toward the water. Suddenly, the woman leaned in and whispered something into the man's ear, and he smiled. They had an aura about them that told me they'd been together for most of their lives, probably had children and grandchildren and maybe even great-grandchildren. Still, they could make each other smile, still wanted to hold hands.

I glanced up at Declan's face, savoring his ice-blue eyes beneath wavy dark hair. A half grin softened the solid planes of his cheekbones and jaw. However, his attention had been snagged by something down toward the River Street Market Place, and he missed the question in my eyes. Would we be like that older couple in fifty years? Would we have children and grandchildren, too? We'd been engaged for a little more than four months but hadn't set a date for the wedding yet. He'd made only a few mild comments, but I could sense he was getting impatient. From the beginning, Declan had been the one pushing our relationship to the next level.

I knew he wasn't at all like Andrew, my erstwhile fiancé of three years ago. He'd never leave me at the altar. Still, how could I know we'd make it together in the long run? How could anyone know? Then my gaze cut to Lucy and Ben, and I had my answer. His gentle brown eyes were full of affection as they met hers. They'd met later in life and been married thirteen years. I couldn't imagine the way they looked at each other ever changing, not if they lived to be a hundred. The chemistry between them was undeniable, the roots of their connection tangled deep and strong.

Declan and I had been through quite a bit in the year and a half we'd been together. It had been touch and go a couple of times—especially after an incident when I'd nearly killed him with magic. It had been an accident, but still . . . it could have broken us. Yet in the end it had helped to strengthen our bond.

The anxiety that had begun to rise within me quieted.

As we continued to walk, I disengaged my hand from Declan's and slid it around his waist. He grinned down at me absently, then looked at the juggler we were approaching. As we watched, he touched a flame to four torches and began tossing them into the air. The spectacle lent a dramatic touch to the festive atmosphere. Ben's and Declan's eyes lit up in appreciation, drawn to the flames as only those of a former fire chief and a current firefighter would be.

Ben either hadn't noticed the dragonfly or didn't care. Unlike Lucy and me, my uncle wasn't particularly interested in such small magical details. He knew we were witches, of course, and fully supported his wife, his niece, and the other members of our informal coven, the spellbook club. Declan had come around, too, especially after a séance in which he discovered he had his own, er . . . gift.

We passed the juggler. A group of children was gathered around a ventriloquist with a wooden dummy on his knee, their mouths open with delight as the dummy appeared to speak of its own accord. The man and his puppet sported the same dark-framed glasses and black hair, the puppet a mirror of its handler.

"What's brown and sticky?" the ventriloquist asked.

Murmurs from the kids, and a few parents exchanged looks of mild alarm.

"A stick!" cracked the dummy in a high voice.

Everyone laughed, and we kept walking.

A redheaded man on a unicycle pedaled among the buskers and spectators in complicated turns and spirals, stopping on a dime and then veering off again. Booths and tables boasted everything from crafts and food products to kitschy souvenirs and funky clothing.

About fifty feet away, a woman sat beneath an arching canopy of draperies. The high back of her chair was elaborately carved and rose a foot above her head, giving the impression of a throne. Her silver braid was coiled on the crown of her head. A small black fedora tied with a scarlet scarf perched on top of the braid. Her long red skirt pooled on the patterned carpet beneath her feet, and silver rings flashed from every finger. Thick eyeliner gave her the look of a wise cat, peering over her tiny half-glasses at the woman sitting across the table from her.

"Katie, look. That's Orla." Lucy turned to me. "She hasn't come into the bakery for ages."

"Maybe she's on a diet," I said. "And I rather suspect that at the moment she's not the Orla Black we know." I tipped my head to the side. I'd never seen our friend in her full fortune-telling regalia.

My aunt nodded. "This is certainly a different look for her. I wonder if she's almost finished with this client."

"Client or mark?" Ben murmured as he pushed his glasses up the bridge of his nose. Even though he witnessed us practicing our mild-mannered magic every day, his eyes were narrowed with skepticism, and his lips pressed together above his short beard.

"Hush, dear," Lucy said. "Orla's the real deal."

A lush velvet cloth the color of the night sky covered the round table in front of the fortune-teller. On it sat a deck of oversized tarot cards and a plain glass sphere on a black stand. Instinctively, I sent out a questioning tendril of intuition and felt an oh-so-subtle current of real power coming from the woman. That wasn't surprising, really, since magic is around us every day if we pause to look for it. However, the elaborate costume and stereotypical trappings seemed a little over-the-top.

Or are they stereotypical? I chided myself. Spellbook club member Jaida French was an expert in all things tarot, and Mimsey Carmichael's pink quartz shew stone had come in handy for our group more than once.

"We should get back to the bakery," Ben said with a pointed glance at his watch.

Reluctantly, I began to follow him toward the stairs that led up to Bay Street.

Suddenly the air was a-whir with the lacy wings of a hundred dragonflies. I heard Declan suck in his breath, and a pang of anticipation arrowed through my sternum as I stopped and turned back toward Orla.

"Katie," Ben said, "what are you . . ."

He trailed off when Lucy gently squeezed his shoulder. Her eyes followed the phalanx of dragonflies as they gathered above the fortune-teller's canopy, hovered in a tight knot, and then exploded in every direction like a benevolent bomb.

I quickly sidled back, drawing Declan with me. We watched as Orla shoved the crystal ball to the side, placed her hands palms up in the center of the table, and nodded for the woman who sat in the rickety metal chair across from her to grasp them with her own. After a moment's hesitation, she did. She flinched as their skin touched, and she drew back. Then she took a deep breath and reached for the fortune-teller's fingers again.

The client looked to be a decade or so older than me, so about forty. Her cream-colored suit and expensive shoes coupled with the blond chignon and haughty expression made her look like an unlikely personality to seek the advice of a sidewalk seer. Still, I knew better than to judge anyone by her looks when it came to magic or any of its ancillaries. No one in the spellbook club looked like a "witch," except perhaps Bianca Devereaux, with her long black hair and piercing green eyes.

We had drawn close enough that I could hear the lilt of Orla's murmuring voice, but not the words. However, the look on the other woman's face had gone from stony to frightened.

Suddenly, the blonde swept the deck of cards off the table and stood. "How dare you say that to me?" she growled. Her hand came up, and she shook her finger in Orla's face. "You are a disgrace. A sad, pathetic disgrace. A complete and utter fraud. And you ask for money for telling people this kind of nonsense? Unconscionable!" Her eyes blazed with anger, but even from where Declan and I stood thirty feet away, I could see the anguish behind her anger.

"Wow," Declan murmured into my ear. "I've never heard anyone actually use that word out loud before."

I nudged him to be quiet.

"Madam." Orla slowly rose to her feet with great dignity. "I'm sorry you didn't like what you heard. However, you did insist that I tell you the truth. It is my gift and my curse that I am able to do so."

"Truth! Ha! I bet what you're doing is illegal. In fact, I'm going to contact the authorities—" She stopped midsentence as a man strode across the brick walk toward her. It was the ventriloquist whom we'd seen earlier, sans dummy. His face, so cheerful when he'd been joking with the kids, was now mottled with fury.

Blanching, Orla's client backed away, then turned and fled. I was surprised at how fast she was able to make her way up the stairway to Bay Street in those heels.

"Hey!" the man yelled after her. "Stop! You haven't paid the fee!"

He appeared poised to run after her, but Orla stopped him with a hand on his arm. "Let it go, Taber."

"But—" He shrugged off her hand and turned toward her. "Mother, are you all right?"

Mother?

She snorted. "Of course. You worry too much."

He regarded her in silence for a few seconds. "Perhaps. Still, you can't allow your clients to get away without paying. I'm only trying to help."

Orla tore off her fedora, which unfastened the braid on top of her head. As it uncoiled, she absently flipped it over her shoulder. That simple act transformed her from being a mysterious reader of fortunes to plain old Orla Black, who loved the peach fritters at the Honeybee Bakery.

"Have you been spying on me?" she demanded.

"What are you talking about?" he countered with a sigh, and ran his fingers through his mop of black hair. Without the glasses, his eyes shone bright blue above a sturdy nose. His generous mouth was slightly turned down.

"I don't think it was a coincidence that you showed up right when you did." Her dark eyes flashed. "You should be in the middle of a show. Where is that doll of yours?"

"Taber! I thought I might find you here." A woman

glided toward us, the ventriloquist's dummy dangling lifelessly from one hand. She was tall, and her chestnut hair was streaked with copper. Without thinking, I ran my hand through my own short auburn locks. She wore her forest green shift with the kind of glamour seen on the streets of Paris. Her voice was silky as she held the dummy out to the man. "You left Cobby behind."

"I just wanted to check on your mother," he said. "Sometimes she runs into some shady characters."

Okay, not her son. Her son-in-law. Now that I saw the newcomer and Orla together, it was clear they were mother and daughter.

Taber took the dummy. As soon as he held it, the thing seemed to come alive. It shrugged and moved its neck as if to stretch out a crick. The mouth opened and shut a few times as if the puppet were limbering up. Then it all fell slack as Taber dropped his hand to his side, the doll dangling from his fingers.

"Yes, I'm sure you're here to protect me from miscreants and thieves." Orla's words were fairly dripping with sarcasm. "More like checking on the day's receipts."

Her son-in-law's jaw set, but his words were mild. "John asked me to keep an eye out."

Orla's eyes widened, and she turned toward her daughter. "Fern? Are you in on this as well?"

Fern shook her head at Taber. "I think Mother can take care of herself down here."

He opened his mouth as if to say something, then glanced over at the four of us watching. "We can continue this conversation at home. In *private*."

Well, good heavens. You're quarreling on a public

walkway, and you don't like that other people are listening?

"Hello there!" Lucy bustled toward the trio. Oh, how my aunt loathed conflict of any kind.

As one, Orla, her daughter, and her son-in-law turned to look. Then Orla's face transformed into a smile. "Lucy Eagel, as I live and breathe. And Katie. I didn't realize that was you standing there. Come meet my daughter." Her nostrils flared slightly. "And her husband."

We shook hands, and I introduced Declan. The tension faded somewhat as Lucy and Orla chatted about the weather. Fern smiled politely and walked to the fortune-telling tent. She began picking up the tarot cards her mother's disgruntled client had scattered on the ground.

"Hey, are you taking off?" a male voice interrupted. It was the fire juggler. He wore board shorts and had the tanned physique of a runner. His dark hair was in a man bun at the back of his head, and a tattoo of Chinese characters wound up one bicep. A tendril of smoke wafted from one of the torches he still carried.

Orla turned. "What? No, of course not. Fern, just put those on the table there. I'm planning to be here for at least two more hours this evening. The traffic is terrific tonight." As she spoke, she coiled the braid back on her head, pinned it in place, and perched the fedora on top.

Fern sighed. "Are you sure, Mother?"

Orla waved away her daughter's concern. "Of

course. Go on home and put Nuala to bed. I'll stop in when I get back."

Fern hesitated, then nodded. "All right. Come on, Taber. Mother doesn't need your help, and your audience has moved on. Finn is still around on his cycle. He'll help her pack up."

Her husband looked as if he was about to argue, but finally gave a little shrug and joined her.

"Nice to meet you all," Orla's daughter called as they walked toward the River Market.

The juggler's expression had hardened into anger. "You know this was my spot first, Orla."

"I know, dear." Her response was mild.

"And that guy was with the one who ran me off." He pointed at her son-in-law's retreating back.

"Ran you off? Oh, now—"

"He threatened me," the juggler insisted.

She looked surprised. Then her face fell. "I'm sorry. I didn't know."

The juggler snorted. "You didn't know? I just bet. This is the best spot on the riverfront."

"Plenty of people walk by where you work now," Lucy protested, to my surprise.

To Ben's, too, because he stepped in and put his arm protectively around her shoulders. Declan went to stand by them.

Ignoring the two men, the juggler took a step toward Orla. "Sure, they walk by to get to the market, but that far away, only half as many people stop to watch. I put on a show, lady, and I need the right stage." He pointed down to the ground. "This one. I have friends, you know. Tomorrow I want this spot back."

Orla's expression hardened. "I rather like it here, and I don't think I'll be moving anytime soon. Go find another place to throw your little balls."

I blinked. This was a side of Orla I'd never witnessed before. The evening was turning out to be quite interesting, but so far nothing seemed to require any magical intervention from me.

His face red with frustration and embarrassment, the juggler turned and stalked away.

"Whew!" Lucy exclaimed. "I had no idea there was so much drama down here in the evenings. We'll have to come to the riverfront more often, Ben." She smiled, but it didn't quite reach her eyes. The tension was spoiling our mellow celebration.

Orla shook her head. "Sorry about all that. Listen, I'd better get back to work. I'll come into the Honeybee soon, and we can catch up then. Okay, girls? Besides, I haven't had a peach fritter for ages." She grinned.

"Of course," my aunt said. "We need to get going anyway. Honeybee and Mungo are waiting." My companions began to walk away.

At the mention of Honeybee—Lucy's cat, who had inspired the name of our bakery—and my own canine familiar, I felt a pang of guilt. Still, I didn't move.

Why the dragonflies?

"See you later, Orla," I said, prolonging my contact with her a few more seconds.

She smiled and held out her hands to me. "Sooner than later, my dear."

I took her hands and squeezed them in farewell.

She gasped. Her eyes fluttered closed. When she opened them, her pupils had eclipsed the coffee-colored irises, almost seeming to throb. Fascinated and a little frightened, I couldn't look away.

Chapter 2

"You have such power." Orla's lips barely moved, and I leaned closer to hear. "I had no idea." Her hands were shaking in mine.

I opened my mouth to speak, but she continued. "So much violence! You've seen so much. More than your share."

Well, anyone who read the *Savannah Morning News* would know I had a tendency to get caught up in homicide cases on an alarmingly frequent basis. Still, I couldn't tear my gaze away from hers.

"No wonder, as it is your calling to help others in the magical community," she breathed.

Okay, *that* wasn't common knowledge. And honestly, I still took issue with the idea that I was somehow obligated to answer this "calling" of mine. Could Lucy have told her?

Orla's voice was dreamy, and she swayed on her feet. "You are particularly gifted at it."

"Er . . ." I finally managed.

Her eyes widened, and the grip on my hands grew so tight it was painful.

"Sacrifice."

"What?"

"There is sacrifice to come. You will have a decision to make."

Uh-oh.

"Katie?" Lucy said. I could hear the alarm in her voice. "Is everything all right?" She started back toward me.

Orla blinked rapidly, and she dropped my hands. "Oh, dear. I'm so sorry!"

"What? Why?" I cried, thoroughly alarmed now as well.

"I can't think what came over me. I never do that! It's a personal rule of mine, to not force what I see upon other people. It's the kind of thing I abhor in those who have my talent, and I'm very ashamed."

"Well, it's not—"

"Please forgive me, Katie?"

"Well, of course, I forgive you. There's nothing to . . . What did you mean by—"

Orla shook her head so hard, her fedora slipped. "I shouldn't have imposed like that. You may decide you want to know more. If you do, let me know, and I'll be happy to officially read for you. But now I have a client waiting."

I looked over and saw that a man was indeed standing by her booth.

"Katie? Mungo and Honeybee will be wanting their suppers," Lucy called.

I gave Orla a quick nod. "I'll let you know."

She sketched a wave as she turned away to tend to her paying client.

What just happened?

"Are you okay?" Declan asked when I hurried over to join them. "What did she say to you?"

I tried to wave it away with a flip of my wrist. "It's nothing. Though, I must say, if that's a sales technique to convince people to pay for more, it's one of the more creative loss leaders I've seen. I'm afraid it makes her look like just another sidewalk charlatan." Yet a part of me suspected I might have been overreacting because Orla's words had disturbed me.

Lucy confirmed it. She and Ben were walking in front of us again, and she whirled to face me. "Katie! I'm surprised at you. If anyone can sense that Orla has real ability when it comes to divination, it's you." As she resumed walking, I heard her mutter, "Better than any of us in the spellbook club—that's for sure."

"Aye, that's a woman who knows her stuff," Declan said in a low voice, the slightest Irish lilt riding beneath the words.

I stopped dead in my tracks, staring at him. When we'd first been getting to know each other, Declan had told me of his heritage and tried to put on a real Irish accent. He'd failed miserably. He was a Savannah boy, through and through, and I loved how the round sounds of the South threaded through his speech.

Declan didn't sound Irish, but someone else we both knew did. Remember that "gift" I mentioned he'd acquired during a séance?

"Connell," I hissed, "you promised to leave him alone."

Several feet ahead of us on the sidewalk, Ben and Lucy paused to look back at us quizzically.

Declan gave an almost imperceptible shake of his head along with a look that said we'd talk about it later.

Great. Just what I need.

I'd thought my boyfriend had tamed the spirit of his not-quite-dead and possibly leprechaun ancestor to the point where I didn't have to worry about its otherworldly interference anymore. Apparently, I was wrong.

And worse, Connell had just confirmed that I should take Orla's fortune seriously. The problem was, I wasn't even sure what she had started to tell me.

Sacrifice.

We'd replaced the blinds in the Honeybee with cozy café curtains the same blue as the bistro chairs in the customer seating area. They were closed against the lowering night as we approached, giving the bakery a snug, put-to-bed appearance. Through the glass of the door, the faint gleam of the shiny stainless appliances and work surfaces in the open kitchen promised passersby tasty treats warm from the oven come morning. A cheery light beckoned from the floor lamp in the reading area as well. Lucy's feline familiar would no doubt be snoozing on her window perch there.

Ben took out his keys and unlocked the door. We followed him inside. It felt strange to be coming in during the evening rather than in the dark of morning, and I resisted the urge to flip on all the lights and ready the ovens for the first batch of sourdough bread. The high ceiling was in shadow, as were the welcoming amber and burnt orange walls. The chalkboard menu behind the old-fashioned register listed our current offerings of pastries and pies, cakes and cookies, muffins, scones, and more. With the Easter holiday approaching, Lucy had added drawings of bunnies and chicks and flowers around the edges. The miniature sandwich board on top of the dark display case was literally a blank slate awaiting the next day's special to be declared in chalk. The tulips sitting next to it in a vase had shuttered their blooms tightly for the night.

Yip!

I smiled. "Hey, little guy. Miss me?"

My Cairn terrier tumbled out of his bed on a bottom bookshelf and ran over to me. I scooped him up, and he licked my chin in greeting. I laughed and set him back down.

"There's my girl," Lucy said. Honeybee jumped down from her window perch to stroll languidly over. Her orange stripes glowed brightly in the yellow lamplight.

I started to reach down to give her a scritch under the chin but decided not to risk it. My allergies had been helped a little by a naturopath and even more by one of Bianca's moon potions, but not enough that I could actually snuggle with those of the feline persuasion. However, as if she understood that now it would no longer send me into paroxysms of sneezing, she'd taken to coming to work with Lucy, like Mungo did with me.

After retrieving the jackets we'd worn on our way to work at five a.m., Lucy and I joined the guys out on the sidewalk, our animals in our arms. Ben locked up again, and I one-arm-hugged my aunt and uncle good night.

"Thanks for dinner, Ben," Declan said, and shook his hand.

"Of course, son." My uncle really did look upon Declan as a son after taking him under his wing as a firefighter years before. I'd never seen him happier than when I'd accepted Declan's proposal.

Ben and Lucy headed down Broughton Street toward Lucy's car, while Declan and I headed to our respective vehicles in the opposite direction.

He kissed me before I climbed into my Volkswagen Bug. "I need to swing by my place for some clothes, but I won't be long."

I kissed him back. "Okay. See you in a few."

Seconds later the Bug was pulling out on the street, Declan's ginormous pickup truck right behind me. He was practically living with me since we'd become engaged—well, before that, really—but our disparate schedules meant we hardly ever rode in the same vehicle.

I wended my way down Abercorn Street, around a few of the famous Savannah squares created by the city's founder, James Oglethorpe, and out of the historic district toward Midtown. Soon I arrived at the little carriage house I'd bought when I'd decided to move south. The down payment had taken all the money I'd saved in Akron, but it had been so perfect, I couldn't see spending money on rent instead. It had been one of the best decisions I'd ever made.

I parked in the driveway and got out. Mungo leaped out of the backseat and headed for the lawn. Immediately, a few fireflies lit up near where he paused to take care of business. They were his totems like dragonflies were mine.

Leaning against the wheel well of the car, I considered. Why had the dragonflies appeared earlier that evening? It had to have something to do with Orla.

Orla Black, fortune-teller. Who'd told me a fortune. Or at least part of one.

Sacrifice.

But what? I wondered if there was anyone who had ever been told they would be called upon to sacrifice something who thought, *Oh, great. I can hardly wait for that. Yay!*

I thought not.

As possibilities ran through my mind, I realized I was staring at my house. It had originally been the carriage house of a large estate, but that was long gone now. A middle-class neighborhood had taken the place of the mansion and grounds, with the carriage house being the only remnant. Though quite small, it sat on a standard-sized lot, so I'd had the pleasure of filling the backyard with gardens and a gazebo. In front, brilliant apricot-colored azaleas bloomed along the wrought-iron porch railing, and the dark magnolia by the corner of the house waved its broad shiny leaves in the moonlight. Declan had left the porch light on that morning, so the little abode seemed to be even more welcoming than usual.

A sudden, heavy sense of loss descended upon me.

This is what she meant. I'm going to have to give up this house to marry Declan.

And I didn't want to. I wanted to marry the man I loved *and* keep this place. But there just wasn't enough room. My brain knew that, even if my heart didn't. We'd already started looking for a new home.

"Yoo-hoo! Katie!"

I turned to see my next-door neighbor hurrying across her front lawn. "Hey, Margie. Haven't seen you for a few days."

She stopped in front of me and stuck out her lower lip to blow a stray lock of fair hair off her forehead. "Lordy, girl. It seems like you're only home in the middle of the night anymore. You get a second job?"

I tried a laugh. "No, nothing like that. Tonight we had dinner with Ben and Lucy, but most evenings lately we've gone to look at houses after work. You know, Cookie Rios is working in residential real estate now." With horror, I realized I was close to tears. Orla's talk of sacrifice had brought home the reality of having to move more than all our house shopping had.

"It's nice that you have a friend in the business," Margie said. "But I hate that you're leaving. Say! There's a house over on the next block that's for sale! Seriously, you guys should take a look. We don't want to lose you," she practically moaned.

Swallowing hard, I pasted on a smile. "How're the kids?"

She rolled her eyes. "My God, Katie. They talk talk talk all the time. Even Baby Bart."

"Baby Bart" was nearly three now and well into

toddlerhood. He'd be Baby Bart to his mother until the day she died, though.

"And the JJs. Heavens. Thank God for first grade. If they didn't go to school every day, I'd lose my mind." Jonathan and Julia, aka the JJs, were the Coopersmiths' six-year-old twins. "Chatterboxes, morning to night—heck, even in the middle of the night sometimes. I swear they talk in their sleep, too. I don't know where they get it from." But her eyes were twinkling. She knew exactly where they got it from, and it wasn't from her husband. "Saw your car pull in and just wanted to say hey. I better get back, though. Redding's orchestrating bath time, and he could use an extra set of hands. Bye!" She took off for her house at a jog as Declan's truck turned the corner.

I waited while he parked at the curb and pulled a grocery bag of clothes from the passenger seat. Then we called to Mungo, and he led us inside. Flipping the switch by the front door turned on the floor lamp with the tasseled shade across the room. In its muted light, I paused to survey the postage-stamp living space.

When I'd moved from Akron, I gave away or sold almost everything I owned. I brought only my clothes, a few treasured possessions like books and family mementos, and my favorite cooking gear and cookbooks. Everything else in my abode had been acquired after the move, and almost all of it was used. The purple upholstery on the fainting couch opposite the front door popped brightly against the peach walls. A Civil War–era trunk served as a coffee table, and two small wingback chairs completed the seating area—and filled the rest of the room. The built-in bookshelves had been gradually filled in the last two years, their dark wood reflected in the worn planks of the floor below and the shutters on the front windows. A short hall to the right led to the bedroom and the bathroom. Near the couch, French doors led out to the patio and backyard. Mungo sat in the doorway to the kitchen on the left, staring at me with an urgent demand for food in his eyes.

Declan went into the bedroom to stash his clothes next to one of the armoires I used as a closet. His bag of dirty laundry that was already in that space would have to go under the bed until he hauled it to the firehouse to wash. He was free to use my washer, of course, but it was a compact, and he said he preferred to use the one at Five House in order to get everything done at once. It was one of many compromises we'd worked out in the carriage house.

Since my familiar was obviously on the brink of starving to death, I went into the kitchen, dropped my tote on one of the two vinyl café chairs, and opened the refrigerator. Minutes later, the terrier was delicately digging into a selection of leftover chicken salad, saffron rice, and honey-glazed carrots. An elite meal for a dog, indeed. But since the moment the little black dog had shown up on my doorstep and adopted me as his witch—it turned out that's how it works; familiars find their witches rather than the other way around—he'd refused to eat a single bite of dog kibble.

Honestly, I couldn't blame him.

My kitchen duties complete, I poured us some red wine and joined Declan out on the patio.

I handed him a glass and sank into a chair.

"So, you want to tell me what the famous—or is it infamous?—Orla Black said to you?" he asked.

"Not much," I said, not yet ready to discuss how painful the thought of moving was. Besides, I couldn't know for sure if that was what Orla had meant by sacrifice.

Tomorrow I'll track her down and find out more. There. Decision made. I instantly felt better.

"It looked like more than that," Declan persisted. "And I saw the dragonflies. That meant something, didn't it?"

I half smiled and nodded. "Usually. I don't know what, though. She said something about my gifts and helping people in the magical community. You know, stuff she might already know from Lucy or even Mimsey." I was pretty sure the de facto leader of the spellbook club, Mimsey Carmichael, knew Orla better than my aunt and I did. "As for the dragonflies, I guess I'll just have to wait and see what happens."

"Well, we were there for less than ten minutes," Declan mused. "Sure seemed to be a lot of drama in that short time."

"Mm. Not to mention that Connell decided to show up right then." I turned to look into his eyes. Their color had deepened to azure in the faint light from inside.

He looked away for a moment, then back at me. "I've been meaning to talk to you about that."

Stunned, I leaned forward. "Are you kidding? It's really happening again?"

In the past, Declan's ancestor had literally taken

over his body, roaring out his opinions in a blazing Irish accent. It had first happened at a séance, and for a while, it had looked like Connell was around to stay. Declan, a solid, straightforward soul if ever there was one, was horrified and embarrassed. His buddies at the fire station still didn't know anything about it.

As for what, exactly, Connell was? Well, that was still up in the air. He'd been married to a distant aunt in the McCarthy family in Ireland more than a century before. Old photos had revealed him to be six inches shorter than his bride, but they'd looked happy. Then the photos showed her getting older, and older, and finally she wasn't in them at all, while Connell still looked as spry as ever as time went on. Given his green garb and tall hat, his sprightly, bearded appearance, along with a few hints that he'd dropped since barging into Declan's life . . . He might have been a . . . leprechaun.

I'd refused to believe it, but it had been pointed out that someone who practices magic should be careful about where to draw the line regarding what was believable and what wasn't. I had to admit it seemed likely that leprechauns—if they did exist—didn't look like their tiny caricatures any more than witches looked like warty hags who rode brooms. Connell himself had told me he wasn't really a ghost because he wasn't really dead. *Or* alive. Instead, he seemed to exist in a kind of no-man's-land with the sole purpose of helping a chosen McCarthy each generation.

This time around it was Declan.

For me, it was disconcerting not to know whether Connell might show up in, shall we say, intimate circumstances. But he'd agreed to behave himself, and

I'd taken him at his word. He'd convinced me that he had good intentions, and he'd helped out in a couple of dangerous situations, too. Then a few months ago, Declan told me he'd gotten Connell to agree to never take over his physical self like that again. I thought that had been the end of it.

Now Declan shook his head. "No, it's not like before. He doesn't actually take control of me like he did. But I've become used to his presence, you know? There in the background. And he's started . . . Well, I guess you could call it *nudging* me about certain things. Like subtle advice."

My forehead creased, and I sat back. "You mean like intuition?"

My fiancé's face brightened. "Yeah, I guess it is like that. I mean, everyone gets gut feelings, right? It's just that I know exactly where some of mine come from. So I really trust them. And you know what?"

"What?"

"I like it."

I felt a grin spread on my face. "I know exactly what you mean." My intuition had grown exponentially as I'd studied the Craft and practiced spell work over the last two years. It made me glad that Declan shared that—and that he appeared to be at ease about it.

He grinned back at me. "I thought you might. There have been a couple of times it's come in awfully handy. No big world-saving type stuff, but when we were called out to that house fire last week? I knew exactly where to look for the owner's dog before it succumbed to smoke inhalation."

Yip!

Mungo had followed us outside and now voiced his approval.

I showed mine by reaching over and squeezing Declan's hand. "That makes me happy. How long has this been going on?"

He shrugged. "A couple of months."

I drew my hand back. "That long? Why didn't you tell me?"

He looked embarrassed. "I guess I didn't know how you'd take it."

I considered that. "Has Connell ever given you any, er, advice about me?"

"Other than telling me you were in that fire last year, no. I think he's kind of intimidated by you. After all, you were pretty rough on him those times he showed up unannounced. Raked him right over the coals." He grinned. "Still, he thought it was important that you know whatever Orla Black told you was real. You're sure there wasn't more?"

"Not much," I hedged. "She stopped herself. I thought it was just a way to get me to pay her for a reading, but I've decided I don't care. I really want to know what else she was going to tell me."

"I'd like to know, too," he said as he stood and stretched. "I'm putting in some overtime doing building inspections tomorrow, so I think I'll head to bed now. Care to join me?" He raised his eyebrows in invitation.

I grinned. "Yessir, I do believe I would."

Chapter 3

I put a piece of cornmeal sheet cake on the table in front of Jaida French. "Here you go. On the house."

She glanced up from the brief she was working on. "What? Oh! Thanks."

"Or I could get you something from the lunch menu," I said. "It's after noon."

"Already?" She sighed. "You know I love this place, but if they don't get our office finished soon, I'm going to gain ten pounds."

I laughed. "Would you rather have a fruit cup?"

She snorted. "God, no. This stuff is amazing. Light and fluffy, not at all like what I think of as corn cake. Er, and if I could get another mocha . . . ?" She looked at me hopefully.

"Of course." I left her to her work.

Jaida was a defense attorney in her early forties. She worked—and lived—with another witch named Gregory, who was her partner in every sense of the word except that he practiced the Craft solitary rather than belonging to a coven. While their office was being renovated, he was working in their apartment, while she had claimed a corner table in the Honeybee.

She was one of the original members of the spellbook club, and her magical specialty was tarot. A vivacious African-American woman with a quick and wry intelligence, she wore a casual skirt and blouse rather than her usual business suit. And, as always, she smelled of cinnamon.

Ben was working the coffee counter, so I asked him to deliver her mocha and went into the kitchen. Lucy was chatting with a customer at the register and gave me an absent nod as I walked by. We'd had a run on the daily special, so our part-time employee, Iris Grant, was mixing up a new batch of cardamom orange muffins to pop into the oven. She turned as I approached, the multiple rows of piercings in her ears flashing in the light that angled through the alley window. Her short hair was parrot green, pink, and blue, in celebration of the upcoming Easter holiday.

"What's next, boss?"

I drew closer and spoke in a low voice. "Did you remember the spell?"

She leaned toward me. "There were people at the register, so I just whispered it. That will still work, right?"

"It's the intention that counts," I agreed, wiping my hands on the brown-and-teal paisley apron I'd selected to match today's skirt and T-shirt.

When I'd first met Iris, I knew she had potential. Since she'd started working at the Honeybee, Lucy and I had introduced her to the tenets of hedgewitchery and encouraged her to participate in giving our baked goods the little oomph of something extra that set them apart—a deliberate sprinkle of spice here, or a scattering of herbs mixed in there, all with encouraging and benevolent results. The cardamom in the muffins promoted love as well as eloquence, and the candied orange peel inspired happiness and creativity.

"Well, we're low on the cheddar sage scones," I said, thinking out loud about what she could do next.

She wrinkled her nose. "I can't seem to get the texture right."

"Okay, we'll work on that. For now, I'll do them, and you can start prepping the rhubarb for tomorrow's special."

She did a little two-step. "Okeydoke, boss."

"Katie?" Lucy called. "Do we have any more of the lavender basil biscotti?"

I turned and met her eyes. She gave a slight nod toward the woman at the register, who already had her coffee drink.

"For Sadie to sample," Lucy explained. I knew that meant, *Sadie's husband is being a jerk again, and I want to give her a little extra psychic protection.* Basil and lavender would nicely fit the bill.

"In the big glass jar, over by Ben," I said.

She smiled her thanks, and I went back to gathering the ingredients for the cheddar sage scones. They'd been on the menu since day one and were the first cooking spell Lucy had taught me.

Sage for wisdom, memory, and to attract money . . .

Iris finished chopping the rhubarb for the next day's crostini, then left for her afternoon class at the Savannah College of Art and Design. The muffins came out of the oven, and the scones took their place. As I was refilling the display case with cherry chocolate chip cookies, Declan and two of his buddies from Five House came in.

Scott was an African-American battalion chief whose hair was threaded with gray. He carried an air of self-possession and moved with an easy grace. Randy reminded me of my father, who was part Shawnee, except the firefighter was much stockier and kind of a gym rat. He was also a bit higher energy than Scott, who had taken the younger firefighter under his wing much as Uncle Ben had with Declan nearly a decade before.

They took the next-to-the-last table, and I waved from the kitchen. Lucy was the one who went over to take their order, though. When she came back to the kitchen, she was grinning.

"They want a pile of fried-chicken biscuit sandwiches."

"Positively loaded with bacon gravy, I bet." I echoed her smile. "Growing boys and all that."

The fryer was already hot, so I breaded the chicken that had been soaking in buttermilk and a dash of Mo Hotta Mo Betta hot sauce overnight. Soon the smell of fried chicken edged into the usual spicy-sweet atmosphere.

I took their plates out myself. "How's it going, guys?"

They wore dark blue T-shirts with the fire department logo on the sleeve. The shirts did little to hide the well-defined muscles beneath, and I had to make an effort not to trail my fingers over Declan's biceps.

There'll be time for that later.

Randy half shrugged. "Building inspections are pretty boring."

"That they are, but catching violations early helps to keep the rest of our jobs a little more boring, too," Scott said.

"Sounds good to me," I said. "Inspect away." Not that most of their calls were to fires—most were to car accidents—but the fewer the better. I tried not to worry about Declan's dangerous job, but sometimes I couldn't help it.

The door opened, and Bianca Devereaux wafted in with two books under her arm. Tall, elegant, her long dark hair pulled into a complicated inside-out braid, she wore a breezy handkerchief skirt in purple chiffon and a gauzy cream blouse. A four-inch-wide silver band clasped her wrist, and a single, giant pearl nestled into the hollow of her neck. Another member of the spellbook club, in her forties, Bianca concentrated on traditional Wiccan and moon magic. Her skill with numbers didn't hurt when it came to her stunning success in the stock market, but some of her income came from Moon Grapes, her popular wine shop on Factors Walk.

"Holy crow," Randy said, so quiet I could hardly hear him.

I turned to see him staring at Bianca, who sketched a wave to Lucy and Ben and made her way over to the table where Jaida sat.

"Who's *that*?" For all his muscles and good looks, Randy looked like a stunned rabbit.

Declan's eyebrow rose, and he exchanged a look

first with Scott and then with me. "That's Katie's friend Bianca."

"Bianca." Randy rolled the name around on his tongue. "Beautiful. Tell me she's not married."

I blinked. "Um, no. Not anymore." Bianca's husband had left her and their daughter, Colette, when he learned she'd started practicing magic.

"Boyfriend?"

"Not at the moment," I answered.

"That's going to make it much easier, then." His eyes were still glued on her.

"Asking her for a date?" Declan asked.

"That's first on the docket," Randy said. "But I'm telling you, man, I'm going to make that woman my wife."

We all stared at him for a few seconds. Then Scott said, "Well, okay, then. Just let me know the date of the wedding, and I'll be there."

"Hang on," I protested. "I think Bianca's going to have a little something to say about that."

Randy looked at me. "Duh. What kind of a guy do you think I am?" He grinned. "I might have some work to do winning her over, but don't you worry, Katie. I'm up for it."

A movement outside the window caught my eye, and I looked up to see Orla Black walking past the bakery. I craned my neck enough to see her go into the bookstore next door.

"Okay, big guy," I said. "I'll see if Bianca wants to meet you, but first I have to talk to someone." Untying my apron as I went, I hurried toward the kitchen.

The front door opened before I got there, and

Cookie Rios, the youngest spellbook club member, walked into the bakery. Four years my junior, she exuded a cheerful sensuality. She was partial to miniskirts, which she definitely had the legs for, and today's was denim with a simple mauve T-shirt. Cookie had been born in Haiti and still carried a subtle accent beneath her words. I'd learned a lot about voodoo from her, as well as some interesting ways to look at the concepts of good and evil.

"Katie!" She approached and gave me a big hug. "What did you think?"

"About . . . ?"

She frowned. "The beautiful house I showed you and Declan on Tuesday! Closer to work, nice big yard, that extra guest room to turn into a nursery." She winked. "It's perfect!"

Cookie had given up trading in a new boyfriend every three months for marriage to Oscar Ruiz Sanchez but still tended to change jobs on a frequent basis. This last switch had been minor, though, from selling commercial real estate to residential. As my neighbor had noted, it was good to have a friend in the business when you were shopping for a house. Maybe a little too good. Cookie had shown remarkable enthusiasm in poring over all the listings in Savannah, and even Tybee Island and Pooler, just in case our dream home existed a little farther afield.

"We like it a lot," Declan said from behind me.

"Excellent!" she said.

"Um," I said.

"But I think we'll keep looking, okay?" Declan said.

I shot him a grateful look. When we'd talked about it, I hadn't been able to articulate what was wrong with it. I only knew deep down that it wasn't right.

Cookie pouted a tiny bit to let us know she was disappointed, but then she smiled. "Okay. I thought you two fussbudgets might say that, so I have another all ready to take you through tonight. Be ready at six o'clock, okay? I'll pick you up at your place, Katie. Oh! And you really need to let me know when I can list the carriage house! We must get it on the market. You don't want two mortgages, even if there are two of you now."

I stifled a groan.

"Okay," Declan said, looking at me for confirmation. "But just so you know, I'll be on my regular forty-eight-hour shift starting tomorrow, so any other candidates might have to wait a few days."

"Noted," Cookie said.

Declan gestured toward Bianca and Jaida, who had gathered their things and moved into the library area. "Looks like the gang's almost all here," he said. "I assume the inimitable Mimsey is on the way. You didn't mention that you guys were having a meeting." He quirked an eyebrow at me, puzzled. The spellbook club didn't usually have meetings at the bakery when it was open, only after hours or at one of our houses.

"It's not a meeting," I said. "More books are going out of our little lending library than have been coming in, so the ladies agreed to supply a few additional volumes."

"Ah. Gotcha." He grinned.

Spellbook club members tended to bring in a disparate and eclectic selection of books for our customers. From self-help to construction how-to, innovative fiction to the occult, they were all somehow meant for a particular patron—though the ladies didn't know exactly whom when they brought the volumes into the Honeybee. I'd benefited from a couple of their contributions myself, as a matter of fact.

"Listen, I'll be right back," I said, and handed my apron to Lucy.

"Where are you going?" she asked.

"Orla just went into the Fox and Hound. I want to try and catch her before she leaves."

Lucy took off her own apron and shoved them both at Cookie, who took them with an expression of mild surprise.

"I'll come with you," my aunt said.

Though I'd hoped to talk to Orla alone, I nodded, and we went out together. Moments later we were in front of the bookstore.

Through the window, I saw Orla at the cash register. Croft Barrow, the owner of the Fox and Hound, reached beneath the counter and brought out a book. He put it in a bag and handed it to her. She said something to him, turned, and came out onto the sidewalk.

"Well, hello, you two," she said when she saw us. "What are you doing out here?" Today there was no sign of the fedora or the swirling skirt. Orla had her hair in a tidy grandma bun and wore a simple A-line skirt, blouse, and espadrilles.

"Waiting for you," I admitted. "I saw you walk by and was wondering if you were going to be down on the riverfront again this evening." My eyes cut to Lucy, who was watching me with interest, then back to Orla. "I'd like to know more about that, er, thing you were telling me last night."

A knowing spark lit behind her eyes. "Of course. If you'd like. But I'm not going to be working down on the riverfront anymore."

"Really?" Lucy asked.

The other woman shook her head. "I don't like how the family has been handling our presence down there, pushing people around, and I've decided to take a stand." Her lips twisted wryly. "John wasn't very happy to hear that, but—" She waved her hand. "Never mind. You don't need to know all that. If you want to come to my house this evening around six, though, I'll be happy to tell you more about what I saw in your future, Katie."

Ignoring the look I knew my aunt was giving me, I said, "That sounds great."

Lucy put her hand on my arm. "Isn't Cookie showing you a house then?"

I shrugged. "I'm sure she won't mind if I reschedule."

"Here. This is my address." Orla reached into the bag Croft had given her and pulled out the receipt. She jotted something on the back and handed it to me.

"Thank you so much," I said, putting the paper in the pocket of my work skirt. "I'll see you tonight."

"We don't have any peach fritters today," Lucy said to Orla. "But we do have apple. My treat, and we'll have a chance to catch up. Mimsey is on her way over for a late lunch as well."

We began walking slowly back toward the Honeybee. "As tempting as that sounds," Orla said, "I'm going to have to pass this time. Just stopped by the Fox and Hound to pick up a book I ordered for my granddaughter, Nuala, before meeting with my lawyer." She looked at her watch. "And I'm going to be late if I don't get going."

"I'll bring you a treat tonight, then," I said.

Orla brightened. "That would be great. Maybe some of those—"

Mungo came barreling out of the bakery as if the hounds of hell were on his tiny tail. A shrill whistle pierced the air, making me wince. My familiar started to bark frantically, high and urgent. I looked down at him, bewildered and concerned.

Katie, quick! Help Orla! The words came out of nowhere, as did the sudden, intense fragrance of gardenias. I knew that voice, that smell, and my heart bucked in my chest.

"What—?" I managed to get out before Lucy's scream cut me off.

Tires squealed. The smell of hot rubber overtook the sweet scent of gardenias. At my feet, Mungo yelped and then fell silent. There were a few seconds of eerie quiet, before a cacophony of voices up and down the block erupted. I felt more than saw Declan and his coworkers rush out of the Honeybee.

They ran past us and out to the street, where Orla Black lay alarmingly still in front of a red car.

Chapter 4

One of Orla's espadrilles sat alone and undamaged by her bare foot. A thin red trickle of blood wound by the shoe. I watched it for what seemed like an eternity, my head swimming.

Then I remembered to breathe. I sucked in a whopping hit of oxygen. Then another. The darkness at the edges of my vision receded.

"Orla!" Lucy cried, and ran out to our friend.

The driver's door of the red Toyota opened, and a very shaken middle-aged man got out. Declan and the other two EMTs, who seconds before had been eating their lunch inside the Honeybee, bent over the body. They murmured to one another as they worked together to check her vitals.

I stood with my hand over my mouth, staring in horror. Even from the sidewalk, I could tell there were no vitals to check.

Declan saw my aunt coming. He quickly stood and met her halfway. Catching her by the shoulders, he said something to her in a low voice. She shook her head emphatically as he led her back over to where I waited. He helped her to sit on the edge of a big barrel planter filled with purple and yellow petunias. Lucy swallowed hard and blinked back tears. My fiancé gave me a warning look and a slight shake of his head, then turned back to the accident.

A sick feeling swamped over me, and I felt my knees buckle. Strong hands gripped my elbows from behind. Uncle Ben murmured, "I've got you."

"I'm okay." I forced strength into my legs and pointed. "Lucy."

He let go of me and moved to his wife. Her hands were on either side of her neck, her eyes locked on the body in the street. They dropped to her lap as she turned to stare at me.

"Did you see that?"

"I wasn't looking—"

Jaida, Bianca, and Cookie rushed out of the open doorway. "What happened?" Jaida asked. "Oh, no. Who's that? Is she okay?" She stood on tiptoe to try and see better.

"It's Orla Black," I said, my voice strangled. "We were just talking, and then Mungo . . . he barked. . . . I looked down . . . and I didn't see."

Bianca put her arm around my shoulders and gave a squeeze.

The driver who had hit Orla stood by the side of his car. Disbelief and horror creased his features, and he blinked rapidly as if hoping each time he'd open his eyes and discover the accident had all been a dream. "She just walked out in front of me. Stepped right off the curb," he said to no one in particular.

"She looked right at me, and then she walked in front of my car."

The alarm bells going off in my mind grew louder. What had really just happened?

The EMTs stood as sirens approached. I'd been too stunned to think of calling 911, but thankfully someone had their wits about them. The police and ambulance arrived first, quickly followed by a ladder truck. Declan and the other two firemen spoke with their coworkers; then my fiancé came over to where I stood, still rooted to the spot where I'd first heard Lucy's scream.

"What happened?" he asked.

"Is she dead?" I countered, even though I knew.

His look was answer enough.

"I didn't see," I said. "Mungo came out and started barking. I was looking at him to see what was wrong."

Next to me, Cookie frowned. "He was in the reading area with us, calm as could be, and then all of a sudden he shot out of his bed and ran out the door. I thought maybe you'd called him."

"Mungo came out *before* Orla was hit," I said slowly. My brain wasn't quite working at full speed. "I wonder if he was trying to warn me." I cleared my throat. "If so, he wasn't the only one."

Lucy whirled to face me. "What do you mean?"

The other spellbook club members and Declan were looking at me, too.

"Nonna," I said. "I smelled her gardenia perfume."

Understanding dawned in my aunt's eyes. "She spoke to you?" she asked quietly.

The spirit of my dead grandmother had reached

through from the other side to warn me of impending danger before. In fact, she'd twice saved my life. She'd also talked to my mother at least once that I knew of, but hadn't ever communicated directly with Lucy in the same way. My aunt kept hoping, though, and now a flicker of sorrow mixed with the curiosity on her face.

Tears threatened, burning my eyelids. "Nonna told me to help Orla. She said to hurry. But everything seemed to happen at the same time. I didn't know what she meant. I didn't—" A sob broke from my throat.

Declan stroked my hair. "It's not your fault."

I nodded, struggling to get myself back under control.

He took a deep breath. "Um, but there's something you . . . Never mind."

"What is it?" I managed.

His look contained such sweet tenderness that it nearly undid me all over again. "Later, hon. There's enough going on right now. Are you going to be okay for a while? I know I was just doing inspections for overtime today, but I want to check in with the crew and see if I can help. As long as I'm here, you know?" He gave me a knowing look. "Maybe accompany the, er, Ms. Black to the hospital."

I ventured a little smile, admiring his dedication. "Of course. I'm fine, really. Stunned, mostly. Numb. And somehow feeling like I should have been able to prevent Orla from walking in front of that car. Declan, I'm still not sure how it happened."

"I know," he murmured. "But trust me, whatever caused Ms. Black's death, it's awfully suspicious—and not your fault." He kissed me on the cheek and walked over to where his buddies were gathered by the ladder truck.

Awfully suspicious? And had I heard a slight Irish accent beneath his words? There was something he wasn't telling me. Was that what his *Later, hon* had been about?

Quickly, the authorities set up a temporary shield, so the gawkers wouldn't have anything to ogle as the emergency personnel worked. As intended, people began to wander away. Croft Barrow's eyes met mine, and his usually gruff expression softened before he shook his head sorrowfully and went back into his bookstore. Annette Lander, the owner of the Fiber Attic yarn shop on the other side of the Honeybee, stood inside her front window with two of her customers, gazing pensively over a pile of fuzzy wool skeins at the scene playing out in the middle of Broughton Street.

"Come on, everyone. Let's go inside," Jaida said. "There's nothing we can do out here."

There were murmurs of agreement.

Uniformed officers were questioning bystanders. Ben went over to one of them and spoke for a moment, pointing to the Honeybee. She nodded, and he came back over to us. "I let them know where we'll be. They have enough of an audience without us adding to it. They'll come speak to us when they can."

I gave Ben a grateful look, sure that none of us had a desire to watch what was coming next. Everyone went inside, and Lucy flipped the sign in the window from OPEN to CLOSED.

Turning to join them, I saw something on the ground.

It was the book Orla had just purchased for her granddaughter at the Fox and Hound. She must have dropped it before stepping into traffic, because it was on the sidewalk, still in a plastic bag with the bookstore logo on the side. I bent and picked it up. Sliding it out of the bag, I saw the title. *Maeve, Traveler Girl.*

Scanning the back-cover copy, I made my way with slow steps to the door of the Honeybee. It looked like the story of a young girl who had been part of a band of Irish Gypsies in the 1950s.

Orla. Taber. Fern. Nuala. All names as Irish as my dear Declan McCarthy.

A flash of color in my peripheral vision caught my attention. A short, stout figure hurried through the remaining crowd. Her bright orange pantsuit and the matching bow on the side of her white pageboy haircut looked like a flame cutting through the darkness. Mimsey Carmichael, the octogenarian de facto leader of the spellbook club, marched toward the hubbub with an air of determination. She was particularly fond of color and flower magic. Orange promoted creativity, self-expression, vitality, and fun, and was one of her favorite colors to wear.

She slowed on the other side of the police screen, looking at the ground. An officer shooed her along, but not before I saw Mimsey's mouth form a tiny O. She bustled over to me.

"Lord love a duck, Katie. That's Orla Black!" she said.

I nodded. "She was hit by a car."

"Horrible." Mimsey squinted at the stunned driver,

who stood nearby speaking with a uniformed patrolman.

"I feel terrible for him," I said. "How awful to be involved in an accident like that."

She eyed me. "What happened?"

"Lucy can tell you more than I can. The others are all waiting inside."

"All right." Mimsey nodded and pushed open the door.

I was right behind her when another car pulled up to the scene, and Detective Peter Quinn got out.

Great.

The homicide detective and I had had a rather strained relationship since the previous November when a visiting author had been killed in the Fox and Hound. I'd reluctantly become involved in clearing the name of his primary suspect, which I'd also done when he'd been ready to arrest Ben for Mavis Templeton's murder. In between, there had been four other investigations that I'd stuck my nose into, each of them with some kind of supernatural connection. And yes, that was all in the mere two years since I'd lived in Savannah, thank you very much.

The last situation had been unique in that Quinn, who'd always pooh-poohed any notion of the occult being real, despite repeated evidence to the contrary, had actually seen me perform magic. Since then, we'd generally avoided each other, even to the point of him giving up his usual Honeybee pastry fix. It was a shame, because I liked the guy. Barring the fact that he'd been willing to think my uncle might have been a killer, he was good at his job—smart, insightful, and more open-minded than he realized.

I paused in the doorway, waiting to see what Quinn would do. He surveyed the scene with his hands on his hips. His more-salt-than-pepper hair caught the sunlight, and his tanned patrician features looked grim. I couldn't see the gray eyes behind the designer sunglasses, but I knew they were judging and assessing everything that was going on.

He looked up and saw me. His lips thinned, but he didn't look away. Then his shoulders squared as if he was about to face something unpleasant, and he walked toward me. He passed the driver, who had turned an increasingly sickly shade of green. I pulled the door of the bakery closed and waited until Quinn stopped in front of me.

"I should have known you'd be out here," he said, pulling off his glasses.

"Yes. How odd that I'd be out on the sidewalk in front of my place of business when there was an accident in the street." I didn't even try to keep the sarcasm out of my voice.

He let a few beats pass, then: "Who's the victim?"

I hesitated. "Victim?"

"Of the accident. Or suicide. From what I heard on the radio, it could be either one."

Suicide? I hadn't even thought of that.

"If you were on the radio, then I bet you know who she is. Was. Whatever," I said.

He waited.

I sighed. "Orla Black. Her name is Orla Black."

His lips twitched in triumph. “Now, how did I know you’d know who she was?”

“She was a regular Honeybee customer,” I said, and couldn’t help adding, “Like you used to be.”

He looked away.

“There’s something suspicious about this, Quinn,” I said, trying for the level of interaction we’d once enjoyed.

His eyes narrowed. “Like what?”

“I don’t know,” I admitted. “Lucy and I were standing right here with her. I didn’t happen to be looking when it happened, but something is off.”

Expression stony, he said again, as if to an imbecile, “Like. What?”

Like my nonna warned me from beyond the veil. Like I’m pretty sure Connell gave Declan an intuitional nudge that Orla’s death was suspicious.

“Like there was no reason for her to step off the sidewalk right then.” I was fully aware of how lame it sounded.

So was Quinn. He gave me a wry look. After a moment, it softened a little. “I’m sorry, Katie. This kind of thing is hard to see. But trust me, it was an accident. Or, at worst, a suicide.”

I shook my head. “Not suicide. She was on the way to a meeting.” *With her lawyer. Why?* “And she’d just bought a book for her grandchild at the Fox and Hound. She seemed just fine.” I took a deep breath and barreled on. “And after all, you’re here. A homicide detective. So you must have some questions.”

“As I said, I heard the call on the radio, and I was

in the area." Which made sense—the precinct was only a few blocks away. "And given your predilection for getting involved in some nasty situations, I had to wonder." He sighed and gestured vaguely toward the street. "But that's no homicide unless someone pushed her. You were there. Who else was?"

"Just Lucy," I said.

"Did either of you push Ms. Black into traffic?"

"Of course not!"

"Well, there you go." Kindness flickered behind his eyes, then was gone. "Not every tragedy gets justice, Katie." He glanced at the miserable driver of the red Toyota. "Or requires it."

"It's just that . . ." I trailed off. There was no convincing him. Heck, I didn't even know what I was trying to convince him of. Just that something was *wrong*.

"Take care of yourself," he said, and sliding his sunglasses back on, he turned away.

"Quinn," I said.

He paused.

"You take care of yourself, too."

He nodded and walked away.

I'd wanted to say something else, something more, but didn't know how.

I turned and went inside. There was something off here, and I didn't know what it was. However, it was evident from our brief conversation that this time Detective Quinn would not be investigating.

All the customers had left. Mimsey and Lucy were carrying trays of drinks and pastries over to the reading area. Bianca and Cookie were seated in the two poufy brocade chairs, while Jaida sat on the sofa. Ben carried one of the bistro chairs over and sat on the periphery of the circle. The books that the ladies had brought to contribute to the Honeybee library sat in haphazard piles on the coffee table. I hurried to move them to the floor in front of the bookshelves, and Mimsey and my aunt placed the trays where they had been. After motioning them to join Jaida on the sofa, I settled cross-legged on the floor. Mungo crawled into my lap and leaned against me.

As if that provided permission, the other familiars made themselves known. First Honeybee moved to sit behind Lucy's head on the back of the sofa. Rafe, Cookie's king snake, coiled out of her bag on the floor. He still gave me the shivers, but she didn't even seem to notice when he wrapped himself around her slim ankle. Puck, Bianca's ferret, poked his white nose out of a pocket in her skirt that I hadn't noticed before, then emerged enough to show the black Zorro mask over his eyes. The only ones missing were Jaida's Great Dane, Anubis, and Mimsey's obnoxious parrot, Heckle.

Mimsey reached forward and took a croissant, held it for a few moments, then set it down on a napkin on the table untouched. She sighed and looked around at us. Her gaze settled on me.

"We saw you talking to Detective Quinn, Katie. Does that mean what I think it does?"

I shook my head. "Not if you think he's investigating Orla's death as a homicide. He only came by because he heard about what happened on his radio." I made a face. "Since it happened on Broughton Street, he wanted to know if I was involved."

"Involved! How?" Lucy sputtered.

I grimaced. "Well, you have to admit I've been around more than a few times when he's been called out to a murder scene. Still, he's sure this was either an accident or Orla committed suicide."

Bianca leaned forward. "Suicide by car? That's horrible." Her voice was soft.

Mimsey emphatically shook her head. "And I don't believe it. I've known Orla for over a decade, ever since her family moved up from Florida. She was a happy person—tough and smart, too. When she had a problem, she'd find a solution."

Jaida looked thoughtful. "Still, you can't really know what goes on in someone else's mind."

I tipped my head to one side. "I agree with Mimsey. I only knew Orla well enough to sell her a treat now and then." And to be hooked by the beginning of a fortune she would never finish telling me. "But the timing was off."

"What do you mean?" Cookie asked. She reached down and scritched behind Rafe's beady little eyes.

Quelling a shudder, I said, "She had just bought a book for her granddaughter." I held up the bag from the Fox and Hound and removed the volume so they could see the front. "It's a story about an Irish Gypsy girl."

I saw Ben raise an eyebrow, but he remained silent, letting us hash out what had happened among ourselves. He usually wasn't involved in our discussions, and I wondered what he thought.

Lucy said slowly, "It was so *strange*."

We all looked at her.

"Did you see her expression right before she stepped off the curb, Katie?"

"Huh-uh. This little guy"—I nuzzled the top of Mungo's head with my chin—"came running out of the bakery and started barking. I was looking at him when I heard you scream." I winced. "It was over by the time I looked up."

My aunt took a deep breath. "Oh. I wish you'd seen her face." She looked around at us. "Her eyes. They went blank. Completely blank. It was kind of scary. And even worse, she was right in the middle of a sentence. Suddenly she stopped talking, she looked across the street, her eyes became empty, and a split second later, she'd stepped in front of . . . that car." Her voice broke on the last two words.

"That's weird," Jaida said, speculation in her voice. I could almost see the wheels turning in her head. She turned to me and said what had been in the back of my mind all along. "That doesn't sound like a suicide *or* an accident."

Lucy met my eyes, and understanding passed between us. "Tell them about Nonna," she said.

Chapter 5

Mimsey slid off the couch to stand over me. "Your grandmother spoke to you? Why didn't you say so in the first place?"

Feeling at a distinct disadvantage with the diminutive Mimsey towering over where I sat on the floor, I tried not to sound defensive. "I haven't had a chance yet!"

Mollified, she sat back down.

"It was right before it happened. Mungo ran out of the bakery, and at the same time, I heard Nonna say, 'Katie, quick! Help Orla.'" Passing my hand over my face, I continued. "I didn't know what she was talking about. I was just so surprised." Tipping my dog's face up so I could look at it, I said, "And this one seemed to know something was going on, too. I only wish he could speak."

Yip!

A small laugh escaped my throat, and my shoulders eased. "Did anyone else's familiar act funny?"

They all shook their heads.

"Maybe Mungo knew because Orla's death has

something to do with your calling as a lightwitch," Mimsey said.

Nods all around.

Great.

Placing Mungo on the floor, I stood. "Well, if Orla did step in front of that car on purpose, I don't know what I'm supposed to do about it," I grumbled. "Same thing if it was an accident."

"What if it was neither?" Ben asked.

"Murder? Quinn is right about one thing. No one else was nearby. No one pushed her into the street. It would have to be something like . . ." I trailed off.

"Magic?" he asked.

My chin jerked up. "Really, Ben?"

He shrugged and said in a mild tone, "I may not be a member of your, er, book club, and no spirits of the dead have ever deigned to communicate with me, but I've been around these last two years since you moved to Savannah. This has all the earmarks of a situation you need to suss out, Katie."

"I have a choice, remember?" I said. "Just because I'm a lightwitch doesn't mean I have a calling I can't refuse, no matter what we thought before."

He nodded. "Of course."

They all watched me in silence. One by one, I looked around at them. Mimsey's blue eyes were distressed, but in them, I saw confidence that I'd make the right decision. Jaida gave me an encouraging smile. Bianca nodded slowly, her face open. Cookie watched me with narrowed eyes, but I knew she'd accept whatever I said. Ben's brown eyes were difficult to read behind his glasses, but his lips softened and turned up.

Finally, my aunt. Dear Lucy. Tenderhearted yet with a toughness most people didn't get to see. Now she gazed at me with wise affection, as if she knew what I was thinking.

I didn't know Orla very well. It's not my responsibility. I like my life nice and simple the way it is right now. I'm supposed to be finding a house and planning a wedding, not investigating a suspicious death. Not to mention that when I've stuck my nose into things like this in the past, I've almost been killed. So have Declan and other people I loved. Including Lucy.

And:

A woman died. A woman we knew. A woman who had seen something in my future, and who might not have been at the wrong place at the wrong time if I hadn't stopped her on the street to find out more. Something is off, something Nonna tried to warn me about, something Mungo sensed. And I haven't even told them that Connell has an opinion.

I nodded slowly. "Okay. I can at least see what I can find out about Orla's death."

"Good for you," Ben said.

"We can help," Lucy said.

Murmurs all around.

I held up a finger. "Hang on. I don't want to go off half-cocked. It still could have been an accident. She could have slipped, or felt dizzy."

Ben nodded. "Yes, that's possible. She could have suffered an aneurysm or something else that would make her behave the way Lucy described." He paused. "In fact, that was my first thought until I heard about your grandmother's spirit warning you and Mungo's behavior."

"That could have been due to a medical condition, too, you know. Nonna might have just wanted me to grab her, and Mungo is certainly a clever, intuitive little beast."

My terrier looked up at me with a worried expression.

Despite what I'd just said, I didn't really think Orla had died because of a medical condition. But it was possible. I needed to talk to Declan to make sure. He'd gone to the hospital, so he might know more on that front. And now I was more curious than ever about what his resident guardian spirit had to say about Orla's death being "suspicious."

"To look into Orla's death, we need to look into her life." Mimsey pointed to the book I still held in my hand. "She got that book for her granddaughter because the Blacks come from a long line of Irish travelers."

I blinked. "Really? Gypsies?"

"Travelers," she emphasized. "But, oh my, yes. Of the modern-day variety."

"Ginnie Black was Colette's teacher last year," Bianca said. Colette was her eight-year-old daughter. "Isn't she part of that family?"

Mimsey frowned. "I think she married into it."

"Well, for travelers, they sure stay put," Cookie said. "They own a whole cluster of town houses. Great investment property. And when I was selling commercial real estate, John Black bought a couple of storefronts from a colleague. Prime locations. He must be making a bundle from them."

"Okay," I said. "This is good. There's a Ginnie Black, who is a teacher, and John Black, who's a real estate mogul. I remember Orla mentioning someone named John. Has to be the same guy."

"He's the head of the family," Mimsey said. "He has a reputation."

"For what?" I asked, curious.

"Probably the same as his son, Aiden," Jaida said. "I worked with him when he was sued by a customer for some concrete work their construction company did."

By that, she meant she'd worked as his attorney. But being attorney of record in a public case was one thing; disclosing any other information about her client would be verboten. I didn't even ask.

"Okay, add in Aiden Black and his concrete business," I said.

But Jaida was shaking her head. "The company is owned by John, Aiden, and Taber O'Cleary."

"Orla's son-in-law." Ben looked around the group. "We met him down on the riverfront last night."

I rubbed my eyes suddenly. It felt as if our celebratory dinner and walk had been weeks ago, not less than twenty-four hours.

But Lucy was nodding vigorously. "And her daughter, Fern."

"Fern has a brother," Mimsey said. "His name is . . . Finn? Yes, that's it. Finn and Fern. He's married to the teacher."

"Fern mentioned that Finn was around last night. Something about a 'cycle.' I think he might have been the one riding the unicycle?"

Ben said, "I wouldn't be surprised. But, Katie, this

might be more difficult that we thought. Remember all the strife in the short time we stopped by Orla's fortune-telling booth?"

"The juggler," I said.

"And the unhappy client," Lucy said.

"Either of them could be a sorcerer or witch of some kind." I looked down at the book. "I'm not sure where to start, honestly. At least I can give this to Fern. Orla meant for her granddaughter to have it." And if I happened to find out a little more about the Black clan, then all the better. "I think I'll wait a bit, though. I'm sure she must be reeling over her mother's death."

Murmurs of agreement all around.

"It may be difficult to get the family to talk about Orla," Mimsey said.

I was about to ask her why when a knock at the door brought Ben to his feet. He let a uniformed policewoman in and moved a chair over to where the rest of us still sat. Unlike when Quinn conducted interviews in a homicide investigation, she was happy to talk to us as a group. I offered her a glass of sweet tea, a bit diluted now that the ice had mostly melted, and a scone. She accepted both with a grateful nod and sat nibbling and sipping while we all told her our stories.

There wasn't much to tell. Lucy was the only one who had seen Orla step in front of the car. I related what I'd told the spellbook club, minus mention of Nonna or Mungo, and they all confirmed that they'd been inside. By the time we were finished, she'd made a few notes and polished off her food.

"Thanks for sticking around, everyone. I'll be in

touch if we need any more information from you." She stood, put away her notebook, and turned to me. "I've heard about the food in here from a friend of mine. He's right. It's excellent. I'll definitely be back."

I smiled. "Who's your friend?"

"His name is Peter Quinn."

Of course it was. At least he wasn't bad-mouthing the bakery, even if he couldn't bring himself to come in anymore.

She left, and the others gathered their things. Bianca approached me with an apologetic smile.

"Do you still want to have the egg-coloring party the day after tomorrow? Colette would understand if you want to cancel."

I shook my head. "That's sweet, but absolutely not. Declan will be working, and it'll give me something to do besides sit and stew. Not only that, but Margie's bringing the JJs. I don't want to disappoint any of the kids, plus it'll be fun for us, too. Right?"

"Right." She reached into her little Coach bag, retrieved a scarlet lipstick, and touched up her lips. "I'll stop by the craft store tomorrow and pick up the supplies we talked about."

"I'll take care of the dyes—regular Easter egg colors plus some natural hues."

She smiled. "We've always just dunked them in dye and plunked them in a basket. I can't wait to try some of your ideas."

Lucy came over. "I'll be there, too. It's been too long since we've seen Colette."

One by one, everyone went on to their respective

evening activities in a somber mood. Before she left, Cookie gave me a quick hug.

"See you in a couple of hours."

I stared at her for a moment, confused.

"The showing, remember? You haven't forgotten already, have you?" she chided.

"No, of course not. Um, do you think we could . . ." I trailed off when I saw her expression begin to morph from happy to disappointed. She'd put in so much effort to find the perfect place for Declan and me. The least I could do was go see this house she was so excited about. Taking a deep breath, I tried to buck up. "Six o'clock, right?"

"Right. I'm driving. All you have to do is enjoy yourself." She beamed. "Oh, Katie. You're going to *love* this one. I promise!"

I smiled weakly. "See you at six."

She left with a bounce in her step the others hadn't possessed. It wasn't surprising, really. She'd lived through a great deal in her life, including having her father, a voodoo priest in Haiti, killed by a curse. At the age of nine, she'd relocated to the U.S. with her mother and brothers. Cookie had earned her resilience.

After locking the door, Lucy cleaned up the virtually untouched food and began wiping down the kitchen. I mixed the sourdough levain for the next day, while Ben shut down the coffee area and cleared out the register. By the time we were ready to leave, it was almost our usual closing hour of five o'clock.

As I made one last swipe through the reading area, I spied the books that the spellbook club had brought.

They were still lying on the floor in front of the bookcase. Dropping to my knees, I arranged them on top of the coffee table to take a look. The titles were eclectic as usual. There was a primer on how to build garden gates, which went into the nonfiction section. The collection of advice columns went on the self-help shelf, but the book on UFOs looked strange enough that I didn't know where it should go. Shrugging, I tossed it randomly into an empty space, faceup, sure that anyone who was meant to find it would. There were two books from the Boxcar Children series, which went into the kids' section, a Chilton's car care manual for a 2006 Accord, a book about modern cowboys, three paperback romances, two mysteries—both hardbacks—and a title that made me pause.

Telling Fortunes for Fun and Profit.

On impulse, I tucked it under my arm. Since I slept very little, I read a lot at night. Perhaps this would be entertaining. Or helpful. After all, I sure wasn't going to learn the rest of my fortune from Orla now.

Declan had texted when he got home, assuring me that he'd prep something for a late supper after we'd checked out Cookie's next real estate option. *He* hadn't forgotten about our house-hunting date, despite the crazy afternoon we'd both had.

When I walked into the kitchen, he was mixing up a simple orzo salad with a lemony vinaigrette and lots of spring vegetables from the garden. Baby carrots, scallions, radishes, peas, blanched spinach, and asparagus, along with chives, parsley, tarragon, and sage blooms studded the ricelike pasta. Next to it was a bowl of deviled crab to serve on top. I checked in the fridge and smiled at the bottle of Pinot Grigio chilling.

"You know I love your deviled crab," I said, coming up behind him and wrapping my arms around his waist. "Among other things."

Yip!

Mungo stepped over to his place mat on the floor and immediately tucked into the dollop of plain crabmeat and crumbled biscuit my fiancé had ready for him.

Declan put the mixing spoon in the sink and turned. "I thought you deserved a little something special after today." Putting his arms around me, he pulled me close. "Of course, I think you deserve a lot of something special no matter what kind of day you've had."

I felt the tension flow out of my shoulders, and I relaxed into him. "I don't know why that was the right thing to say, but it was," I said. I wasn't usually one to feel sorry for myself, but I'd really been hoping the last murder I'd investigated would be exactly that: the last. A part of me really hoped that Orla had been felled by something like a heart attack or a dizzy spell, rather than someone deliberately killing her.

Wait. Could the driver of that car have known her? He'd looked so miserable that I assumed he hadn't meant to hit her. And his story did jibe with Lucy's. Still . . .

Then I realized that here, enveloped in the arms of my sweet fiancé, who had just said a sweet something to me, I was thinking about murder suspects.

It was getting to be a bad habit.

I tipped my face up and gave Declan a nice long kiss to make up for being distracted. He, of course, didn't know I'd been distracted and moved his hand to my back, sliding it under my T-shirt.

"Whoa there, big guy. Cookie's going to be here any minute." Stepping back, I pointed to the round flea-market clock on the wall over the kitchen window.

He grinned. "We don't have to open the door."

"Oh, yes, we do. She'd have a fit. I tried to get out of this thing tonight, but she looked like I'd taken away her candy." I sat down on one of the kitchen chairs.

"Well, at least you can have this while you wait." He retrieved the wine from the refrigerator and poured a couple of inches into two glasses. Putting one in front of me, he sat down across from me. He looked uncomfortable jammed into the corner by the window on the little chair.

"Have you thought about what kind of table you want to get?" I asked. "A big dining table where we can entertain twelve people? Or something smaller with leaves?"

He cocked his head and gave me a slightly puzzled look. "Don't you think that's something we should figure out once we find the right place? I mean, what if there isn't a formal dining room? Wait. Do you *want* a formal dining room?"

I took a drink of wine, feeling the sweet yet acidic liquid flow down. My throat loosened a little. I hadn't realized how tight it had been all afternoon, as if I had been unconsciously holding back tears. Or frustration. Maybe both. I took another drink.

"I don't know," I said. "Do you?"

He took a sip. "If you do. I don't really care."

"How long were you at the hospital?"

Blinking, he changed gears. "A little over an hour."

"Did you hear anyone talk about whether Orla could have suffered from some kind of underlying physical problem, like a heart issue? Or an aneurysm?" I licked my lips, thinking. "Or even a brain tumor. Will there be an autopsy?"

Declan sat back, a strange look on his face. "Funny you should ask."

I quirked an eyebrow at that.

"The victim's family arrived at the hospital just before I left. I kind of, you know, made myself unobtrusive and listened in."

A small laugh escaped my lips. "You? Unobtrusive?"

He looked insulted.

Declan was six foot four. He had a dimple, for heaven's sake. In my book, he was anything but unobtrusive. Of course, that might have just been my book. But tall, dark, and handsome is still tall, dark, and handsome. However, grief was a big leveler. When I'd first met him, I'd been worried sick about Uncle Ben, and Declan's good looks had just irritated me. It was the way he'd taken care of Lucy that first started to melt my heart.

"Was it Fern who came to the hospital?" I asked.

He shook his head. "Someone named John," he said. "I think he was Orla's brother-in-law."

"That name came up earlier, and I remember Orla saying he wasn't happy about her decision to stop working at the riverfront. I hadn't realized he was her brother-in-law, though."

Orla's deceased husband's brother? Must be, because they shared the same last name.

Declan nodded. "Then Fern got there right before I left. John told her he'd already requested an autopsy."

"Well, I guess that makes sense," I said. "A sudden death like that."

"Right. The medical examiner probably would have done one anyway."

"Then why do you look like that? The family wants to understand what happened. Heck, *I* want to understand what happened."

I was about to ask him whether Connell had any inside information in that regard when a speculative look crossed his face. "You may be right, but this John fellow seemed a lot more concerned that the insurance company would need the autopsy than he was about asking questions about exactly how his sister-in-law died."

The alarm bells that had grown quiet over the course of the afternoon started ding-a-linging in my head again. "Insurance company? As in life insurance? Or is the brother-in-law planning to go after the driver and *his* insurance company for damages? Either way, they'd probably need an autopsy, but it seems awfully cold that he'd be asking about that right away."

"That's what I thought, too." One side of his mouth turned up in a half smile. "A guy that used to work at Five House has a job with the Chatham County medical examiner's office now. Seems like a good time to touch base with him, don't you think? See how the new job's going and all."

"By all means," I said. "You have to stay in contact with old friends, you know."

His eyes flashed with humor.

Sobering, I said, "You mentioned something to me right after Orla was killed. Something about it being suspicious. Was that from Connell?"

Declan nodded. "He gave me the distinct impression that Orla did not die by accident. Someone was responsible for her death."

My shoulders slumped. I rubbed my hands over my face. *Great.* Then a shiver ran down my back, and I looked up. "But *how*? What else did he say?"

"Nothing."

"What do you mean, 'nothing'?" I demanded.

He shrugged. "I mean that's all I got from him."

"Well, ask him for more information!"

"That's not the way it works," he said.

"Can't you try?" I wasn't proud of the whiny undertone in my voice.

A sigh, then Declan dipped his chin. "Sure. I'll give it a go."

He closed his eyes, and his breathing quieted. The seconds stretched out to a minute, then two. Finally, he looked up with an apologetic expression. "Sorry, hon. No go. I get what I get from Connell. It's also possible he doesn't know any more."

"Maybe," I grumbled. What good was having a resident guardian spirit if he just teased with hints and whispers?

The doorbell rang.

Chapter 6

Declan drained his glass of wine before going into the living room. Moments later I heard Cookie's voice. I put our supper in the fridge and went to join them, Mungo trailing at my heels.

Cookie stood in the doorway. She'd changed into black slacks and a sleeveless lime-colored shell. Since she'd started working in residential real estate, she'd gotten rid of the purple—or blue, or green, depending—streak in her long black tresses. Now they tumbled down her back, the angled light bringing out just the slightest hint of red in their depths.

"Katie! Are you ready to see the absolutely most perfect place you can imagine?" She bounced a few times on the balls of her feet. "I can't wait to show you what I found!"

I smiled and walked to the row of hooks by the French doors where our coats hung. "Sure thing. Let me grab a jacket."

She put her hand on her hip and looked around the room. "You know, you keep this place neat as a pin, and it doesn't really need any repair work. Is there any reason I shouldn't go ahead and list it? I'm sure I could start showing it right away."

The pang of impending loss that I felt every time I thought of selling the carriage house struck beneath my sternum, but I kept the smile on my face. "Let's see how we like this new place, first. Okay? You're right that we don't want two mortgages, but we don't want to be out of a place to live, either."

As Mungo and I walked out to the yard, I heard her say something to Declan about contingencies. Ignoring them, I hurried to the dark blue Lexus she'd parked in the driveway behind my car. I couldn't ignore her excitement, however. It fairly oozed out of her pores.

Maybe this really will be the perfect place. Maybe I'll like it even better than the carriage house. It's possible. I just have to keep an open mind.

Declan and Cookie chatted about a recent television series in the front seat, and Mungo and I buckled up in the back. I was grateful for their meaningless chatter, which was entertaining enough to keep my mind off the memory of Orla Black lying in Broughton Street, but unimportant enough that I didn't feel a need to offer my own opinion.

She drove with a deft hand for someone who had for years relied on public transportation, guiding her recently purchased vehicle in and out of traffic. After a while, I realized the route was familiar. In fact, I frequently drove these streets to get to Lucy and Ben's town house in Ardsley Park. A few minutes later, Cookie made the turn into their neighborhood.

"Are we going to the Eagels' first?" Declan asked.

A grin broke out on her face as she met my eyes in the rearview mirror. "Nope! This is the surprise! A town house right down the block from your aunt and uncle's place is up for sale, Katie! You always talk about how much you love their home, and I know you stayed with them for a while when you were getting the bakery going and looking for your own place." She practically vibrated with delight. "The layout is even the same. Lots of light from those big, two-story windows in the living room, and, Declan, you can have a man cave just like Ben's."

"Wow" was all I could think of to say.

"Man cave," Declan repeated. He turned to give me a questioning look as we drove by the walkway that led up to Lucy and Ben's front door. I could tell he was trying to gauge whether I liked Cookie's surprise.

Two blocks later, she pulled to the curb and bounded out of the car. "Come on!"

We followed her up the stone walkway more slowly. She had the front door open by the time we got there. The three of us stopped in the foyer to look around, while Mungo ran into the living room.

Yip!

His bark echoed off the bare walls and high ceiling.

The layout was, indeed, identical. The spacious kitchen was to the left, and a staircase led from the far end of the living room to the second and third floors and the rooftop above. But instead of Lucy's dark cherrywood floor, this place had a nondescript mottled carpet. There was a white marble mantel instead of warm brick, and I could see cold granite and white cupboards in the kitchen rather than Lucy's welcoming butcher block and glass-fronted cabinets, where she displayed her casual stoneware and rows of home-canned produce. The staircase was metal rather than wood, and the paint throughout was standard eggshell white.

But mostly, the difference was that there was no flora. Lucy had plants *everywhere*. She was, after all, a hedgewitch. They lined the front walk and flowed from pots on the steps. Inside, ivy twined up the brick fireplace facade, palms towered near the windows, and vines trailed from hanging planters.

"Can't you just see yourself here?" Cookie gushed. "Of course, you'll need new furniture. Get rid of that old stuff of yours and start all over. Maybe hire a designer. The sellers just did the kitchen over, and the baths, too."

"Nice," I said, noncommittally.

Declan looked over at me. "Cookie, this is a terrific place. I mean, what a nice idea, moving in so close to Ben and Lucy. And we do love their home. But I'm pretty sure Katie and I want a real yard." He glanced down. "Mungo, too."

She waved away his words. "Oh, I know Katie likes to garden. It's part of her gift. But Lucy is the same way, and she has that terrific space up on the roof where she grows all her herbs and magical plants. Katie can do the same thing."

"But I don't—" I began.

"Sure, Lucy makes that work for her," Declan said in an easy manner. "But you see, I like to garden, too.

Katie and I put in most of those beds in her backyard before we were even officially a couple. I really enjoyed the work. I don't think it would be the same, growing tomatoes in pots."

A quick frown flashed across Cookie's face, but she wasn't giving up. "Well, let's go upstairs. You need to see the view from the roof. It's terrific." There wasn't as much bounce in her step as we went up the stairs.

I gave Declan a grateful smile. It was true that he liked to garden—he'd grown up gardening with his mother and four sisters—but his current apartment didn't have room, either. He knew I wasn't crazy about living in a town house, in this neighborhood or any other. And since he was so good at reading my feelings, he probably understood why.

While I adored Lucy and Ben's place, it was because it was theirs. They'd put their own mark on it, making it cozy and welcoming, verdant and rich with texture and atmosphere. Of course, I had done the same thing with the carriage house but in my own style. And that style didn't seem like it would translate well to this high, wide, and handsome space.

Get rid of my "old stuff" and start all over, indeed.

Also, while Lucy had created an oasis on her rooftop, with built-in planter boxes, trellises all around the exterior, and pots attached to the brick walls and wrought-iron railings, I didn't want to do the same thing. I wanted my wending garden beds, flowing from one to the next. I wanted the little stream that cut across the corner of my backyard. I wanted to see my rowan tree grow tall and beautiful. I wanted—

Stop it. You have to give up on seeing that rowan

tree mature. Can't have everything. This town house might not be the right place, but some place will be.

"This is where Lucy has the guest room," Cookie said on the second floor. "You can make that room on the third floor that she uses as a hobby room a guest room instead, and use this as a nursery." She winked. "And your aunt and uncle will be close by for babysitting."

What's with her obsession with nurseries? Let us get hitched before we start talking about babies.

I looked at Declan with eyebrows raised. "Gosh, hon. Cookie's thought of everything."

"Darn straight," she muttered as she turned to go up the stairs again.

We went out on the rooftop. The view was of stately mansions mixed in with Craftsman bungalows, punctuated by a sea of green lawns and leafy treetops. The owners had installed Astroturf and a putting green on the roof. Mungo ran out and sat by one of the tiny flags, tipping his head to the side as if to fetch any balls that came his way.

"Now, Ben would love this," I said with a grin.

"It would be easy enough to take out," Cookie said, knowing neither Declan nor I golfed. "You could replace it with rows of raised beds relatively inexpensively."

"That's true," I agreed.

Back downstairs, I dutifully checked out the details in the kitchen and the brand-new bath. The front door had been open as we looked around, and Mungo was waiting on the step when we went back outside.

"You're not going to buy it, are you?" Cookie's voice was heavy with disappointment.

"Oh, sweetie," I said, "I'm sorry. We're the worst clients ever, aren't we?"

She laughed. "Of course not. But you're a challenge—that's for sure. I'll find something you love, though. Don't worry."

We got into the car. She started the engine and pulled away from the curb—in the opposite direction from home.

"There another place for sale in this neighborhood. As long as we're here, let's do a quick drive-by."

"Sure," I agreed, and Declan nodded his head.

After a few turns, she slowed in front of a three-story brick house complete with antebellum-style columns, gabled windows, a three-car garage, and a sprawling lawn. "What do you think?"

"I think we could never afford this. It's enormous, Cookie!" I said.

She stopped smack-dab in the middle of the street and turned around in her seat so she could see both Declan and me. "Tell me again exactly what you're looking for."

"More space," I said. "But not nearly this much. A yard, but not like this."

"Garage?"

I shrugged at the same time Declan said, "That would be great."

She listed another dozen items, and we did our best to answer. Finally, I said, "I'm sorry, Cookie. I'm still a little distracted by what happened at the bakery today."

"Oh, gosh. Of course you are. Let's table the house hunting for a couple of days and come back to it fresh."

She started driving again. I looked out the window in time to see the sign for Paulsen Street going by.

"Hey, hold on," I said.

"What is it?" Cookie asked, slowing the car.

I pulled out of my skirt pocket the receipt from the Fox and Hound that Orla had given me. I'd glanced at it after she jotted her address on the back, and sure enough, her house was less than a block away. If she hadn't died that afternoon, I would have been there at that very moment finding out what the heck she'd seen in my future.

"Do you mind going by this address?" I read the street number.

"Oh . . ." Cookie said as she whipped a U-turn. "Remember those town houses I told you the Black family owns? That sounds like it's one of them."

"It's Orla's," I said. "I was supposed to go see her tonight."

Oops. But Cookie didn't appear to put it together that I had been going to cancel our showing.

Declan frowned. "You didn't mention that."

"We made the arrangements right before she was killed," I said.

"Oh." He ran his hand over his face.

"This is it," Cookie said, and stopped across the street. "There are six of them, connected in a row. They share a common space in the back. There's a nice swimming pool."

"How do you know all that?" Declan asked.

Her white teeth flashed in a smile. "I sold a house on the street behind them. There's a fence, but it was easy enough to take a peek over the top."

I suppressed a laugh. *Sheesh. She's getting to be as nosy as me.*

The Black compound took up a whole block. The three-story town houses were constructed of gray brick, and each had a veranda rimmed with an elaborate wrought-iron railing on the top floor. Ivy crawled up the corners and spread like fingers to the middle units. The front doors on the ends were red, and in between them, bright orange-, blue-, green-, and yellow-painted doors brightened the otherwise somber building.

The blue door opened, and a stocky, dark-haired man came out. He looked to be about sixty. Two younger men followed behind. They appeared to be arguing. The older man pointed to a flatbed truck parked at the end of the block, and the taller of the others scowled but took a set of keys out of his pocket. He walked down, got into the truck, and drove away. As the other one turned to go inside with the older man, I saw it was Orla's son-in-law, Taber.

Then the orange door opened, and a woman came out. I recognized Fern by the way she moved and the color of her hair. A girl who looked to be about ten years old ran out and took her hand. Fern ruffled the child's brunette locks and led her over to the two men.

Right then, the older man looked over at Cookie's car and frowned. He put his arm around Fern, gestured toward us with his chin, and led her back to the door she'd come out of. Taber followed behind. Moments later, everyone was inside, and we were left staring at curtained windows.

"Any idea who those guys were?" I asked Cookie.

She shook her head. "I don't know any of them."

"The woman is Orla's daughter," Declan said, catching my eye.

"She's quite beautiful," Cookie said, putting the car in gear and pulling away.

"And that must have been Orla's granddaughter, Nuala," I mused.

Silence descended in the car on the way home, each of us thinking our own thoughts. Mine kept going back to the book Orla had bought at the Fox and Hound. I turned over the receipt I still held in my hand and scanned the front. Beside me, Mungo leaned over to take a look, too. I shifted the paper so he could see, then mentally chided myself. Still, I wouldn't have been entirely surprised if my familiar could read.

Apparently, Orla had asked Croft to order another book for her and had prepaid for it when she'd picked up the book for Nuala. It was a guide to the best places to live in northern California. Had Orla planned to move away from Savannah? Or was it a gift for someone else?

Back at the carriage house, I invited Cookie in to share our light supper.

"No, thanks. Oscar made up a mess of Dominican braised chicken and stewed beans. I need to get going."

"Sounds delish," I said, and got out of the Lexus. "See you soon."

She waved out the window as she drove away. Declan and I headed inside for our own meal and an early night. At least for one of us.

* * *

Declan snored quietly in the bedroom. Not quite ready for sleep, I settled on the couch near the floor lamp. I picked up the first of two books on the cushion beside me.

Maeve, Traveler Girl was aimed at middle-grade readers and was an easy skim. It told the tale of an eleven-year-old girl who was born into a family of travelers in Connemara, Ireland. She grew up moving from place to place in a caravan, discriminated against by the "settled," and being educated by her mother and older sister. Then the family made the move to the United States, and themselves "settled" in northern Florida.

I'd heard of Irish Gypsies, and Maeve's fictional journey made me want to know more. However, the story focused on her family relationships and having to overcome the difficulty of getting used to a new country after a very rural existence in 1950s Ireland, rather than the history and details of her subculture.

Mimsey seemed to know about Orla's connection to the travelers. Perhaps she can tell me more.

I put that book aside to take to Fern later and picked up the volume that one of the spellbook club members had brought into the Honeybee library, *Telling Fortunes for Fun and Profit.* A quick look at the table of contents revealed an extensive list of possible methods of divination, including tarot, runes, palm reading, pendulums, dowsing, dreams, dice, tea leaves, and crystal balls.

The sections on tarot and scrying with a crystal ball made me think of the cards Orla's client had furiously swept to the ground and the clear glass sphere the fortune-teller had pushed aside to do her reading. They also reminded me of Jaida's expertise in tarot reading and Mimsey's shew stone. Jaida preferred the classic Rider-Waite deck for spell work but had a collection of unique and beautiful decks for her own use. And Mimsey's shew stone looked like something out of a bad movie, but it did the job. It was a polished pink quartz sphere atop a rather gaudy bronze stand studded with what looked like glass jewels but were real precious gems.

Still, the idea that you could simply look at a spread of cards or into a chunk of crystal and see your future, or anyone else's, wasn't exactly how it worked in real magical divination. It was more like murky hints and hazy visions ripe for interpretation. Being able to accurately make those interpretations turned out to be as much a part of the Craft as invoking elemental forces in the course of casting a spell. The others in the spellbook club had been schooling me for two years, but I was still lousy at it. I'd had a little luck with a dowsing rod Lucy had given me, but I didn't know how to use it to find out what Orla had been going to tell me about my own future.

But I have tarot cards. I can at least see what they say.

Chapter 7

Leaving Mungo to snooze on his favorite wingback chair, I quietly climbed the stairs to the loft that overlooked the living room. Opening the secretary's desk that Lucy had given me revealed my small altar—always ready and yet out of view most of the time.

Nonna, who'd also been a hedgewitch, had knit the lace shawl that served as my altar cloth. I liked to think of her energy and love being intertwined in the stitches, supporting my own magical intentions. The items arranged on it were my personal versions of classic tools of magic, each reflecting one of the four elements. For water, my chalice was a small, swirly glass bowl I'd unearthed at the flea market. For air, an antique kitchen knife served as a ritual athame, nestled next to a bright azure feather I'd found in the gazebo. For earth, a small tumble of smooth stones gathered over the years, as well as an Indian arrowhead my father had given me. And for fire, a garnet necklace from Declan twined around the wand I'd made from the witch hazel bush in the backyard.

From one of the cubbyholes above the drop lid, I removed a deck of cards wrapped in a silken cloth. Taking them over to the futon in front of the television, I moved aside a few cushions and considered my options. Despite its listing in the book on fortune-telling, Jaida had explained to me that the purpose of tarot wasn't really to tell the future. It was rather to indicate how things were currently going, and the possible general outcomes if your life continued on the same course. But life is changeable, and a day later the same spread would have different results. The cards held power when a person infused them with intention and were useful in spell work, especially burning magic. However, when it came to prediction, the cards were best at pointing out things a person might not have noticed, or for interpreting the past, present, and future in ways one hadn't thought of.

I didn't know of a spread I could do that would tell me the exact sacrifice that Orla had said I'd have to face. Nonetheless, I decided on a quick three-card spread to try to gain a little perspective.

With a question held firmly in my mind, I unwrapped my cards. The Kitchen Tarot by Shie and Fairchild, which I'd gravitated toward, was abbreviated, but still contained cards that echoed the major arcana of more traditional decks, as well as some unique additions. I liked it because the artwork was fantastic, it reflected my love of cooking and food, and the thoughtful messages were affirming and helpful. After shuffling, I laid three cards down.

In the position of the past, I turned over the Kitchen Timer—postponements, delays, second thoughts, secrets, and decisions. Well, that made sense. Deciding to marry Declan had certainly taken me a while, to everyone's chagrin. And me being a witch, secrets were a part of my everyday life.

The card representing the present was the Food Scales. The interpretations for that one included accountability and poetic justice, cause and effect, being true to yourself, favorable outcomes with legal issues, and objectivity.

And maybe more than mere poetic justice. That one certainly is a nudge toward finding out exactly how—or why—Orla died.

I hesitated before flipping the future card. Taking a deep breath, I laid it on the futon.

The Silverware Drawer.

I smiled. That was encouraging. It predicted my faith and perseverance would be rewarded, that there was a light at the end of the tunnel, and that by justified means *and* ends, problems would be resolved.

There was nothing in those cards about sacrifice. Maybe Declan and I would find a new home that wouldn't make me feel like I was giving up a part of myself by selling the carriage house. Maybe Orla had gotten her signals crossed.

Either way, I felt even more urgency to solve the puzzle of why she'd suddenly stopped talking midsentence to step in front of a car.

The next day, Declan would start his forty-eight-hour shift at the firehouse at seven, but as often happened in our close quarters, my predawn showering and breakfasting woke him. He rarely complained, but I knew that he fell back to sleep only half the time, and I felt guilty for robbing him of much-needed rest—especially right before he went to work. It was yet another reason we needed to find a place where the rooms weren't practically on top of one another.

I have to stop putting it off, I thought as I gazed down at his sleepy face, and promised myself that I'd give the next house Cookie showed us a real chance.

Thankful that today appeared to be one of the mornings when Declan would be able to get a little more shut-eye, I kissed his rough cheek, and Mungo and I trundled off to the bakery at five a.m. By the time Lucy arrived a little after six, loaves of fragrant sourdough bread were sitting on racks, the crusts still audibly crackling as they cooled from their high-temperature baking. I'd rustled up the varieties of muffins and cookies currently on offer on the chalkboard menu, and the baguettes left over from the day before were sliced and ready to toast for that day's rhubarb crostini special. We would top them with the sweet stewed rhubarb that Iris had whipped up the day before, along with a dollop of ricotta cheese and a drizzle of local honey.

"Morning, Lucy!" I said.

Smiling, my aunt returned my greeting, then grabbed a bright yellow hostess apron from the vintage selection hanging on the back wall and tied it around her waist. I wiped my hands on my own skirt apron, a green gingham that I'd chosen to complement my pink skirt and white T-shirt.

"If you want to start filling the tins for the mini-pie special, I'll get to work on a batch of croissants."

She nodded briskly. "Better you than me."

I grinned. The long process of folding and rolling croissant dough over and over again to achieve the delicate, flaky layers could be tedious, but I chose to see it as meditative instead.

Iris came in a bit before seven. Ben arrived right behind her, loaded with supplies from an early-morning run to the bulk grocery. I stored the items while he opened the bakery. Three customers were already waiting. He cheerfully whipped up their morning doses of caffeine and armed them with sweet treats to face the day. People might come in for Lucy's and my baked goods, but I would have bet that just as many came in to visit with my gregarious uncle.

The midmorning lull hit about ten thirty. I set Iris to work cleaning out the refrigerator, an unpleasant job that she dove into armed with rubber gloves and a cheerful smile. Then I went into the office to check e-mail. An inquiry about a wedding cake was waiting in the in-box.

"Hey, Lucy," I called from the desk. "Are you around?"

Moments later, she rounded the corner of a cabinet to stand in the doorway. "What's up?"

I showed her the e-mail. "What do you think? It's just over a week away. She wants a simple three-layer red velvet cake with candied roses and lilacs on it."

"Shouldn't be a problem," my aunt said. "I'll get Iris to help me. Ever since we did a few for that Christmas party last year, we're starting to get more and more orders for our candied flower cakes. She needs to learn how to sugar the petals."

"Sounds good. Say, I was about to run over to Mimsey's anyway. Since it's slow and all. I can make sure she'll have the right blooms for this cake when we need them."

Lucy cocked her head to the side. "You need to see Mims?"

Shrugging, I said, "I want to talk to her about Orla."

My aunt's puzzlement cleared. "Ah . . ."

"She mentioned that the Blacks were Irish travelers. I'm curious. Maybe she can tell me more."

She made a shooing motion with her hands. "Get going, then. I need you back here before the lunch rush, because Iris has to leave for her creative business class."

I reached for Mungo's leash. "Come on, little guy. Let's go for a walk."

On the way, I paused to pack some muffins into a waxed paper bag. Out on Broughton Street, there was no evidence of the accident the day before. Cars passed and pedestrians crossed, and I wondered if any of them knew what had happened. There had been a mention of it on page three of the *Savannah Morning News*, but I'd had to search for it.

We set off for Bull Street at a brisk pace. Mimsey had owned her flower shop, Vase Value, for decades. Even at eighty, she still went in to work most days. She said it kept her young. Lucy had assured me Mimsey did not use glamour spells—or any others—to maintain her sparkle and youth, so I believed that her work kept her spry and interested. It also fit perfectly with her affinity for color and flower magic.

As we approached Vase Value, the smell of gardenias

filled the air. My footsteps slowed as I probed my surroundings. Then I saw several of the glossy-leaved plants sat in stair-stepping pots outside the open door. Both relieved and disappointed that the fragrance came from actual blooms rather than my dead nonna's signature perfume, I continued to the shop.

A canvas canopy shaded a plethora of galvanized tubs filled with choose-your-own stems on the sidewalk. Next to them, wooden produce crates were arranged in tiers. Houseplants, blooming tropicals, miniature roses, hydrangeas, and arrangements of succulents marched along the rustic shelves and tumbled down the edges. I breathed in the verdant atmosphere and felt my muscles loosen. Together, Mungo and I went inside.

More potted plants lined the shelves along the interior walls. Displayed among them were garden- and floral-themed gifts. I spied a birdhouse that would have been a perfect addition to the gazebo behind the carriage house, and two cutwork lanterns that would have looked great on my back patio. I stopped to examine a set of the cutest stained-glass plant markers, sorely tempted to buy them even though I shouldn't until I knew what kind of garden I'd have.

Reluctantly, I returned them to their place and led Mungo to the back counter. On the far side, Mimsey's assistant, Ryan, stood at a wide table. He was working on an arrangement of white lilies, ferns, and stems of burgundy-colored grasses. Behind him, floral foam, wires, tapes, vases in various shapes and sizes, decorative ribbons, and cutting tools were neatly arranged in cubbyholes. At the very rear of the store, Mimsey worked at the desk in her glass-walled office.

Ryan saw me and smiled. "Katie Lightfoot. Haven't seen you for a while."

He was in his midtwenties, with a shock of yellow hair, laughing brown eyes, and skill working with flowers that Mimsey claimed was supernatural. When she'd hinted to him about it, though, he'd made it clear that he found such an idea to be nonsense. She was content to let that lie, counting herself lucky to have him working for her.

"There's too much temptation to buy out the place when I come in," I said with a grin.

"I know, right? I swear I spend a third of my paycheck in here."

I handed him the bakery bag. "A few goodies to get you through to lunch."

His eyes lit up. "You really should come by more often." He reached under the counter and brought out a low-rimmed dish like the ones that held succulent gardens outside. It looked clean, but he laid a couple of paper towels on the bottom before reaching into the bag and arranging the muffins I'd brought. "You here to see the boss lady?"

"If she's not too busy," I said, nodding toward the office. Mimsey was intent on her computer screen and hadn't seen me yet.

"Just going over outstanding accounts receivable. She'll welcome the interruption, believe me." He stepped over and knocked on the door.

She looked up, then jumped to her feet and motioned

me in. Mungo and I went around the counter as she opened the door. "You're doing a lovely job with that arrangement, Ryan. They will be so pleased," she said to her assistant before shutting the door behind me. "Funeral pieces can be quite tricky."

I grimaced.

"Sit down, dear."

I sat in the chair across from her. Today Mimsey wore flowing slacks and a tunic the color of moss. Green was one of her favorite colors to wear to work, as it represented money as well as plant magic. It could also be used to counteract jealousy and greed.

She hadn't stopped with employing a little color magic to help Vase Value's bottom line. A pot of bamboo—again, to attract money and good fortune—sat on her desk next to the computer, and next to it a fluffy arrangement of pink peonies encouraged abundance and gratitude. A huge chunk of amber-colored citrine hunkered on a pedestal in the corner, so well-known to promote prosperity that it had been dubbed the shopkeeper's stone. On the wall behind her, blackberry brambles had been twisted and woven into an attractive star that was actually a pentacle of protection.

Mimsey peered at me over the top of her half-glasses. "I'm guessing you weren't just in my neighborhood in the middle of a workday."

I shook my head. "No, ma'am. Though we do need to order some deep red roses and dark purple lilac blooms for a cake next week."

She made a note, then sat back. "Done." Her eyebrows raised in a silent question.

"Thanks," I said. "The other reason I stopped by

is because you mentioned that Orla belonged to a group of Irish travelers. I read through the book she bought for her granddaughter, and it's about a young Irish Gypsy who emigrates from Ireland to the U.S. I was wondering what you might know about that aspect of Orla's life."

Mimsey removed her glasses. "Well, first off, Irish travelers aren't exactly Gypsies. I mean, some have Romany heritage, but most are ethnically Irish."

"Do they dislike being called Gypsies?"

"Let's just say it's inaccurate. The Rom, or Romany Gypsies, are descended from peoples in India. No one knows for sure how the Irish travelers came to live the nomadic lifestyle they do, but Orla told me it was probably a combination of things that pushed folks out of their homes and made them into wanderers. Cromwell's policies in England in the 1650s and people being discriminated against for their religion—the flip-flopping between whether Protestantism or Catholicism was the accepted religion of the land was dangerous for a lot of citizens of Britain for centuries. The Potato Famine forced many people onto the road as well."

"That was in the 1800s, though," I said. "From what I understand, there are still groups of travelers in Ireland—and apparently in the U.S. as well."

"Indeed, there are. There was a massive influx of Irish immigrants into the U.S. back then. They weren't exactly welcomed with open arms, either. The travelers certainly suffered as much here as they did in their native land. Still, they retained their culture. And I think 'families' is more accurate than 'groups.'"

"And the Blacks are one of those families? Orla seemed pretty normal," I said. "I mean, other than when she was all dressed up to tell fortunes."

Mimsey shrugged. "What's 'normal'? She functioned in the mainstream quite successfully, but make no mistake, the Blacks live by many of their own rules. Like other cultural groups—Mennonites, Hutterites, the Amish—they have retained what they can of their cultural identity by keeping to themselves. However, unlike those other groups, their primary identity isn't related to religion."

"What's it related to, then?" I asked.

She tipped her head to the side. "Other traditions. Other skills."

Seeing the twinkle in her eye, I asked, "Magical skills?"

"Could be," Mimsey acquiesced. "Different groups live differently. The Black clan is insular and almost secretive. For all I know, they still speak the traveler patois, called Cant or sometimes Gammon. It won't be easy to find out about Orla's personal life. She spoke out more than the others about their lifestyle and beliefs, especially after her husband died, but she still didn't tell me much."

"Well, you sure seem to know a lot."

Her eyes danced. "I am a born and bred Savannahian, darlin'. Some things just soak in by osmosis over eighty years."

The sound of a raised voice reached us through the glass wall, and we turned to see what was going on out front. Ryan was speaking to someone. When he moved to the side, I was surprised that I'd seen his customer before.

"Oh, dear," Mimsey said as she stood up and moved toward the office door. "I was afraid this might happen."

"Wait," I said.

She gave me an impatient look.

"Do you know that woman?"

"Vera Smythe. She's a regular customer."

"Can you introduce me?" I asked.

Glancing out at the disgruntled woman, Mimsey asked, "Whatever for?"

"Because she's one of the last people whose fortune Orla told before she died. We saw her down on the riverfront, and Vera was one unhappy camper."

The older witch shot me a frown and nodded. "I'll see what I can do. Vera, dear!" she called as she breezed out to the front of her store. "Whatever is the problem?"

I followed behind her, sending out tendrils of intuition to see if I could get any kind of a hit from the blonde. Whether it was from intuition or deduction, I couldn't know for sure, but Vera Smythe struck me as nervous and sad. Her shiny hair was in a simple ponytail today, and her pale face and red-rimmed eyes gave the impression she'd been crying. She wore black ponte pants, a drop-shouldered T-shirt, and ballet flats.

"Mrs. Carmichael. Thank heavens. Your so-called assistant here can't seem to locate my weekly bouquet of carnations."

Mimsey smiled easily. "Let's take a look. Ryan,

perhaps you could check for the order on the computer?"

"But—" he started, until she cut him off with a pointed glance.

He smiled a tight smile. "Sure." He went into the office and sat down in Mimsey's chair.

"In the meantime, let me whip up a quick arrangement for you to take with you." Mimsey bustled over to the refrigerator and lifted out a bucket of white carnations and one of red.

"Can I help with those?" I asked, moving out from behind the counter.

"Thank you, hon, but work like this keeps me fit. Vera, this is my friend Katie Lightfoot."

"Hello," she said, her displeasure apparently smoothed by Mimsey's deft touch.

"Katie, Vera has a salon. You were mentioning that you were thinking about changing your hair, weren't you?" As she spoke, she began pulling out stems and putting them in a clear vase.

Vera's expression became less pained as she focused her attention on me. She gestured. "Come over here. Let me look at you."

Feeling slightly foolish, I complied.

She looked me over with an expert eye. "Excellent bone structure. Beautiful skin tone."

"Um, thanks," I said.

"Have you ever tried to do anything about those freckles?"

"I like my freckles," I said, trying to keep from sounding defensive. "They're from my mother's side."

"Good for you," she said, reaching up and fluffing my short hair. "Who dyes your hair?"

"No one," I said. "It's my natural color."

She looked surprised. "Really. Well, that's an unusual shade of red." She laughed. "Don't scowl. It's gorgeous. You're a very lucky woman."

"Thank you," I said, mollified. And then, because I really had no interest in changing my hair, I said, "You look familiar."

Vera stepped back. "Hmm. I wonder why."

I snapped my fingers. "The other night. Down by the riverfront. Didn't I see you at that fortune-teller's booth?" I braced for an angry response, mentally apologizing to Mimsey.

Her expression turned hard; then she looked like she was about to start crying. "*Fortune-teller.* Ha." The words dripped with dread. "She's a charlatan. I'm going to report her to somebody. The Better Business Bureau or maybe the Downtown Business Association."

I frowned, debating internally. When I spoke, I watched her carefully. "I don't know if she was a charlatan or not, but she was in an accident yesterday. She didn't survive."

Vera blanched. "That's horrible. I didn't like what she told me about my husband, but I'd never want . . ." Her hand flew to her cheek.

Mimsey carried the vase of flowers out. She'd added baby's breath and spiky bear grass to the red and white blooms. "Here you go, dear."

Slowly, the blond woman tore her gaze from mine and settled it on the flower arrangement. She started to reach for it, then stopped. "He didn't order them this week, did he?"

"Ryan is checking on that," Mimsey said in a kind voice.

A quick glance revealed the young man still at the computer.

Vera sighed. "He didn't."

Mimsey handed her the flowers. "Take them anyway. Oh, and Katie brought some of her special goodies from the Honeybee Bakery. Katie, hon? What do you recommend for Vera here?"

Clever woman.

"I think you might like a blackberry thyme muffin," I said, hurrying over to retrieve one for her.

She juggled the flowers and her purse to take it. "Sounds unusual."

"If you like it, you should drop by the Honeybee Bakery for more."

"Mm. We'll see." She was looking sadly at the vase of flowers in her hand.

When Vera had left, Mimsey turned to me. "Blackberry thyme?"

"You know I like a little savory with my sweet," I said. "Thyme complements blackberry well."

She raised an eyebrow.

"And," I continued with a grin, "it's good for strength and courage. It's also known to attract the opposite sex." I sobered. "It seemed like Vera might benefit from those aspects."

Mimsey nodded. "Her husband used to order carnations for her—red for deep love and white for pure love—every week for three years. He hasn't ordered them for the last two weeks."

"Hmm," I mused. "And Orla told her something about her husband that upset her a great deal."

Enough for her to kill the fortune-teller, though? And if so, how?

Chapter 8

I glanced at my watch on the way out the door. "Uh-oh. Mungo, we need to hurry. The lunch rush is already in full swing."

Yip!

We set off for the Honeybee at a brisk pace, dodging pedestrians, dog walkers, strollers, and café tables. As we neared the bakery, I could hear the murmur of voices and the clatter of dishes through the propped-open door. Inside, the tables were all full, and a line had formed at the coffee counter. Lucy stood behind the register, looking harried. When she saw me come in the door, she shot me a grateful look and seemed to relax.

We tried not to let customers—or the food police—see my dog in the kitchen. I hadn't brought my tote bag, so there was no hope of smuggling Mungo back to the office, where he often spent the afternoon snoozing on the club chair.

"Library," I murmured to my familiar, who obediently jogged through the crowd and hopped into his comfy bed on the bottom bookshelf. A few people noticed him passing and smiled, and as soon as he'd curled up, a little girl went over to pet him. He half closed his eyes in pleasure, and I left him to his adoring fan.

In the kitchen, I quickly donned my apron again and joined Lucy. "What can I do?"

"There are several tables that need busing," she said. "And three people have ordered croissant sandwiches that I haven't gotten to."

"I'll make those first," I said, and grabbed the order slip she held out to me.

Quickly, I assembled a caprese sandwich with homemade mozzarella from the local dairy, tomato from a nearby farm, and basil Lucy had grown. Then I smeared a healthy dose of tangy chicken salad studded with pecans on one croissant and layered thin slices of Tasso ham with sharp cheddar and spicy whole-grain mustard on another. Lucy pointed out the threesome of ladies waiting for their lunch at a table by the window, and I delivered it with an apology for taking so long.

"No worries," one said before taking a big bite.

"It's worth the wait to get croissants this light and flaky," said another with a smile.

"You just made my day," I said. It was true. A nicely placed compliment went a long way, especially when things were busy.

I grabbed the coffeepot from behind Ben and went out to top off a few cups. Jaida had settled into her usual spot and was typing away on her laptop. I stopped by the table and asked, "How are you getting anything done with this din?" At that moment, the espresso machine let out a long, shrieking whine.

She looked up at me for a few distracted seconds, then reached up and took out an earplug that I hadn't noticed. "What?"

Patting her on the shoulder, I said, "Never mind. Sorry I bothered you."

As I began gathering detritus a few inconsiderate customers had left behind—or, to be fair, they might not have noticed the two self-busing stations—I saw a couple sitting at a table near the front door. She had short graying hair and was dressed in light slacks, oxford shirt, and blazer. He wore black dress pants and a light blue shirt with a sedate tie. His hairline was so crisp he may have visited the barber that very morning, and his heavy-framed glasses gave a geek-is-the-new-hip flavor to his appearance. At first, I thought they might be mother and son, but I revised my assessment as I realized he was well into his thirties, while she was probably still in her forties.

What drew my attention to them among all the other patrons was that, though seated, they weren't eating or drinking anything. Dodging two teenage girls, I approached their table.

"Hi," I said. "I'm afraid we don't have table service, but if you place your order at the counter, I can try to bring it out to you."

"We're not here to eat," the woman said. "Are you Lucy Eagel?"

I blinked. "No. I'm Katie Lightfoot."

She held out her hand to her companion. "File?"

"Of course." He picked up a briefcase and opened it on the table. Withdrawing a manila folder, he handed it to her.

Flipping it open, she peered at one of the pages it contained. "You're the niece, then." She nodded toward the register. "That must be Ms. Eagel."

I frowned. "May I ask who you are?"

"My name is Nancy Carter, and this is Nick Barker. We'd like to talk to you when you're free."

"Katie," Lucy called, "I need you in the kitchen."

Nodding back at my aunt, I told Nick and Nancy, "It might be a while. We're pretty busy right now."

She settled back in her chair. "That's fine. We'll wait."

As I hurried back to fill an order of chicken and biscuits, I paused by my aunt. "How long have those two been here?"

"Maybe fifteen minutes. They haven't come to the counter, though."

"I know. They say they want to talk to us when things slow down."

Now it was her turn to frown. "Why?"

"No idea," I said, moving into the kitchen behind her.

Half an hour later, the rush petered out. Ben was able to take over the register, and Lucy and I went over to the waiting pair. It looked like they weren't nearly as sanguine about waiting for us by then, while we were curious as all get-out.

Nancy introduced herself and Nick to my aunt, then said, "Can you sit down for a few minutes?"

We looked at each other and slid into the two other chairs at the table.

The woman said, "I understand you witnessed the death of Orla Black yesterday."

Lucy licked her lips. "Yes."

Nick and Nancy exchanged a look. "Would you

mind relating what happened?" Nick asked in a formal tone. He reached into the briefcase that was still open on the table and drew out a notebook and a fancy-looking pen.

"Hang on," I said. "We already told the police everything we saw."

"Hmm," Nancy said, flipping through her file. "Yes, we have the police report. That's how we got your names in the first place. But we like to talk to witnesses ourselves."

Nick nodded eagerly, his eyes bright behind his glasses.

"Why?" I asked. "Who, exactly, are you? And why should we talk to you at all? What happened yesterday was awful." Could they be reporters?

Nancy carefully selected two cards from inside the briefcase and handed them to us. "We're investigators for Firststate Mutual Life Insurance." She looked over at Nick. "We should have explained that in the first place."

He nodded and took a note.

Realization dawned. "And Orla had a life insurance policy," I said.

He made a noise. "More like five."

"Nick!" the woman admonished. His boss, I guessed, or perhaps his trainer.

Ducking his head, he muttered, "Sorry."

But I was reeling. *Five* policies? Orla had been in her late fifties, like Lucy. Could she have been suffering from some terminal illness? My mind scrambled for an explanation.

"We need to talk to anyone who witnessed her death before we can pay her beneficiaries," the woman said. "Will you help us?"

"Um, sure," Lucy said. She went on to relate what she'd seen, leaving out the blank look in Orla's eyes that she had mentioned to the spellbook club, but including the fact that Orla had stopped right in the middle of a sentence before stepping into the street. I explained that I had been distracted at the time and hadn't seen the actual accident.

The veteran insurance investigator frowned, and Nick scribbled another note. "So, you were speaking to her out front here. Were you a friend of Ms. Black's?" she asked.

"Orla was a customer," I said. "I'd call her a friend, and I think Lucy would, too. But we weren't close, if that's what you mean."

She sat back and folded her arms. Eyeing us, she asked, "Do you think it's possible that she committed suicide?"

Lucy shook her head. "No. No, I don't. She was taking a book to her granddaughter. And didn't she say something about being late for a meeting with her lawyer, Katie?"

Something flickered in the woman's eyes when Lucy said the word "lawyer," and Nick jerked his head up to look at her.

I nodded. "She did. And there was nothing about her demeanor that hinted at depression or any kind of low mood."

Nancy huffed out a breath. "Okay."

"So, the policies won't pay if Orla killed herself?"

"Nope," Nick said.

She glared at him, and he ducked his head again.

"Have you checked with the medical examiner?" I asked. "Someone suggested that Orla might have suffered some kind of medical event that caused her to act oddly."

The older woman's eyes narrowed. "We will, of course, take any such findings into consideration. Thank you very much for talking with us. Did you get all that, Nick?"

"Yup." He beamed at her.

"Well, sitting here watching everyone eating those delicious-looking pastries has convinced me to go off my diet for one afternoon," Nancy said, and stood. "Nick, what can I get you? We'll call it lunch and put it on the expense account."

He stood as well. "Let me see what they have."

Lucy went across the room to the counter and began pointing out possible selections.

Looking around, I saw the bakery had mostly emptied. Jaida still sat at the table in the corner, and our resident author was immersed in whatever tale he was telling himself on his laptop, noise-canceling headphones firmly in place. I rose and casually looked inside the briefcase. The cream-colored folder Nancy had referred to regarding Orla's insurance investigation still sat on the table, shielded from the investigators' view by the open lid of the case. After another quick glance around, I flipped it open with a fingertip. Lifting the edges of the pages, I saw the police report, and then a list of names with the heading BENEFICIARIES.

"This looks like just the thing to break a diet for," Nancy said, turning away from the display with a hefty cinnamon roll on a plate.

I flipped the cover of the file closed and moved quickly away from the table. As I did, my wrist hit the edge of the briefcase lid, which thudded down and created enough air current to blow another page half out of the folder. I barely had a chance to glance down at it before the older investigator was at my side.

"Oops," I said, pasting an apologetic expression on my face.

Nancy gave me a long, assessing look before scooping up the file, returning it to the briefcase, and placing it on the floor. Then she set her roll on the table and sat down. "Do you have an interest in life insurance, Ms. Lightfoot?"

I smiled, feeling the heat in my cheeks. "I'm getting married soon. I suppose we should start thinking about such things."

"I can put you in touch with an agent if you like," she said.

"Maybe you can just tell me—could I buy a policy on my husband without him knowing?"

She'd taken a bite of cinnamon roll and now chewed it with slow appreciation. When she'd swallowed, she said, "It doesn't work like that. He'd have to take a physical and agree to the stipulations set out in the policy."

"Makes sense," I said cheerfully. So much for the old movie trope of killing someone for life insurance they didn't even know they had.

"Here's one of our sales agents' cards." She handed

it to me as Nick came back with a selection of cookies and two cups of coffee. He set one in front of her.

"Thanks." I took the card and backed away.

"Katie," Jaida said from behind me.

I whirled. She pointed to the chair beside her. I went over and joined her.

"What were you thinking?" she asked in a low voice. "She almost caught you."

"You saw?" I whispered.

"And heard." She nodded at the earplugs now sitting on her keyboard. "Did you find anything out?"

"You heard Orla had five life insurance policies?" I barely breathed the words.

She nodded. "Crazy."

"I saw a list of beneficiaries." Quickly, I grabbed her legal pad and jotted down the names from memory.

Fern O'Cleary, Finn Black, John Black, Nuala O'Cleary, and Aiden Black

Jaida looked over my shoulder, and I turned to see the insurance investigators packing up and leaving. Once the door closed behind them, we were able to speak in normal tones.

"All family, I take it," Jaida said, perusing the list I'd made. "That makes sense. There's viable insurable interest in each case."

"Which is . . . ?"

"When the death of the insured person would cause financial loss for the beneficiary. Or another kind of loss that might be compensated for by money—caregiving, for example. Close family is automatically considered to have an insurable interest." She sat back, looking thoughtful. "Five policies seems excessive, but I wonder if each was relatively small. That would be a way to break up the payments among several people."

"And create a lot of people who might want their money sooner than later," I said.

She made a face. "I still don't see how it could be murder."

I held up a finger. "Someone could have been across the street and beckoned to her."

Jaida rolled her eyes. "Right."

"It's possible."

"Okay, what else?"

I held up a second finger. "Poison of some kind. Slow acting."

"Hmm."

The third finger came up. "Or some kind of drug. Hallucinogenic. A plant derivative like nightshade or oleander could have the same effect."

My friend was looking interested now.

"Or it could have been some kind of magical spell or curse." I dropped my hand. "I know how that sounds, but it wouldn't be the first time we've run into murder by magic. Even Ben thought of it."

"True," she agreed.

"I saw something else in that file," I said. "And I bet you can help."

"Really? How?"

"At the last second, I also saw a name. Michael Barrion. Is it familiar to you?"

She shook her head. "No. Should it be?"

"It was followed by the letters A, T, T, and, I think, Y. An attorney?"

"Hold on a sec," Jaida said, and began typing on her laptop. "Here it is. Yes, Michael Barrion is a lawyer in Savannah." She met my eyes. "I haven't run into him, though, probably because he specializes in divorce and insurance cases."

I leaned forward. "Orla told us she was on the way to see a lawyer. Do you think that could be him?"

Slowly, Jaida nodded. "It's possible." She licked her lips, and I could practically see the thoughts ping-ponging in her brain. "Especially if Orla wanted to cancel a life insurance policy that someone else held on her."

Surprised, I asked, "Couldn't she just tell the insurance company?"

"Once she signs the papers, whoever pays for it owns it. She couldn't have taken it away from them."

A group of tourists came in the door then, and I rose. "Listen, what are you doing after we close?"

"Supper with Gregory, but not until seven."

"Want to take a walk down to the riverfront with me a little after five, then? I'd like to talk to a few people down there, and could use the company."

"Sure. I'm heading over to the courthouse to file some paperwork now, but then I'll pop home and pick up Anubis. He hasn't been getting out as much since he can't come to the office with me. We'll meet you back here at five."

"Perfect," I said, and went to help Ben with coffee orders.

Chapter 9

A little after three o'clock, Bianca came into the Honeybee with her daughter. Lucy and I spied them from where we were working out a new recipe for peanut butter cake in the kitchen. My aunt dropped everything and hurried out front.

"Colette!" she exclaimed. "We haven't seen you for so long. How have you been, honey?"

"Pretty good," she said. She was slim, and tall for her age. Her eyes were a lighter green than her mother's, and fringed with long lashes. "And how are you, Mrs. Eagel?"

"Pshaw. I keep telling you to call me Lucy. And I've been just peachy, thank you very much for asking. Now, what can I get you to eat?"

The eight-year-old looked up at her mother with a question in her eyes.

Bianca smiled and tucked an errant brown curl behind her daughter's ear. "You can have anything you want. We'll have a light dinner."

Colette grinned and went to stand in front of the

display case, carefully perusing each tray for the perfect after-school snack. Lucy joined her, pointing out the different choices.

Bianca left them to it and came back to the kitchen with a canvas bag. "I had this stuff in the car and thought I might as well bring it by for tomorrow night." She opened it enough that I could see inside. "Four colors of glitter, spray glue, and feathers," she said. "I also found some old-fashioned rickrack and a bunch of tiny, fun stickers. I know you mentioned you'd get the dyes, but I saw some Paas kits on sale and picked up a few—regular, metallic, and neon. While I was at it, I grabbed some crayons. Remember doing that as a kid? Writing your name—or whatever—in wax and then dyeing the egg?"

I nodded. "That was as fancy as it got back then. This egg-dyeing party is going to be a lot of fun." I pulled out a set of shiny flower stickers. "And perfect for all ages. Margie's twins can do some of the simpler decorations, and Colette can try some of the more complicated stuff. And I want to try to give a marbled effect to a few using oil in the dye." I returned the stickers to the bag. "Oh, and I have the natural pigments all ready to go. Turmeric, beet powder, and two kinds of tea. I even got some annatto from the dairy. They use it to color their cheddar cheese."

Bianca leaned forward. "I think we might be more excited about this than the kids."

I grinned. "I won't tell if you won't."

The bell over the entrance dinged. I glanced out and saw that Lucy and Colette had moved to the reading area, and Colette was rubbing a very happy Honeybee behind the ears.

I handed the bag back to Bianca. "Thanks for getting all this stuff. Can you stick it back in the office until we need it tomorrow night?"

"Sure," she said.

Adjusting my apron, I went out front to help the new customer. "Well, hello there," I said when I saw it was Randy from the firehouse.

Had he ever come into the bakery without Declan? I couldn't remember ever seeing him out of uniform, either. Today he wore pressed khakis, a stonewashed T-shirt with a soft-looking collared shirt over it, and loafers.

"Hi," he said, looking around. His eyes finally settled on me. "I thought your friend might be here."

Then I remembered when he'd first seen Bianca. "Oh, gosh. I totally forgot to tell her that you wanted to meet her," I said.

Right then, she came out of the kitchen. Randy gaped at her. She shot me a questioning look, and I saw her hand go into the pocket of her jacket where Puck the ferret had no doubt tucked himself out of sight.

"Um, Randy, this is Bianca Devereaux," I said. "And, Bianca—"

He cut me off. "I'm Randy Post. I work with Declan McCarthy." He stuck out his hand.

She hesitated before shaking it. "Hello."

"Hello," he breathed. "I saw you in here the other day."

Right before Orla died, I thought.

"And I knew then that I needed to see you again."

She looked confused.

"Please tell me that you'll go out with me," he said.

Subtle. I bit my lip to keep from smiling.

"Oh, gosh. I don't—" Bianca began.

He held up his hand. "It doesn't have to be a date date. Just a drink. Or coffee! I love coffee. We could have coffee here, if you'd like, just to talk and get to know each other. You know, so it's not weird or anything."

I coughed to cover a laugh. This guy had it bad. I couldn't blame him, of course. Bianca was gorgeous, smart, kind, and wealthy. But he knew only the first part.

Wait. Was that true?

"How did you know she was here?" I asked.

"I saw your car," he said to her as if she'd asked the question.

"My car." Her tone was flat. "Yes, men do seem to like that car." She drove a red Jaguar.

"How do you know what Bianca drives?" I asked.

"Declan told me. He told me all about you," he said.

Her eyes widened.

Randy continued. "About your little girl, and your work with charities in the community, and your wine shop. In fact, I was on my way there to introduce myself when I passed by and saw your car parked on Broughton Street. I figured you must be in here."

"I'm sorry," she managed. "I don't remember ever seeing you before."

He waved that away. "Oh, that's okay. It was just one time. But you'll like me if you give me a chance."

Well, at least he doesn't lack for confidence.

But Bianca was shaking her head. "I don't think so. I mean, I'm very flattered, but I'm going to pass. . . ."

"Mom," Colette said, coming up behind us with Lucy at her side.

Bianca turned and put her hand protectively on her daughter's shoulder.

"Can I take this home? It's a new Felicity story." She held up an American Girl book that she'd found in the library area. "And it's a choose-your-own-path, so I can pick my own ending!"

"I like Felicity, too," Randy said. "But I like Caroline just as much."

"Me, too!" Colette piped, then tipped her head to the side and looked up at him. "Wait. You don't read American Girl books, do you?"

He laughed. "I've sure read a few. I have a niece who's a little younger than you are. I know more than you might think about those books, not to mention Disney princesses and how to make friendship bracelets."

I looked over to see Bianca smiling at him.

Randy saw, too. His eyes flashed. "Come on, Bianca. Declan can vouch for me. And if you're feeling adventurous, there's a gallery opening tomorrow night that I think you might like. We can have that coffee date afterward if you enjoy yourself."

Colette raised her eyebrows and looked between them.

Bianca looked down at her, then back at Randy. "Okay."

"Okay!" he echoed. Then, to Colette: "By the way, my name is Randy."

"I'm very pleased to meet you," she said formally. "I'm Colette Devereaux."

They solemnly shook hands. Then he said, "Bianca, may I pick you up tomorrow? Around seven?"

She looked at Lucy. "Would you mind hanging out with Colette tomorrow after we dye eggs?"

My aunt's eyes twinkled. "Of course not. We'll have a grand time together."

Bianca and Randy arranged for him to pick her up at the bakery. He said good-bye to all of us and left with a bounce in his step. Colette went back to look for more books and finish up her toasted coconut cupcake. I poured out sweating glasses of mango sweet tea and joined Lucy and Bianca at a table.

"You do know him, don't you, Katie?" Bianca asked. I could tell she was wondering what she'd gotten herself into.

"Just through Declan. Seems like a good man, though."

"Easy on the eyes, too," Lucy observed.

Murmured agreement all around.

"But how old is he?" Bianca asked.

"Mid to late thirties?" I guessed.

She frowned. "That's what I thought, too. He's way too young for me."

"Oh, pooh," Lucy said. "You don't look a day over thirty-eight."

"Thank you, but that's not the point," our friend said. "I'm still forty-five. And that's not all. You know I have terrible luck with men. Even if I do end up liking him, I'll eventually tell him that I'm a witch, and he'll freak out like all the rest."

Lucy and I exchanged looks. "Not necessarily," she said. "There are men who are okay with it."

"Yeah, for all the rest of the spellbook club," Bianca muttered. "But apparently not for me." Puck stuck his head out of her pocket, nosed her wrist, and then slithered up her arm to comfort her.

My aunt shook her head. "Now you're just feeling sorry for yourself. You're never going to meet the right man if you don't give any of them a chance."

"Sounds like kissing a bunch of frogs," Bianca said wryly.

"Aphorisms exist because they're true." Lucy stood. "And no one said you have to kiss them all."

At five o'clock, we closed the bakery. In the office, I found Mungo had already climbed into my tote bag, ready to go.

"Nice try, buddy," I said. "But I'm afraid you're going to have to get a little more exercise before the day is out." I held out his leash.

His mouth turned down in a doggy frown, and he didn't budge.

"Come on," I coaxed. "It'll be a nice walk down by the water. You like walking by the river, remember? There are lots of birds to pretend you want to chase."

The terrier buried himself into the tote so far that I could see only his black nose and shiny brown eyes peering up at me.

"Anubis is coming," I said.

Yip!

He bounded out of the bag and to the floor, his back end wiggling with excitement.

I laughed. "That's better."

Jaida and the Great Dane were waiting for us out on the sidewalk. He was a regal beast, his coat a gorgeous brindle, and his intelligent eyes watched everything around him. When he saw Mungo, his mouth opened in a wide grin, and he bent his square head to touch noses with my little guy.

Greetings complete, we set off toward the river. Soon we reached the stairs that led from Factors Walk down to the river. Though it was only a bit after five o'clock, the pedestrian traffic was starting to increase. I led everyone down the tabby sidewalk, stepping around Bermuda-shorts-clad tourists and professionals heading to the local watering holes for an after-work cocktail. We had passed Rousakis Plaza and the waving girl statue before I spied the tattooed juggler.

He was already at work. Sure enough, he'd moved into the spot where Orla had told fortunes, and his audience was already twice the size of the one he'd had two nights before. As we approached, he dropped the four batons he'd been casually tossing and picked up seven balls. He began juggling them in a circle, then added in a few rolls across his neck, bounced a few off the top of his head, then behind him, continuously keeping in rhythm and never dropping a one. It was impressive, and he appeared to be enjoying himself.

We joined the edge of the crowd. Anubis sat beside Jaida, his enormous head even with her elbow. A few people looked at him sideways, but she didn't seem to notice. It probably happened to them all the time. Mungo sat beside the bigger dog, mimicking his posture in a comical way. My familiar had always respected the spellbook club's animals—except Heckle when he was particularly obnoxious—but I was pretty sure Mungo looked up to Anubis more than literally.

"Wow," Jaida said.

"Yeah," I agreed. "The guy's good. And he was right when he said more people would stop to watch him if he worked in this spot."

"This is where Orla was telling fortunes when you saw her, then?"

I nodded. "She told Lucy and me that she didn't want to work down here any longer. That she didn't like how her family had handled things with the other buskers and vendors. That's one of the reasons I want to talk to this guy."

With a flourish, he caught all the balls and dropped them dramatically into their case. A smattering of applause erupted from his audience.

He bowed and then straightened with a big smile on his face. "Thank you very much! I hope my humble abilities have entertained and amused you." He wiggled his eyebrows. "And if they have, I hope you'll drop a coin or two in the hat." He removed the porkpie hat from his head, revealing his hipster man bun, and tossed it brim up on the ground in front of him.

Several people filed by, dropping more dollar bills than coins. I hung back until everyone was gone. He'd started arranging the torches to light when I added my own dollar to the hat.

He looked up. "Thanks!"

"You bet. It looks like things are going better on this part of the riverfront."

"True that. This was my original spot. . . ." He

trailed off, and the smile dropped from his face. "You were here with them the other night."

"Only briefly. Having my fortune read, you know. I did see you confront Orla Black, though."

"She had it coming," he growled.

The way he said it made my stomach clench. I held up my hand. "Relax. What's your name?"

He scowled.

I waited.

"Spud."

I blinked. "Seriously?"

His chin came up. "Yeah."

"Okay, Spud. You said that someone in Orla's family threatened you."

Jaida, who had hung back, now walked up next to me.

Spud's eyes widened when he saw Anubis. "Is that your not-so-subtle way of telling me you're going to sic this monster on me if I don't move back to my old spot?"

Jaida looked at me. "What's he talking about?"

"I'm not sure," I said. "Spud, you can't really think *we're* trying to threaten you."

"You weren't 'having your fortune told,' honey. I saw you guys talking. You're friends." His chin came up again, and his shoulders squared. "Well, I'm not moving. You'll have to put me in the hospital first. And you can tell Orla Black and her goons that."

"Oh." I exchanged a glance with Jaida. "You haven't heard." *Or you're an excellent actor.* Watching him carefully, I slowly said, "Orla was hit by a car yesterday."

He stared at me for a long moment. Licked his lips. Looked away.

"And you're right—we were friends. She told me she wasn't going to work here anymore because she didn't like what her family had done to you."

Spud's shoulders slumped, and he looked down at the ground. When his eyes met mine, he seemed . . . frightened? "Really?"

"She didn't like it when you said you were threatened."

Jaida's head tipped to the side. "Who was it?"

"John Black and a couple of other guys. One of them was here the other night."

"What did he do?"

The juggler hesitated for a few beats. Then: "Told me if I didn't move to another spot, he'd make sure I did. Then he—" Spud made a face. "I know it sounds stupid, but he threw my balls all around. I had to go chase them down. A couple of them I never did find." His voice had lowered as he spoke, and his face was two shades pinker.

"That's horrible," I said. *And humiliating. The kind of thing that could spark a desire for revenge.*

But Spud the juggler hadn't been anywhere near Orla when she'd died. Still, he could have been closer than anyone knew. Lucy said Orla had looked away and stopped talking before stepping out. Had she seen Spud on the far side of Broughton Street? She'd just been talking about him, in a way. If he'd gestured for her to cross, she might have done so without checking traffic first.

Simple? Definitely. Possible? Maybe. Intentional? Unlikely.

"Listen, I'm not the only one those people threatened," Spud said.

My attention veered back from my speculations. "What do you mean?"

"Hannah. She makes jewelry and sells it down here most evenings. Sometimes during the day, too." He pointed at a young woman arranging shiny objects on a table a few hundred feet away. "She was set up nearby, but that guy Taber? He wanted her spot for his creepy ventriloquist act. He and some other dude told her to move. She didn't give them any argument." He shook his head. "That bunch is bad news."

Not all of them, I thought. I said, "Well, good luck with your show." We turned to go.

"I don't need luck," he said to our backs. "And hey?"

I paused and looked over my shoulder.

"I'm sorry about Ms. Black. I mean, we had our problems, but I didn't wish her any harm."

I nodded. "Thanks."

"Shall we have a chat with Hannah?" Jaida asked.

"Can't hurt," I agreed. "You think that guy's name is really Spud?"

"Maybe his parents liked to drink Bud Light," she said with a snort.

I grinned. "Or he was a really chubby baby." Then I sobered. "What do you think about Orla's son-in-law threatening him? Is he telling the truth?"

Jaida looked thoughtful. "I wouldn't be surprised. The competition for tourist dollars is fierce down here during high season. If the Black family worked together to get the prime spots, it would benefit them all."

"Hmm. I don't think Orla realized it was going on."

"I didn't really know her, but I trust your judgment. Honestly, the whole idea that they worked down here at all is kind of odd."

"Why?" I asked.

"Well, Cookie mentioned that the family has property here in town. And some of it is commercial, so they have an income from that. And then there's their concrete business. Construction is on the rise, so a business like that is bound to be doing well."

"Right. The concrete business. You said it was sued by a customer."

"It was. However, Aiden Black had done the subpar work, so he was the one who had to deal with the fallout. He's one of the owners, and he's the only one I worked with during the lawsuit."

"Huh. Aiden was on that list of beneficiaries."

"Yup," she agreed.

"Can you tell me if they lost? As in, does the business owe someone a bunch of damages?"

She shook her head and grinned. "I'm a better attorney than that. Aiden had to redo the work for free and pay court costs."

I shrugged. "Well, maybe it's more than a little lucrative to work down here. I have no idea how much Orla charged, but Spud already had fifty bucks, and it's still early."

But was it lucrative enough to kill for?

Chapter 10

Hannah, the jewelry maker, was young and fresh-faced, with a bright, hopeful smile. "Hello, ladies! Are you in the market for a bauble or two? Or perhaps you're hunting for a gift. No matter the occasion, I'm sure I have something that will suit."

A pair of silver dragonfly earrings glinted up at me from a bed of black velvet. "Those are gorgeous," I breathed, forgetting for the moment why we were there.

"Here, try them on." She handed them to me.

Jaida shot me an amused look as I held them up to my ears and looked in the mirror.

"I'll take them," I said.

"Terrific!" She beamed at me and reached for an old-school receipt book.

"You're Hannah, right?"

"Um, yeah?" She didn't sound too sure of it.

"Spud down the way told us about you," Jaida explained, fingering a chunky turquoise necklace.

"Oh! That was sweet of him."

"How's business?" I asked.

"Um, it's good," Hannah said, putting my purchase in a small bag.

I handed her a bill. "As good as it was before Taber O'Cleary made you move?"

She stopped what she was doing, and the smile faded from her face. "Spud has a big mouth."

Jaida ignored her. "Can you tell us what happened? He must have been pretty convincing."

"I, uh . . ." Suddenly she looked over our shoulders, and her eyes grew wide. "Um, hi, Mr. Black."

I turned to see the stocky, dark-haired man who had been standing in the yard with Fern the evening before when Cookie had taken us by Orla's house. My hand shot out.

"Mr. Black? Oh, gosh. You must be a relative of Orla's," I said a little too brightly.

Alarm crossed his face. "What would that be to you?" he asked.

My hand dropped like an anvil.

Jaida stepped forward. "We were friends of hers. Please allow us to extend our deepest sympathies for your loss." Unlike my birdlike chirp, her smooth voice was warm and confident.

Hannah looked confused, evidently unaware that Orla had died.

The man hesitated; then his expression softened, and he gave a single nod. "Thank you." Then he turned his attention to the young jeweler and his eyes narrowed. "Best be minding your own business, Hannah. Understand?"

She nodded vigorously, obviously intimidated. "Oh, yessir. Don't worry, sir."

He held her frightened gaze for a few more seconds, gave us another small nod, and strode away.

"Good Lord," I said when he was far enough away not to hear. "Who is that? The godfather of the Savannah riverfront?"

"That's John Black," Hannah said in a small voice. "And you're not far off."

With Declan on the first night of his shift, Mungo and I were on our own for supper. It happened every week, but I still missed my fiancé. I'd texted him after Bianca and Colette left the bakery, curious about whether he might have mentioned anything to Randy about Bianca's practice of the Craft. He responded that he hadn't felt it was his place—but that his friend seemed so smitten that she could have been on the FBI's most wanted list and he probably wouldn't care.

I hoped Declan was right, and Randy's infatuation wasn't just a flash in the pan. I wished I knew him a little better.

Let's just hope things work out and you get a chance to know him better.

The Coopersmiths were grilling in their backyard when I got home. As I unlocked the door, I heard Margie call something, then the high voices of the twins in response. The sound of Redding's deep, booming laugh followed me inside. I thought about dropping over and mooching a burger, but it was rare that he was home from his over-the-road trucking job for so many days at a time, and I didn't want to interrupt their family time.

Still, the smell of hot dogs and hamburgers made

my mouth water, inspiring me to fire up the little hibachi on my patio. I blended a sprinkle of Old Bay Seasoning into some hamburger. Then I chopped a red potato into chunks and tossed them with olive oil, finely chopped rosemary, salt, and pepper. I bundled the potatoes into a foil packet and tossed it on the hibachi, then went back into the kitchen to form the meat patties and make a green salad.

My familiar definitely approved of burgers for dinner. I topped his tiny version with cheese, pickle, and ketchup, as he preferred, and loaded mine up with leftover bacon and mashed avocado. After we'd eaten, I cleaned up the dishes and got out the ingredients for my favorite thinking food: peanut butter swirl brownies. They used to be my go-to sweet treat at home, but I'd fallen out of the habit of making them since I baked all day at the Honeybee.

My phone rang. When I saw it was Declan, I picked up right away.

"Hey, you," I said. "Everything all right?" We usually spoke later in the evening when he was working, unless the crew was out on a call.

"Everything's fine here. Slow day so far," he said.

"My favorite kind," I said with relief.

"I heard from my friend at the medical examiner's office about Orla Black's autopsy," he said.

I sank into a kitchen chair. "They've finished so soon? It must be slow over there, too. Which is good, of course . . ."

"Could be, but it also sounds like there was some pressure to complete the autopsy in record time and release the body."

"Pressure? From whom?"

"From higher up. Maybe they're just trying to be more efficient," he said.

"Or someone pushed for it. Orla's family, or maybe the insurance company." I told him about our visit from the insurance investigators that afternoon.

"Five policies? That's crazy," he said.

"No kidding. It makes you wonder—"

"Hey, hon, I'm sorry to cut you off, but we just got called out. But I thought you'd want to know the ME didn't find evidence of a heart attack or any other condition that could explain why Orla walked in front of that car."

"Oh. Wow. Okay, thanks."

I heard a ruckus in the background, and Declan said, "Gotta run. I'll try to call later. Bye." And he hung up.

His call had given me even more to think about as I mixed up the brownies and poured the batter into the pan. Then I dribbled the peanut butter topping on top and drew a skewer through it to create a swirly pattern and distribute it more evenly with the dark chocolate goodness beneath. As I worked, I pondered what I knew so far about Orla's death.

It wasn't much. She'd died suddenly, right in front of Lucy and me, and without any kind of warning. She'd had no reason that we knew of to step into the street, and I absolutely believed she hadn't killed herself intentionally. I'd listed the possible ways someone could have killed her to Jaida, but they were all long shots. I mean, what kind of magical spell could make someone walk into traffic? A voodoo curse, maybe?

Maybe it wasn't anything but a simple accident. I racked my brain. Maybe Orla suffered from attention deficit disorder and stopped talking in the middle of her sentence because she suddenly thought of something else. Or saw something across the street. Or someone. Maybe she'd lost her balance or slipped on the edge of the curb. I hadn't seen the exact moment when it happened, but it was possible.

Except . . .

Lucy would have noticed something like that, and she hadn't. The look she'd reported seeing in Orla's eyes before she stepped off the curb had really disturbed my aunt. Add in Mungo's behavior, the warning I'd received from my ghostly grandmother, and Declan's/Connell's assertion that there was something suspicious about Orla's death, and I really had to believe she had somehow been killed.

When I'd sneaked a look at the Firststate Mutual investigators' file on Orla, I hadn't seen how much each of the life insurance policies on Orla had been for. Still, several people were going to receive at least some money as a result of her death. And she'd been on the way to see a lawyer. Had it been the one who specialized in insurance cases? What had that been all about? Had she been trying to find a way to cancel one or more insurance policies on her own life?

Fern O'Cleary, Finn Black, John Black, Nuala O'Cleary, and Aiden Black.

Not Taber O'Cleary, but presumably, he would benefit from anything his wife, Fern, inherited. Plus, his daughter was the beneficiary of another policy. Mimsey said Ginnie Black was married to Finn, so she'd benefit, too. My unpleasant encounter with John Black earlier that evening would have put him smack-dab in the middle of the suspect list even if he hadn't been one of the five beneficiaries. And what about his son, Aiden, whose only claim to fame so far was that he'd been sued for shoddy concrete work?

I put the brownies in the oven and went up to the loft. This time, I chose an unopened deck of Rider-Waite cards that I'd purchased for spell work rather than the Kitchen Tarot I loved so much. Another spread wasn't going to tell me anything about Orla's fortune, but I wanted to see what the cards said regarding whether I should continue to look into her death.

Back in the living room, I settled on the couch. Mungo jumped up beside me and watched with interest as I opened the deck. As I shuffled the stiff cards, I deepened my breathing and tried to calm my mind. When I felt ready, I formed a clear question in my head.

Will I discover the truth about Orla Black's death?

I laid three cards out on the trunk that served as my coffee table.

The first card, which represented the past, was the Star. *Hope, renewal, inspiration, and the five senses.* The female figure on the front had one foot on land and one foot in the water—practical abilities and common sense on the one hand, and intuition and inner resources on the other.

Well, that fits me to a T since I moved to Savannah and began practicing the Craft. A down-to-earth witch, that's me.

The middle card, for the present, was the Hanged

Man. *Surrender, restriction, attainment of knowledge, letting go . . .*

And *sacrifice.*

I stared at the upside-down figure hanging from the tree of life for several seconds.

It's not a negative card. It's an opportunity card, one that may mean finding the truth. Sooner than later. At least that's what Jaida had taught me.

Sighing, I took a deep breath and tried to think positive. Then I turned over the third card and stopped cold. The Tower stared up at me. The white tower had flames shooting out of the windows, and people were leaping out of them, falling headfirst toward earth.

Danger. Crisis. Change. Destruction. Lies discovered through shocking truth. But ultimately liberation as a result of all that. For me? For Orla? For someone else entirely?

I silently cursed the murkiness of divination and my lack of skill with it. With a sigh, I packed the cards back into their box and rose to check on the brownies.

They were cooling in the pan when a knock sounded on the door. I opened a shutter and looked out the window to see Margie waving at me from the front step. She lifted a ginormous bottle of pink wine and waggled her eyebrows. Grinning, I unlocked the door, and she blew in.

"Hey, darlin'. I know your lover boy's gone for the night, and I didn't want you to get lonely."

"That's sweet of you," I said, immediately heading into the kitchen for glasses.

"Oh, who am I kidding? I need to take advantage of Redding being home for a whole week. He loves spending all kinds of time with the kiddos, and I love that he's doing it. I need a break sometimes, too, you know." She stooped and scratched Mungo on the head. "Hey, sweet pea. How's the dog's life?"

He grinned up at her and panted.

"And here I thought mothering was effortless," I said.

"Ha!"

"Actually, you do make it look that way. You're a great mom." I placed the glasses on the coffee table, along with a plate of still-warm brownies.

She grinned. "Thanks. But right now, I'm going to let Redding be a great dad while I have a drink with my friend. Maybe two." Then she spied the brownies. "Oh, you're kidding. Not the peanut butter kind." She picked one up. "Mm. Still warm? You knew I was coming?"

"I had a feeling." I gave her a little smile, unwilling to admit I'd made an entire pan of brownies for myself.

I gestured toward the couch, but she plopped into one of the wingbacks, put her half-eaten brownie on a napkin, and reached for a glass. As she poured her favorite libation, I scooped up the deck of tarot cards to put on a nearby shelf.

Not before she saw them, though. "Oooh! Do you read tarot, Katie?"

"Not really," I hedged, accepting the glass filled to the brim with sweet pink wine. I took a quick sip so it wouldn't spill.

"Well, you must, if you have the cards and all."

"I just like to get hints about things," I said, reaching for a brownie. "Sometimes a card will make me think differently about a situation, you know?"

She nodded and took a healthy swig. "Sounds good to me. But does that mean you won't read my cards?"

I sighed. "Bad idea. I'm not exactly qualified." Despite Jaida's training, I wasn't lying. Heck, I apparently wasn't even good at reading my own.

"Please?" She raised her eyebrows in playful supplication.

"What kind of reading did you have in mind?" I asked.

She looked blank.

"Do you have a question that you want answered?" I clarified.

"Oh. Let me see. . . ." Her forehead squinched in thought. Then her face cleared, and she beamed at me. "I guess there's nothing I'm too worried about."

"That's great!" I said, and started to put the cards away.

"So I think I just want to know my future."

My lips parted in surprise. "Your whole future?" I rolled my eyes. "Sure, Margie. No problem."

She grinned. "Okay, how about just next week?"

"Maybe you should just call dial-a-psychic," I said.

My friend sobered a little. "Come on, Katie. It's just for fun."

I considered. "Okay, I'll do a quick three-card reading." After all, if that was all I was ready to do for myself, how could I presume to do a more elaborate spread for Margie?

She shrugged and swallowed some wine. "M'kay."

I handed her the cards. "Shuffle."

She set down her glass and shuffled the deck with the surprising expertise of a dealer in a Las Vegas casino. Then she handed it back to me and retrieved her wineglass.

Taking a deep breath, I laid out the cards. This was the first time I'd read for anyone besides myself or Jaida as part of my tarot instruction.

Quickly, before I could back out, I laid the three cards on the coffee table. Then I turned the first one up. It was the Ten of Cups.

I smiled.

"Ooh. Is that good?" she asked.

"This is your past," I said. "And here I see a happy family."

She blew a raspberry. "That's not very interesting."

I gave her a stern look. "To those people who don't have a happy family, it's more than interesting. It's the holy grail."

Margie blinked, then looked pleased. "You're right. That Redding and I and the kids are happy as clams isn't news, but I really need to pay more attention to being grateful for it."

"Every day," I said.

"Every day," she agreed.

I turned over another card. It was the Judgment card.

She frowned. "That doesn't look good."

"Hmm. There are a lot of meanings, of course, and I'm no expert. But have you been thinking about making a change in your life lately?"

Her eyes widened. "How did you know that?"

I shrugged and stayed quiet. If she was happy with her family, it wouldn't be anything to disrupt that.

"I've been thinking about getting a part-time job

now that the JJs are in school. I thought maybe my mother-in-law could watch Baby Bart a few times a week if I find something that I like."

I couldn't help but grin. I was doing pretty well for a neophyte. "Sounds good. Let me know if I can help." Feeling cocky, I turned over the third card.

It was Death.

"Oh, no!" Margie said, standing so suddenly her pink wine sloshed in her glass.

I waved my hand. "Stop it. Death can be a great card. Sit."

She sat but still looked pensive. "I don't know how death can be a good thing."

"Well, it can be death of a situation you want to get out of—"

"I don't want to get out of my situation!" she wailed.

Grabbing her glass, I filled it again. "Drink this and listen to me. The Death card simply signifies change." I didn't mention how big the change might be.

"Change?"

I nodded. Then I had it. Tarot wasn't always about the huge things. "It might just be that you end up getting that part-time job you mentioned."

Visibly relaxing, she grabbed another brownie and sat back. "Whew. You had me worried there for a minute."

I gathered up the cards and returned the deck to the box. Then I took it over and put it on the shelf. No more readings for me tonight.

Margie cocked her head as I came and sat back down. "You seem kind of down tonight. Is everything okay?"

"Sure," I said, then paused. "Well, actually, there

was an accident in front of the Honeybee yesterday. I guess I'm a little shaken up about it. A woman was killed."

Her eyes grew round. "Oh, Katie, that's terrible! Tell me it wasn't someone you knew."

I grimaced. "Actually, that's why I had the tarot cards out. Her death made me think of them. See, she was a fortune-teller who worked down by the riverfront. Orla Black. She was one of our customers."

My neighbor was staring at me. "She died in a car accident?"

I blinked. "You knew her?"

Her head slowly bobbed. She looked down at the wineglass in her hand, then lifted it to her lips. After she swallowed, she said, "A little. One day a few years ago, my sister and I had lunch together. Afterward, we walked along the river, and Ms. Black was there. On a lark, I had her read my fortune. Oh, Katie, she was wonderful!"

"She could be quite theatrical," I agreed.

"No, that's not what I meant. She told me I was pregnant."

I leaned forward. "And you were?"

Margie nodded. "Baby Bart. It was too early for me to even think such a thing." She blushed. "I'm pretty sure he was conceived just two nights before she told me."

"Wow." I sat back and took a drink of wine myself.

Margie stayed for another hour, but bringing up Orla's death had taken the fizz out of the evening. The wine bottle was nearly as full when she left as when she arrived.

Outside, she lifted a hand in farewell. "The JJs are super excited about the egg-coloring party tomorrow night."

"It'll be fun," I called to her as she crossed my driveway to her house. Then I went inside to see what else I could find out about Irish travelers on the Internet.

And to very carefully avoid the image of the Death card that lurked in the back of my mind. Everything I'd told Margie was true. Or could be true. But usually the Death card boded more than just change. It predicted transformation on a large scale. Sometimes that transformation was for the best—and sometimes it wasn't.

Now I understood Orla's predicament when it had come to telling her clients' future. What if it was something they didn't want to know? And what if you didn't know enough to properly interpret the bits and pieces that came from the cards or anywhere else?

From now on, I'm sticking to good old spell magic. This divination thing blows.

I had a restless night fraught with dreams of tarot cards with no faces and the roar of car engines. At three thirty, I finally rose, dressed in running clothes, and stretched. Soon I was out on the street, pounding through my neighborhood in the cool darkness. Stars still glinted overhead in the deep velvet of the sky, fading from view near the almost full moon. It hovered above the horizon, its oblique light sufficient to illuminate the patches between the streetlamps.

A dog barked. A raccoon family perched along a front fence, the mother and two cubs my sole audience. There was no traffic, no cooking smells, only the fading fragrance of dryer sheets from someone's late-night laundry binge and the slightest hint of wood-smoke from the ashes of a hearth fire.

The silence quieted my dream-scrambled brain, and soon my steady footfalls triggered a flood of endorphins. By the time I'd completed my favorite four-mile loop, my mind was clear and my mood considerably brighter.

I showered and fixed Mungo's and my breakfast while my short hair air-dried. Luckily, he liked steel-cut oatmeal as much as I did. He preferred a splash of milk, while I added banana, roasted cocoa nibs, and smoked sea salt to mine.

A little before five, we were bopping downtown, the windows down in the Bug and rock music rolling out of the speakers. At the bakery, Mungo trundled into the office to go back to sleep on his club chair. I flipped on lights, found the same station I'd been listening to in the car, set the volume on the stereo system a little louder than we kept it during business hours, and started preheating the ovens.

When I was a little girl, Nonna had once told me that whatever happened, it was up to me to decide what to do with it. So for now, this morning, I was going to enjoy doing the work I loved so much in my very own bakery.

Chapter 11

"So how do you want me to cut out the centers?" Iris asked. "I could try a sharp paring knife."

"Here, try this," I said, handing her a one-inch circular cookie cutter. "It should be about the right size."

"Okay." Carefully removing the top knot off the muffin-sized brioche bun, she gently worked the cookie cutter down into the center and drew out the core to leave a tidy pocket. Then she reached for the pastry bag of lemon curd and piped the hole full of creamy goodness.

"Put a little more inside," I said, peering over her shoulder. "It will give the top something to adhere to."

Sure enough, when she put the top of the brioche back, it stuck nicely.

"Do I smell cinnamon?" she asked, sniffing the core she'd just removed before popping it in her mouth and slowly chewing. "Yep. Cinnamon," she mumbled around the rich mouthful. "Ummy."

"Cinnamon for healing and love, and lemon for . . . ?" I prompted.

She swallowed. "Lemon for purification and protection."

"Excellent."

"Cookie!" I heard Lucy greet our friend.

I waved from where Iris and I were working. "Hey."

"I'll start your breve," my uncle said from behind the espresso counter.

"Hi, Katie. Oh, no coffee for me this morning, Ben. I'll have herbal tea today."

"Really?" he asked. Cookie was known for her coffee consumption.

"Ginger, if you have it," she said.

"Uh, sure," he said.

"Thanks!" Cookie called as she wended her way back to the kitchen.

Having worked at the Honeybee for a few months soon after it opened, she appeared right at home as she leaned against the wall by the apron hooks. Today she wore a slightly longer skirt than usual and a sleeveless tie-dyed tunic. Her hair was woven into a loose braid that fell over one shoulder.

She grinned at me. "I'm on my way to show that town house over by Lucy and Ben's place. Sounds like this couple is really interested."

"You looked at a place in Ardsley Park?" Lucy asked as she joined us.

"Er . . . yeah. Another town house," I fumbled. I shot Cookie a look.

She returned it with an apologetic twist to her lips.

Lucy frowned. "That one down the street? Isn't that just like ours?"

Cookie and I nodded in unison. Iris' eyes darted between us.

"You didn't like it?" Lucy asked.

"I . . . um . . . we . . . of course we liked it," I stammered. "It's just that—"

"Declan really wants a yard," Cookie broke in. "So do Katie and Mungo, of course. I knew that ahead of time, but I thought I'd take the chance, you know. Some of those town houses have open areas behind them, but not that particular one."

Lucy smiled. "Of course. Don't worry, Katie. You'll find just the right place for your new life."

But I don't want a new life. I want the life I have, only married to Declan. I kept the thought to myself, though.

"And speaking of the right place, I have another one to show you," Cookie said.

"Declan—"

"I know he's on shift right now. But tomorrow he'll be free, right? I'll take you over there after work. It's on the edge of Paradise Park."

I nodded. "Sounds good. I'll let him know."

Iris let out a long sigh. "I don't know how you can pick, Katie. Decisions like that are so hard."

Turning to her, I asked, "Are you looking for a place to live?"

"Nuh-uh. I'm still living with Patsy." Patsy was her stepmother. "I have the whole basement to myself, so that works out fine. I can't afford a place of my own right now anyway. Not going to school. I was just talking about how hard it is to make any decision, you know? Like, major ones that you'll have to live with forever."

"Does this have anything to do with having to decide what program to settle into at SCAD?" Lucy asked. Iris had been attending classes at the Savannah College of Art and Design for three quarters and had yet to decide what to focus her considerable talents on.

She grimaced. "They want me to make a decision. So does Patsy. Says I need to stop being such a—a flibbertigibbet, she calls it—and focus on something I can turn into a career."

"Have you narrowed it down?" Lucy's voice was kind.

"A little," Iris said. "To photography or maybe motion media design. Or graphic design. Or maybe interior design." She rolled her eyes.

I laughed.

Cookie folded her arms. "You know you'll have to sacrifice."

My head jerked around so fast my neck popped.

"Every time you make a choice," she continued, "you sacrifice something. Usually more than one thing. It's just the way it works, Iris."

"Well, I don't like it," Iris said, her brow furrowed.

"Doesn't matter. And getting stuck in not liking it simply means you're not making a choice." Cookie smiled. "Which is, of course, also making a choice—and that means you're sacrificing something even if you don't see it. It's good that you tried a little of this and a little of that in school. That gave you information to base your decision on. But now you're just stuck, and by not committing to a major course of study, you sacrifice learning about something deeply, the satisfaction of accomplishment, overcoming challenges, and embracing the results."

I stared at the younger witch. Everything she said made perfect sense, of course. However, I had the feeling she wasn't trying to convince Iris so much as herself. As she spoke, Cookie seemed to be looking into the distance at something the rest of us couldn't see.

Was she thinking about how she'd dated so many men before deciding on Oscar and getting married? Or all the jobs she seemed to go through, trying to find the right one? She'd committed to marriage. Maybe real estate would turn out to be her long-term calling professionally.

"But it's going to change my life!" Iris wailed. "What if I end up hating what I choose? I won't be able to go back."

"Nonsense," Lucy said. "If you find you don't like whatever you decide to go into, you can make the decision to pursue something else. People do it all the time."

Cookie looked over at me. "It's true. There are very few things that you can't change your mind about."

I nodded, holding her gaze. "Like marriage?"

Iris said, "What about divorce?"

Cookie shook her head. "Marriage is a big decision, and you'd better be ready to stick with it. Still, divorce might be an option for some people."

But not for her, if I understood the subtext. Was something wrong between Oscar and her?

She broke into my speculation. "I was thinking more along the lines of children. That's one thing you really can't change your mind about."

"Well, that's true—" I began.

"Oh, my Lord! That's *it*!" Lucy exclaimed, her hands flying to her cheeks. Her gray eyes danced. "I've been trying to figure out what's different about you. How did I not see it before!"

My gaze sharpened, homing in on Cookie. "You're pregnant?"

A slow, shy smile blossomed on her face. She nodded.

"Ohmagod!" I rushed across the kitchen and hugged her.

Lucy was right behind me, and Iris did the little two-step she did when she was happy.

"What's going on in here?" Ben boomed in the entrance to the kitchen. Behind him, customers were staring.

"Cookie's expecting!" Lucy said.

"No kidding!" he said, striding over and enveloping Cookie in one of his signature bear hugs.

"I was going to wait to tell everyone together," she said once she'd extricated herself from our demonstrative congratulations. "So don't tell the rest of the spellbook club, okay? I want to do it myself."

"Deal." Lucy nodded decisively.

"Cookie has a bun in the oven?" a loud voice brayed from beside the register.

We all turned to see Mrs. Standish standing there, a delighted grin on her broad-featured face. One of our first customers and an avid supporter of the Honeybee, she wore a zebra-print turban over her gray curls and a Merlot-colored caftan over patent leather heels. She was brash, kind to animals, and one of the worst—or best—gossips I'd ever met.

"I do hope you'll invite me to the shower, girls!"

"Of course," Lucy said, hurrying out to serve Mrs. Standish her daily pastry.

Cookie, however, looked stricken.

I half smiled. "Sorry, hon. Some things you get to decide and some are decided for you. Good luck keeping a lid on your condition now."

After the lunch crowd had petered out, Lucy pulled me aside in the kitchen. "This morning you said you wanted to go over to Fern's and give her the book Orla bought her daughter. Iris is here all day, and the three of us can handle anything that comes up. You might as well go now."

I took off my apron and hung it on its hook. "If you're sure."

"Positive. I'm tempted to go with you myself."

"Why don't you?" I said. "You knew Orla better than I did, and you know Fern as well."

She hesitated, then gave a decisive nod. "I'll do it. And then we can stop by my house and pick up Honeybee. I left her at home this morning."

"Ben, Iris? You guys okay with us leaving for a while?" I called.

Iris waved her hand absently. "Sure."

Ben came over to where she stood at the coffee counter reading something. "What's that?"

"School catalog," she said, and glanced up at me. "Today I'm deciding what to focus on at school."

"Good girl," he said, and patted her on the shoulder. Then he looked up at us. "We'll be fine."

I gathered Mungo into my tote bag and met Lucy

on the sidewalk out front. Once we were all settled into the Bug and on our way, I asked, "Actually, how well do you know Fern?"

"She came into the bakery with her mother a few times. We chatted a bit—weather, books, cooking. She was always pleasant."

"So she and Orla got along?"

Lucy looked at me sideways. "I think so. Why?"

I half smiled. "Oh, you know. Sometimes mothers and daughters don't see eye to eye on everything."

"Like you and Mary Jane?" she asked.

It was true that my mother and I had had a bit of a falling-out when I started practicing the Craft. She'd spent a lot of time and even sacrificed her own practice to protect me from what she thought would get me in trouble in our little town of Fillmore, Ohio. When I'd learned she'd kept my heritage a secret, I'd been furious. At the same time, she'd been angry at Lucy for telling me, and unhappy when I embraced my gift. It had taken a while, but since then we'd made peace with each other.

"You know, if anything, Mama and I are closer now than ever before," I said.

"Mm."

I laughed. "Oh, I know that sister of yours isn't exactly easy to get along with." With a pang, I thought of how awful it would feel if she was suddenly taken from me as Fern's mother had been from her. Silently, I vowed to give my parents a call soon.

She patted my knee. "I'm glad you two are getting along."

I guided the car into her neighborhood, and Lucy's head turned as we drove by her town house. "Yes, there's Honeybee in the window. She'll be happy to come back with us for a few hours this afternoon."

Sure enough, I saw the tabby cat's orange-striped head swivel as my aunt's familiar watched us go by.

I pointed out the town house Cookie had shown us, glad that Lucy hadn't taken offense that I didn't want to live there. Then we turned onto Paulsen, and I pulled to the curb across the street from the Black family compound.

"Love the bright doors," Lucy observed as we exited the vehicle. "That looks like Fern in front of the orange one."

She was sitting on the front steps, elbows on her knees and chin cupped in both hands. The man sitting next to her could have been her twin except for his redder hair. He'd been the unicyclist we'd seen on the riverfront.

"It is," I said. "And I assume that adorable little girl on the front walkway is the reason we're here."

My aunt nodded. "That's Nuala."

"Do you know who that is?" I said, referring to the woman kneeling beside Nuala. Their heads were close together, and I spied lengths of chunky sidewalk chalk in their hands.

"I don't think I've seen her before."

Mungo hopped down to the floor and out to the street as I reached into the backseat for my tote. The book Orla had bought Nuala lay nestled on top, wrapped carefully in the bag from the Fox and Hound. Together, the three of us crossed the street and started up the walkway.

Fern straightened when she saw us, but didn't get up. She looked over her shoulder at the screen door behind her, then leaned toward her companion. Her lips moved slightly, and he shook his head. His expressionless eyes never wavered from our approach.

We paused beside the sidewalk artists. They'd drawn an elaborate forest scene, with green trees filled with vividly colored birds, butterflies, bees, beetles, and even a spider in the middle of its web. The woman tipped back on her heels and raised her face to us, but Nuala barely gave us an unsmiling glance before continuing to apply bright azure chalk to an insect wing.

Then I realized she was putting the finishing touches on a dragonfly. Lucy gave me a nudge as she noticed the same thing, and Mungo padded over to sit beside it.

That got the girl's attention. A noise of delight escaped from her throat, and she dropped the chalk in order to pet my familiar. The blue hue immediately transferred to the fur on his head, giving him a punk look.

I laughed.

"Hi." The woman smiled. "What can we do for you?"

My aunt smiled back. "I'm Lucy Eagel, and this is my niece, Katie Lightfoot. We knew Orla, and wanted to offer our condolences to the family."

She stood and stuck out her hand. "I'm Ginnie Black." She had friendly blue eyes in a wide square-jawed face, smooth tanned skin, and a slight cleft in her chin. Her hair was the color of pine straw. She reminded me of Margie, and I wondered if she had the same Scandinavian genes. "And this is Nuala."

My aunt nodded. "Hi, Nuala. Do you remember me? We met at the Honeybee Bakery."

The little girl nodded, but she didn't say anything. Her dark eyes were huge beneath the shock of black hair, and when she unhinged from her cross-legged position to stand beside her aunt, she was all elbows and knees. She crowded next to Ginnie and watched us with careful eyes.

"And the little black dog is named Mungo," I said.

A smile broke onto her narrow face as she looked down at where he stood, inches away from her sneaker. "Mungo. That's a good name."

His mouth opened in a doggy grin.

Ginnie said, "I take it you know Fern and Finn?"

We followed her to where the siblings sat. They were on the top step, so we were nearly at eye level. "Hi, Fern," I said. "We met down by the riverfront the other night."

She nodded. "I remember. Hello, Lucy."

"And, Finn, I don't believe I've had the pleasure," I said.

More introductions were made, followed by murmurs of sympathy. I watched Finn. He looked even more like Orla than his sister did, with pupils the color of dark-roast coffee and an echoing tilt to his upper lip. He watched me back, eyes probing. And perhaps more than his eyes. When I tried to get a hit from him, there was nothing. Same with Fern. Had they inherited their mother's gift? It wouldn't have surprised me a bit.

"Thank you for stopping by," Finn said. "We appreciate it."

Was he dismissing us?

Chapter 12

I needn't have worried.

Finn turned to the screen door and opened it. "I have some business to attend to. If you'll excuse me?"

"Of course," I said. He held eye contact for a few more seconds than necessary, then smiled a perfunctory smile and went inside.

Lucy turned to Nuala. "I love your drawings. Would you show me more?"

The girl looked to her mother, who smiled and nodded. "She's very talented."

"I can see that," Lucy said as she and Nuala went out to the yard with Mungo.

I took Finn's place on the steps by Fern. Ginnie left us to join the others. I turned my head to look at Orla's daughter. The tip of her nose was red, and the skin around her eyes was pinched with strain. I caught a wisp of nervous energy under her calm mask. Grief, of course. Or guilt? How much money would she be getting from her mother's life insurance policy?

The thought made me feel mean and dirty. I pushed it away and reached into my tote bag.

"I know it's early days to drop by like this, and I hope it's not too much of an imposition. I wanted to give you something, though."

Curiosity sparked behind her eyes.

I handed her the wrapped book. "Orla had just picked this up at the Fox and Hound when . . . when Lucy and I saw her. It's a present for Nuala. I didn't know whether it was for an occasion, like a birthday or something, so I thought you should have it. I know Orla was excited about giving it to her."

Fern's eyes welled, and she blinked rapidly. Drawing out the book, she looked down at the cover for several seconds without speaking. Then: "Mother was always telling Nuala stories about the old country." She gave a little laugh. "Not that she ever lived there. Only visited once. But her heritage was very important to her." Her head came up, and she met my eyes for the first time. "You were there when she died, weren't you?"

Slowly, I nodded. "Lucy and I both."

"Did she suffer?"

"I don't think so. Truly."

She looked out at her daughter. "That's good." She took a deep breath. "You know, I'm trying to remember how Mother always thought we never really died. That we only moved to the next stage of things."

Tentatively, I put my hand on her arm. "My family believes something very similar."

Something rustled on the other side of the screen

door behind us. I craned my neck to see, but couldn't make out anything through the mesh.

Fern sighed and gently disengaged her arm, then rubbed her temples with her fingertips.

Yip!

A giggle erupted from the front lawn. Nuala and Mungo were running in circles. Her arms were flung open, as if she was trying to fly. She ducked and weaved, and my familiar ran around her.

Beside me, her mother smiled. "Just what she needs."

Lucy and Ginnie returned to where we were sitting. My aunt said, "Your daughter really is artistic. You know, this evening after we close the bakery, we're having an egg-coloring party. Perhaps she'd like to come."

"That's a great idea!" I said.

"Colette Devereaux will be there," Lucy continued. "Ginnie here was her teacher last year, I think."

Ginnie nodded. "Colette's a good kid."

Fern looked torn. "I don't know. . . ."

Her sister-in-law plopped down beside her. "I know you don't feel like going out. But Nuala needs to do something fun with other people. Why don't I go with her?"

"Would you?" Fern sounded relieved. "I know it would be good for her, but I just can't bring myself . . ." She trailed off.

Ginnie bounded up. "No worries. Just tell me where and when. Nuala? Can you come here?"

Mungo leaning against her leg, the girl looked shyly at Lucy and me when Fern told her about the egg-dyeing party.

"We have all sorts of glitter and stickers and ribbons, plus other stuff," I said.

Finally, she looked at her mother, then offered a little smile. "It sounds like fun."

Lucy gave Ginnie the details as I gestured Mungo into the tote and stood. "By the way," I said to Fern, "your mother ordered another book from Croft over at the Fox and Hound. I think she prepaid for it. You might want to check with him."

"For Nuala?" Fern asked.

Shaking my head, I said, "No. I think it was some kind of travel guide? No, not a guide. *The Best Places to Live in California* or something like that."

The door opened, and John Black stood on the threshold. A huge bullmastiff filled the rest of the space. Fern's husband, Taber, hovered behind him.

When John saw me, his eyebrows rose just a fraction, but the rest of his face remained impassive. Fern scrambled to her feet and introduced us.

"You're the one who was asking questions down at the riverfront yesterday," he said without so much as a hi-how-are-you. The bullmastiff bared his considerable teeth. In the tote beside me, a low grumble issued from the back of Mungo's throat.

Putting my hand on my familiar's back to calm him, I tried to keep my voice casual. "I don't know about questions. But yes, that was me at the jewelry booth."

His lips twisted, and he turned to Fern. "We have a whole backyard for Nuala to play in. Why is everyone out here on the street?"

Fern's jaw set, but Ginnie stepped forward and said

cheerfully, “We wanted to draw with chalk. There’s no sidewalk in the back.”

“Want to see what we made?” Nuala asked. She tugged at his hand.

John’s face softened. “Sure.” He looked down at his dog. “Sit. Stay.”

The dog sat, right there in the doorway. Taber had to maneuver around it to come out on the step.

“Hi. I’m Taber,” he said to Lucy and me. I could tell from his expression he was trying to place us.

“We’ve met,” I said. “Down at the riverfront.”

He snapped his fingers and smiled. Then the smile dropped, and he put his arm around his wife. “The night before Orla left us. If only we’d known. Let me tell you, ladies. Hold those you love close, because you never know what might happen.”

Fern put her arm around his waist and laid her head on his shoulder.

We took that as our cue to leave. After offering to help with anything if we could, Lucy, Mungo, and I went back to the car.

“What did you think?” I asked my aunt as I drove to her house.

“Hm. Ginnie is nice. One of those open-book sorts, you know.”

I nodded. “More than the others.”

“They’re grieving Orla’s loss. Besides, didn’t Mimsey say it would be difficult to get the family to talk to you?”

“She wasn’t wrong. They didn’t even ask us inside.”

“That doesn’t mean anything,” Lucy admonished.

“Then why do I have the feeling that if we hadn’t

caught them out in the yard, no one would have answered the door when we knocked?"

One side of Lucy's mouth pulled back in a half grimace. "And I bet you're not wrong about that."

"Do you think any of them could have killed Orla—or somehow arranged for her death?"

My aunt looked sorrowful. "I hope not."

"Well, I hope not, too. But every one of the beneficiaries of Orla's life insurance policies was right in front of us today, except for John's son, Aiden. Greed is an awfully good motive for murder."

She frowned. "And blood is thicker than water, Katie. Maybe you should be looking for someone besides Orla's family."

"Who? Vera Smythe, the woman who was so mad about the fortune Orla gave her?" I'd told Lucy about encountering her at Vase Value. "Spud the juggler? Really? The guy . . . huh. Maybe he *is* someone to follow up on."

"Who?" she asked.

"The man who was driving the car. Maybe he did it on purpose." I pulled up in front of her house. Inside, Honeybee disappeared from the window, leaving the curtain swinging in her wake.

"Why would he hit her on purpose?" Lucy asked.

"I'm not sure. What if they had some kind of connection? Or . . . what if someone hired him to kill her!"

Lucy looked skeptical. "That seems a little far-fetched."

"Do you have a better idea?" I snapped. "Because I'm starting to wonder why I'm investigating this at all. No one else seems to think Orla was murdered."

She smiled at me. "The spellbook club does, honey. I know it's frustrating. Is there any way I can help?"

"Sorry," I muttered, feeling like a heel. "I'll let you know if I think of anything."

"Good." She nodded and went inside to retrieve her feline familiar.

We were halfway back to the bakery when the sneezing started. First, it was just once, then twice in a row. Within minutes, I was snorting and sneezing and sniffling like crazy. We rolled down all the windows, and I soldiered on.

Mew.

The plaintive sound broke my heart. I looked in the rearview mirror through watery eyes and saw Honeybee crammed into the corner of the backseat as far away from me as possible. She regarded me with a worried expression furrowing her striped brow.

"Don't worry," I told her, and sneezed again. "I'll be okay. I have some medication at the bakery that'll clear this right up."

"Have you been taking your potion?" Lucy asked, looking as concerned as her cat.

I shook my head and pulled into a parking space. "I ran out. Was going to make more tonight." Opening my door, I staggered out.

Lucy exited more gracefully. She picked up Honeybee, who crawled up to drape around her shoulders. I reached in and pulled out my tote, with Mungo inside.

"The perfect night for it," my aunt said as she

strode toward the bakery with her tabby stole. "Full moon and all. The full Pink Moon, at that."

"Uh-huh," I said, and sneezed.

Back in the office, I rummaged through the desk drawer to find my over-the-counter allergy medication. I popped a couple of pills and dropped the bottle into my tote bag so I could access it whenever I needed it. Then I settled in at the computer while I waited for the drug to take effect. Everything had been copacetic out front when Lucy and I had walked in, and it wouldn't do for customers to see me sneezing and sniffling in the kitchen. They'd think I was ill or, worse, assume I'd sneezed in their food.

I checked e-mail, paid a few invoices online, and ordered some bulk spices. And sneezed. Twice. The worst was over, but I still had an excuse to hole up with Mungo for a few more minutes. So I typed "John Black" into the search engine and waited.

And got approximately sixty thousand suggestions. It was a common name. Trying again, I typed in "John Black, concrete, Savannah, GA." That resulted in a link to the Web site for Black and Sons Concrete. The Web site itself was just as boring as one might expect from a construction contractor. There were testimonials from customers extolling the skill with which their foundations or driveways or patios had been poured. Sighing, I scrolled down through the other offerings.

Most didn't have anything to do with the John Black I was interested in. Then I saw a reference to a lawsuit against the company. There was only the one, but that didn't mean there weren't more instances of disgruntled customers who had settled. Aiden Black wasn't named personally, but Jaida had mentioned that he'd been the one in court.

Still, no matter how I tried, I couldn't see how it could have anything to do with Orla's death.

I flipped over to the image results for John Black. There was only one that showed the man Lucy and I had encountered an hour earlier. Grinning widely, he had his arm thrown around another man with similar features. I clicked on the image, and it took me to another site.

It was almost exclusively photos, but I could cobble together some sense from their content and captions. Someone had created the Web site to chronicle a gathering in Florida eight years before. There were ancient Winnebagos and shiny Airstream trailers along with a few high-end RVs. Scattered among them were caravans much like in the pictures in the book *Maeve, Traveler Girl.* They could have come from centuries before. There was even a photo of a makeshift paddock with milling horses and donkeys.

It was, for lack of a better term, an Irish traveler convention at Lake Kissimmee State Park campground. In general, the people looked like any other campers. The shocking thing was that John Black looked really happy, his head thrown back in laughter. According to the caption, his arm was around his younger brother, Mike.

Orla's husband.

But as interesting as that was, it didn't give me any

new information about Orla's death. Frustrated, I clicked through a few more pictures.

I paused at the one of Ginnie Black standing on the edge of a clearing, surrounded by children about the age that she taught at Gould Elementary. She had on a silly hat with a funny striped flower springing out of the side, and her eyes were dramatically wide as she held out a bouquet of flowers toward her audience.

I zoomed in. Correction. A bouquet of paper flowers.

Okay, so she was putting on a show. Apparently, they all had their skills in that regard. A few more clicks confirmed it, as the camera had caught Taber and his ventriloquist's dummy. What was its name? Cobby, Fern had called it. And there was Orla in her fortune-telling regalia—only with the grandma bun and no fancy fedora. She looked like our Orla, all dressed up. I wondered whether she told the fortunes of her own tribe. There was a picture of Finn on his unicycle, and a woman in mime makeup who I thought must have been Fern. Finally, another picture of John Black, this time in tails and a top hat. He was swinging a pocket watch in front of a woman's face, and his other hand was splayed wide in a theatrical gesture. The woman was laughing, her hand out as if to playfully push him away.

A few more clicks revealed another picture of the woman, this time with "in memoriam" in the caption beneath.

Like Orla, John Black had lost his spouse.

I sighed, starting to feel like I was no better than a stalker. I shut down the computer and went out to help the others.

Chapter 13

As soon as I stepped out to gather the tubs of dirty dishes from the busing station by the reading area, I heard a familiar voice and looked up.

Steve Dawes and Angie Kissel were standing by the coffee counter. They'd been dating ever since I'd cleared her of murder in November. I'd met both Steve and Declan within days of moving to Savannah, and I had to admit that for a while I'd been very attracted to the blond-haired, brown-eyed reporter for the *Savannah Morning News*. Not to mention, he was a druid and still maintained that he'd known I was a witch even before I did. Maybe he was right. Either way, he'd pursued me for months, even after I'd chosen to date Declan exclusively. Indeed, Steve had crossed a few lines to try to get his way, and while I was willing to forgive, I wasn't dumb enough to forget.

His excuse was that we were supposed to be together because we both practiced magic. Well, it turned out Angie did, too. In fact, she'd been Mungo's former witch before he'd become my familiar. It made for some complicated emotions when she and Steve were around, but mostly I was just glad that Steve and Angie had found each other.

Ben started up the espresso machine, and I knew he was making Steve's dry cappuccino. I'd never seen him drink anything else. It looked like Angie had opted for a simple Americano and a raspberry muffin.

With her elfish features, petite build, and dark spiked hair, Angie wouldn't have looked out of place in *The Lord of the Rings*. Steve gazed down at her with warm adoration. I remembered being on the receiving end of that look, and a slight pang went through my sternum at seeing it directed at her. Funny, I hadn't been upset when Steve had been engaged for a short time. I'd been concerned, of course. Samantha had obviously been wrong for him. I mean, I *knew* something was off about her. And I'd been right.

But Steve hadn't ever looked at her like that, I realized with a jolt. He and Angie were the real deal.

Good. It'll keep them both out of my hair. Steve's persistence was nice for the ol' ego, but remember that it was a pain in the patootie, too.

Besides, I'd chosen Declan. And I was happy that I had. More than happy.

I heard Cookie's voice in my mind. *Choice always comes with sacrifice. It's the way of the world.*

Well, that was one sacrifice I'd make over and over again. Even now, a year and a half after Declan and I had been together, hearing the sound of his voice or seeing him walk into a room made my pulse quicken and my heart smile. It was one of the reasons I knew I wanted to spend the rest of my life with him.

I could only hope I'd feel half as good about the sacrifice Orla had predicted.

Angie looked up and saw me. "Oh my! Katie, are you all right? We heard what happened. Have you been crying?" A worried frown creased her face.

I smiled. "It's just allergies. The medication has kicked in, though. I'll stop sniffling any minute."

"You sure?" Steve asked, his voice deep with concern.

Angie gave him a sharp look, and Ben gave me one. Always Declan's advocate, he didn't care for Steve.

"Yup. Just fine." I changed the subject. "How're things with you guys?"

Steve ignored the question. "So, this accident out front—as Angie said, we heard what happened. Then I learned that the victim was a fortune-teller." He quirked an eyebrow. "Are you at it again?"

I debated for a moment, then moved closer. "The police are calling it an accident."

Steve and Angie exchanged a look. "That doesn't exactly answer his question," she said.

I licked my lips. At least I didn't have to explain myself to these two. "There are a few aspects to what happened that make me think it wasn't an accident at all."

Angie's eyes grew round. "Murder?" she whispered.

"It's possible. I'm trying to find out."

"Is there anything we can do to help?" Steve asked.

I thought for a moment. "Don't suppose you know anything about Black and Sons Concrete."

Steve grinned. "Not yet."

I couldn't help grinning back as Ben handed him his drink.

The two lovebirds went to find a seat, and I turned toward the reading area again. A woman sat curled in one of the poufy brocade chairs, a steaming cup in her hand and a half-eaten blackberry thyme muffin on a plate beside her. Her head was bent over the book in her lap, but when she raised it to take another bite, I recognized Vera Smythe.

Surprised, I went over to her. "Hi there. Looks like you enjoyed that muffin enough to stop in and get another."

She blinked, then recognized me. "Oh, they're delicious."

I saw the book that had captured her attention. *What to Expect When You're Expecting a Divorce.* My heart sank.

She saw me looking and tucked the book down in the cushion next to another one, whose title I couldn't make out. A wan smile played on her lips. "This place is lovely. I'm so glad you told me about it. And all these books are really here for the taking?"

"Absolutely." I nodded. "If you have something you want to donate, that's fine, but it's not required."

"What a handy thing to have in a bakery. I'll certainly be back."

That loud voice I knew so well came floating over from the register. "I forgot to ask when I was in before! When is Cookie's little darlin' due?" Mrs. Standish boomed.

"I'll leave you to your reading," I said to Vera before hurrying over to help Lucy.

"Mrs. Standish!" I exclaimed. "Fancy seeing you here twice in one day!"

"Oh, Lord, Katie. I couldn't stay away. I simply must have another half dozen of those chocolate chip cookies I picked up this morning. They are something else! So good that I finished off the first six before Skipper Dean even got a taste." She was referring to her paramour, a short, slight man who managed her excesses with remarkable aplomb. She waggled her eyebrows. "And I wouldn't want to deny the skipper such a treat."

"Let me wrap them up for you." Lucy reached for a bag with the Honeybee logo of a stylized tabby cat on the side.

"Now," Mrs. Standish said to me. "I understand the other day there was an accident out front."

I made a face and nodded.

"Did you see it?"

Lucy frowned and silently began retrieving Mrs. Standish's cookies from the display case.

Mrs. Standish was nice as pie, but she did have a salacious streak. Over her shoulder, I saw Steve and Angie watching. Wisely, they were staying out of the conversation.

"It was tragic," I said flatly.

"Oh, heavens. Yes, tragic. Horrible, horrible."

"I'd just seen the woman who was killed the evening before," Vera said from behind me.

I turned to see her clutching the two books she'd chosen.

"She had a booth down on River Street," she said. "She read my fortune."

"Really! Oh, my goodness," Mrs. Standish exclaimed. "Do you think it will come true?"

For a moment, I thought Vera was going to cry. Then she rallied. "It already has."

Ugh. Poor thing.

"Well, I must be going," Vera said. "I'll be back, though."

"Glad to hear it," I said.

She began to leave but stopped herself. Digging in her purse, she extracted a card and handed it to me. "Give the salon a call next time you're looking for a haircut. We can help with those eyebrows, too. See you later." She walked to the door and pushed it open.

I stared after her, then turned to Lucy. "What's wrong with my eyebrows?"

"Nothing, honey. Your eyebrows are lovely."

Mrs. Standish peered into my face. "Well, that left one is a little shaggy. Might as well take the woman up on her offer."

I felt my face grow warm. Had Steve and Angie heard? They didn't seem to be paying attention.

"Here you go, dear." Lucy held out a bag to Mrs. Standish.

The other woman took it and said conspiratorially, "I must ask—what on earth makes a simple chocolate chip cookie taste like something the angels sent down from heaven?"

I looked around as if the walls might have ears. "You promise you won't tell?"

She made a zipping motion over her lips.

Leaning close, I whispered, "We brown the butter that goes into the batter."

"Oh!" She shuddered with delight. "That's ingenious." Beaming, she paid Lucy and said good-bye.

"You know she's going to tell everyone our secret now," my aunt said.

"Probably. Better than obsessing over Cookie's 'bun in the oven,' though."

Lucy laughed.

"Or giving me grooming advice," I grumbled.

We closed the bakery at five, and Ben got ready to leave. "I'm stopping by Sweet Spice to grab my supper, then spending the whole evening camped in front of the television watching the Braves," he said with a grin.

"I'm jealous," I said. "I love their food." Sweet Spice had fantastic Caribbean dishes.

Lucy gave him a kiss. "Enjoy yourself, my love. I'll be home in a few hours, and Colette will be with me. We'll be sure not to disturb you."

He gazed down at his wife with evident adoration. "Don't be silly. I forgot she was coming over. Do you want me to pick up some extra food for you?"

Her eyes danced. "Well, if you insist. How about some jerk chicken?"

"You've got it," he said.

Bianca and Colette came in then.

"Hello, young lady," Ben said to Colette. "I understand you'll be spending part of the evening with us."

"Yes, sir. My mother has a hot date."

Bianca bit her lip to keep from laughing.

My uncle, on the other hand, didn't hold back. "Ha! Well, you're in luck, because I'm cooking tonight. And that means takeout from Sweet Spice. How does some jerk chicken sound?"

"Actually, I prefer their curried shrimp," the little girl said.

Ben raised his eyebrows. "All righty, then. I'll see you two ladies after your egg-dyeing party." He kissed Lucy again and left.

Margie and the JJs were the next to arrive. "Hi, Katie! Hi, Lucy!" the twins said in unison as soon as they came in the door. They grinned up at me, identical eyes bright and their cheeks tan from running around in the sunshine. White blond hair like Margie's stuck out from under Jonathan's baseball cap, while Julia's was drawn back into a ponytail that bounced every time she moved her head.

"Hey, guys." I gestured to a big table in the corner. "You can toss your stuff over there. Everyone can."

The entrance bell jingled. We turned to see Ginnie Black and Nuala in the doorway. Nuala's eyes were wider than ever in her thin face as she looked around at the group.

"Come on in," I said. "We're just about to get started."

Lucy took a step but then hung back as Bianca's daughter walked over to the newcomers. "Hi, Ms. Black," Colette said.

Ginnie nodded. "It's good to see you. How's third grade going?"

"Okay. I like my teacher." She turned to the older girl. "Hi. I'm Colette. You must be Nuala." The way she said it, she might have been the older of the two.

Nuala nodded. "Hi."

"Don't be scared. Everyone's real nice. And Katie and my mom—" She pointed. "That's my mom. Her name's Bianca. She told me you were coming. Anyway, they have all sorts of fun stuff set up in the back."

"Okay," Nuala said with a little smile.

"Have you ever been in the kitchen of a professional bakery?"

"Huh-uh."

"It's pretty cool. Come on." The two girls went into the kitchen. They could have been sisters from the back, with their slight figures and dark hair.

Jonathan and Julia exchanged glances, nodded at each other, and followed.

"Well, I guess Colette took care of her own introductions," I said with a smile. Ginnie had been watching her niece with an indulgent smile. Now she said, "She's a good kid. A gem in class, and smart as they come."

My eyes cut to Bianca. Quiet pride shone on her face.

I introduced Margie to Ginnie, and they exchanged pleasantries as we followed the kids back to the egg-dyeing stations.

"Okay, everyone," I said. "Over there in the corner, we have natural colors set up. Here in front, the regular egg dyes from the store. Then at this end, lots of decorations for the eggs once they're dry." I walked over to another counter. "And we have some other experiments to try here."

Colette and Nuala craned their necks to see.

"I thought we could try some tie-dye and marbling," I explained. "Now, everyone grab an apron and put it on. Don't worry about staining them—I chose them just for tonight."

"Green," Jonathan said.

I turned toward him. "Sure. We have green dye."

"That's all I want. Green. Lots and lots of green eggs. All colors of green."

Lucy's head tipped to the side, and I could tell she was amused. "How come?"

"For the ham."

Margie said, "He rediscovered Dr. Seuss on National Reading Day a few months ago."

My aunt's face cleared. "Of course. Sam-I-am. Okay, buddy. Let's go get you set up with some green dye. How about making some of the eggs striped?"

Jonathan nodded, the picture of seriousness. "That would be good. As long as they're green."

Margie rolled her eyes and led Julia over to the cups of dye mixed with vinegar that I'd already set up. Nuala and Colette had already started dunking eggs in the metallic versions. Vaguely, I recalled my magpie stage as a tween, when I loved anything that shone or shimmered.

"You said you have some natural dyes?" Ginnie asked. "I've seen eggs dyed with green or black tea. Like that?"

I nodded and waved her over to the corner. "Like that, only with a few other colors. I did brew up some tea, and I like the results, I guess. Only . . . they're kind of dull."

She peered over my shoulder at the eggs I'd already dipped a few times. "They look like they came from the farmers' market. Like eggs actual chickens would lay."

"Right. That's it. They're white eggs that look like

brown eggs now, or those green-blue eggs Araucana chickens lay. No wonder they don't seem like Easter eggs."

"Well, Araucanas are also called Easter egg chickens," she said.

I looked at her sideways.

She shrugged. "My mom grew up on a farm."

"And your dad?" I asked, stirring the mess of purple cabbage leaves that were soaking in hot water and vinegar. They were supposed to give off a blue dye. Weirdly, the red onion skins produced a green color once the vinegar was added.

"Detroit," she said. "Three generations of automobile workers on that side."

Putting an egg into a wire holder, I said, "So you're not part of . . . the . . . uh . . ."

Ginnie balanced an egg in another holder, then dunked it into a yellow-orange mixture of turmeric and paprika. "The 'family'? Nope. I'm the black sheep of the Black family. Of my own as well. My parents acted like marrying Finn was the same as running off and joining the circus or something."

"Well," I said, treading carefully. She seemed willing to talk about her in-laws, but I didn't want to alienate her. "They do have, er, circuslike aspects to them."

I needn't have worried that she'd take offense, because she laughed. "You mean the sideshows? Ventriloquism and unicycles, shell games and"—she sighed—"fortune-telling. Poor Orla."

"Poor Orla," I echoed, remembering how her face had lit up when she spoke of Nuala. I dipped my egg into the pink dye I'd made from crushed amaranth flowers.

"As if I didn't earn my spending money in college with a magic act," Ginnie said. "They sure didn't seem to mind that."

"Who?"

"My parents," she said. "That's how I met Finn. In Florida."

I must have looked confused, because she said, "The magic act. I worked onstage a bit, but I had a street show, too. Made more money working the tourists, you know."

Magic . . .

I sent out a few tendrils of intuition but didn't get a hint of any unusual magical power. That didn't mean she wasn't developing abilities in the Craft. Could she have killed Orla somehow in the process of a spell? On purpose or even by accident like when I'd almost killed Declan? I considered my next words carefully.

"Magic, huh. So you're some kind of sorcerer or witch?"

Chapter 14

Lucy, who was bent over helping Colette and Nuala decide what kind of ribbon to apply to their drying eggs, heard me and stood upright. The JJs had been carrying on a constant, tumbling commentary on their activities in the background, and it continued unabated as Margie mopped up a mess they'd made on the counter.

Ginnie blew a raspberry. "A witch? Good heavens. Of course not. I'm a street magician—or was one. Sleight of hand, card tricks, a little hypnotism. That kind of stuff." She leaned a little closer and grinned. "Some of those skills still come in handy in the classroom, though."

"Ah," I said.

"Anyway, Finn had a mime act with his sister. We got along right away. Next thing I knew, we were dating. Then we eloped."

"Eloped?"

"Well, my parents didn't approve of my marrying a mime, and his family didn't approve of his marrying outside of . . . well, tradition. The exception was Orla. She was great, right from the beginning. John wanted Finn to get the marriage annulled—can you believe that? But Orla stood up for us. For love, she said. She told him we were destined to be together."

"Good for her," I said.

I retrieved my pink egg and set it on a rack to dry. Then I placed a bottle cap in the bottom of a ramekin, balanced an egg on top of it, and carefully poured dye made from beet powder a quarter of the way up.

Ginnie watched with interest. "What are you doing?"

"Ombré egg," I said. "Saw them on Pinterest. I think that must just be a fancy way to say 'striped.' In a few minutes, I'll add some water to dilute the dye and so it's halfway up the egg, then do it again and again. When I'm finished, one end will have a dark stripe, and the other end will have a pale stripe, with increments in the middle."

"Cool."

"Was the fortune-telling more than a sideshow for Orla?" I asked. "I mean, could she really predict someone's future?"

"Hm. Maybe. John certainly thought so. He consulted her about any big moves the family made."

My mouth turned down in thought.

"And she gave the family a lot of good advice. They would have missed her. A lot."

I paused in stirring the grape juice dye. "Would have? What do you mean?"

She pressed her lips together and looked over at Nuala. Her niece and Colette had moved on to the tie-dye station, where Bianca was showing them how to wrap eggs in paper towels and dot food coloring on the outsides.

Finally, she shrugged. "Well, I guess you already know she was looking at going to California."

The book she ordered from the Fox and Hound.

"What did her brother-in-law think about that?" I asked casually.

"I, uh, I'm not sure he knew yet. He would have gone ballistic, though." She took out the orange egg, put it on the rack, and reached for another. "See, John was in love with her."

Stunned, I put down the egg I'd been about to dunk. "His brother's wife?"

Another shrug. "The heart wants what the heart wants. At least I think he was in love with her. He kept asking her to marry him. John couldn't convince her, though."

"Uncle John says he can convince anyone to do anything," Nuala said as she walked over. Thankfully, she seemed to have heard only her aunt's last sentence. "He says that's why business is so good."

Ginnie ruffled her hair. "He does say that."

Oh, does he, now? Could he convince someone to walk into traffic? How would that work?

Then I remembered the pocket watch he was swinging in the online photo I'd found earlier. Was John Black a hypnotist? And what about Ginnie? Only moments earlier she'd implied that she used hypnotism in the classroom.

Nuala peered into the natural-dye pots and wrinkled her nose. "That doesn't smell very good."

My thoughts snapped back to the here and now,

and I laughed. "That's the cabbage. Tell you what. Go grab anything you want from the display case, and it'll take that smell right out of your nose."

"Okay." She skipped back to Colette.

I poured more water into my ombré egg and then checked to see whether our earlier efforts were dry yet. I was debating whether to ask Ginnie one more question about the Blacks, but it was risky.

Well, no one else is going to tell you, so you might as well give it a try.

But before I could ask it, Colette said, "You know why the Easter bunny lays colored eggs, don't you?"

Everyone turned. Nuala shook her head. Colette hopped up on a tall work stool and looked around. "Well, then I'll tell you the story. See, there was this goddess. Her name was Ostara. Sometimes she was called something else, right, Mom?"

"Eostre," Bianca supplied, exchanging looks with Lucy and me.

"Right. Anyway, Ostara was a spring goddess. She was all about the flowers coming up, and trees getting green, and lots of spring babies. Lambs and bunnies and chicks, you know? Anyway, there was this bird who came to Ostara and said it really, really wanted to be a rabbit instead of a bird."

"Wait. Why would a bird want to be a rabbit?" Margie asked.

Colette shrugged. "I dunno. Maybe the bird just identified as a bunny."

Margie looked amused. "Okay. Sorry I interrupted."

"That's all right. So anyway, Ostara took pity on the bird and granted her wish. The bird—who was now a bunny—could still lay eggs, though. And she was so grateful that every year she came back in the spring to lay special colored eggs to celebrate Ostara and spring and baby lambs and flowers and stuff."

She hopped off the chair and looked around. "Pretty cool, huh?"

We all nodded.

Ginnie said, "I'd never heard that. But I always wondered about that egg-laying rabbit."

"I hadn't heard it, either," Margie said. "And you did a good job telling the story, too, Colette."

"Thank you, Ms. Coopersmith."

I was glad Colette hadn't mentioned—and probably didn't know—that in medieval times, hares were thought to be witches who had transformed into animal form to take the cows' milk and could be killed only with a silver bullet. Kind of like werewolves, but way cuter.

Ginnie looked over at the tie-dyed eggs that were now on the rack. They looked kind of messy, but interesting. Afraid she wanted to try one herself, and I'd lose my chance to talk with her alone, I asked, "Do you mind if I ask you something? About Orla?"

Her eyes narrowed. "You seem awfully curious about her."

I smiled, trying for disarming. "What happened to her right out front was, well, *strange*. Tragic and sudden, but also strange. And it bothers me. Then there were the insurance investigators who came to see Lucy and me."

Her hand jerked, knocking an egg off the counter. It hit the floor with a sick, cracking thud. Everyone turned to look.

"Oh, darn. I'm sorry. What a klutz," she said.

I waved away her attempts to pick it up and grabbed a paper towel. "I've got it."

When I had disposed of the egg, I went back to where she was still standing. She seemed to have lost interest in coloring any more eggs.

"What did you tell the insurance people?" she asked.

"Mostly they seemed to want to know whether Orla could have stepped in front of that car intentionally. Lucy and I told them that we didn't think that was possible."

She relaxed.

"Seems like she had an awful lot of life insurance, though. I mean, five policies?"

Ginnie grew still. Her eyes probed mine. Then she let out a long breath and glanced over at Nuala. I realized Lucy and Bianca were intentionally steering the others away from Ginnie and me so we could talk.

"There's nothing suspicious about it," she said. "Every one of us has multiple policies on us. It's one of the ways the family has made money over the years."

I blinked. "Insurance fraud?"

She shook her head vehemently. "It's not fraud. They are all valid policies. At a wedding, a family member might give the couple the gift of letting them take a policy out on him. Or when a baby is born. Or for any reason. A lot of the families do it. It's perfectly legal."

And perfectly profitable. Did that make it any less of a murder motive?

My face must have revealed something, because Ginnie scowled and said in a defensive tone, "I don't know what you're trying to do. Maybe John is right. Maybe it's better not to socialize outside the family."

"Oh, gosh. I'm sorry. I don't want you to—"

"Nuala! It's time to go. Sorry, honey, but I told your mom I'd have you home early."

The girl seemed surprised but didn't question her aunt. She shrugged into her coat, and Ginnie hustled her out the door.

"Oh, no!" Lucy said. "They forgot their eggs."

"What happened?" Colette asked.

Bianca hugged her daughter to her side. "They just had to go. You had fun, didn't you?"

The girl frowned. "Sure. I like Nuala, even if she's already in fifth grade. Or would be if she went to school."

"What do you mean?" her mother asked.

"She's homeschooled."

"Ah. She's still in the fifth grade, then," Bianca said. "Come on. Let's go gather up this evening's masterful creations."

Before we dumped all the dyes down the drain and cleaned up the party, I had to try marbling a couple of eggs. With everyone crowded around to watch, I mixed twenty drops of food coloring—green for Jonathan's benefit—into a cup of cool water along with two teaspoons of white vinegar. Then I melted a tablespoon of butter in the microwave and stirred it into the vinegar solution. I dunked an egg once, twice, three times, then submerged it completely for four minutes.

When I removed it, the oil had created a lovely effect very similar to the veining in marble. Once it was dry, I'd wipe off any oil that was left on the surface of the egg.

Bianca and Colette had to try a few. While they played with the technique, I started to clean things up.

Looking around, I asked, "Where's Lucy?"

The back door opened, and I saw she'd parked her big blue convertible in the alley. She had a basket in each hand. "Surprise!"

I took one and looked inside. She'd planted grass in the bottom, and now it provided the perfect bed for decorated eggs.

"I didn't know we'd have extra people," she said. "I was going to give mine to Nuala."

"Nuala can have mine," I said. "I'll drop it by her house tomorrow."

A knocking on the front door drew our attention. Seeing it was Randy, I hurried to let him in.

"How's the party going?" he asked. This evening, he wore jeans and a sport coat over a collared shirt. He smiled broadly, but I sensed a little nervousness.

Colette waved at him from the kitchen. "Come see what we did."

"Okeydoke," he said, and went back to admire the racks of eggs ready to go into Lucy's baskets.

Bianca sidled over. "She likes him already." She sounded worried. "I try to be so careful, so she doesn't get hurt."

"Don't worry. It's better that Colette likes him, don't you think? She's not going to get attached that fast."

"No. You're right. I'll try to remember to take it one step at a time."

"You ready?" Randy asked, returning. "The gallery opens at seven. We can walk if you'd like."

"Lucky for you I wore comfortable shoes for this little shindig," she teased.

"Or I can drive," he said quickly. "My car is out front."

"What kind of car?" she asked.

A defensive look crossed his face. "It's a—" Then he caught on and stopped himself. "It's a perfectly serviceable Durango that will get you from point A to point B."

Bianca smiled. "Sounds perfect. Colette, you have fun with Lucy. I'll pick you up in a few hours."

"Okay, Mom." She was busy arranging eggs in her basket.

Jonathan loaded his green-lined basket with his multitoned green eggs while Margie helped Julia with her more traditional array of colors. Soon they were on their way, and Lucy and Colette left for home and Caribbean food. I gathered Mungo into my tote bag, put Nuala's eggs into the last basket, and tucked it in the fridge, then locked up.

Chapter 15

The second night of Declan's forty-eight-hour shift at the firehouse was always harder for me than the first. That was one of the reasons why I'd lobbied to have the egg-coloring party this evening. But now it was just Mungo and me at home. Luckily, it was also a full moon, and the perfect time to make more of the antiallergy potion Bianca had worked out with me. I missed that man of mine, but it was sometimes difficult to find the privacy for spell work when he was around the carriage house.

First, I dug out some leftover orzo salad, already regretting that I hadn't followed my instinct to pick up some Caribbean takeout like Ben had. However, a witch needed to stay light on her feet for moon workings, and a big order of brown gravy chicken would have made me sluggish and dull. So Mungo and I split the salad, and then I gave him a baby carrot to chew on. I promised myself a big, fat brownie when I'd finished making the potion.

Stomach no longer growling, I changed out of my

workaday skirt and T-shirt, donning sleek leggings and a navy blue tunic covered with depictions of stars and the moon in various phases. It was symbolic, of course, but, more important, comfortable and warm enough to ward off the evening air of April.

After gathering my tools and herbs, I turned off the lights inside the carriage house and took Mungo out to the backyard. He romped in the grass, chasing the fireflies that flocked around him, and I continued on to the small gazebo. I'd had it built soon after moving in, and it had become my sacred space for garden spells and herbal magic.

I set the jug of water, the big glass jar, cider vinegar, a jar of local honey, a cedar frond I'd cut from the tree across the street in the dark of night the week before, and two bay leaves on the small round table in the middle of the gazebo. A few mismatched chairs from the thrift store were scattered around the outside. After all, Declan and I sat out here in warm weather, sacred space or not. Still, the table stood over a ten-inch, five-pointed star outlined in white and colored purple in the middle. It was a barely disguised pentagram, around which I cast my salt circles. The besom broom in the corner served to sweep out the salt when I was done.

Tonight, there would be no salt circle. Tonight, I needed to be in the open.

Leaving the ingredients for the potion, I checked on my gardens in the light of the moon. Declan had helped me cut away the sod and amend the soil for all of them. There was a vegetable patch, an area devoted to herbs, and a bed of plants used for magic beyond the inherent energies of herbs and spices. Among other flora, it boasted the witch hazel from which I made my wand, the young rowan tree that protected an ancient talisman, and dittany for healing spells. It also had a small patch of red clover, which I needed for tonight's work.

The house aside, how could I leave these carefully tended plants, this area that had become so personal to me?

I can start again. I can create more gardens. Declan helped with these, and he will help in the new house. I adore that man, and our relationship is more important than this place.

With renewed resolve, I harvested enough clover for the potion and returned to the gazebo. I twisted the lid off the empty half-gallon jar. On the side, I'd roughly drawn vertical wavy lines to represent air and the outline of a cat's face. It wasn't art by any means, but it did help set the intention behind the incantation. Carefully, I crafted that intention—clear air passages and an immunity to cat hair and dander—and held it in the back of my mind as I placed the bay leaves, the fresh red clover, a snippet of cedar, a dollop of honey, and a splash of cider vinegar in the bottom of the jar. The combination would have been effective for a tea to treat congestion, but with Bianca's added suggestions the herbs, honey, and vinegar had enough power to tame my rampant allergy to cats.

Most people make sun tea. I was making moon tea.

The water in the jug was from the stream that cut across the corner of the yard. I'd liked the idea of a piece of my very own stream when I'd first looked at the property, completely unaware that having access to live spring water would become important to my witchy activities. However, since I'd be drinking it, I'd boiled the water to purify it. Now I poured the cooled water over the other ingredients, put on the lid, and carried the jar out into the yard.

Sinking down on the grass, I checked my watch. The moon had risen far enough to cast a bright, silvery light where I sat. Mungo trotted over and flopped down by my side. I gave him a pat, then turned my attention back to the potion. Opening my consciousness to the lunar energy flowing down on me, I whispered,

Lunar potion, magic true,
Fill with healing
This herbal brew
To breathe the air
Without a care,
Enjoy feline charm
With zero harm.
So mote it be.

I made a note of the time and made myself comfortable. After exactly thirteen minutes, I lifted the jar and swirled it deosil, or clockwise, thirteen times. Arms aching, I settled it into the middle of the yard, where it would receive moonlight for the majority of the night.

Then I rose and went over to the stream. The moving water glittered, and I imagined it freshening under the face of the full moon.

Purify deeply, I invoked the moon as I traced a star in the air over the water and imagined any negative energy being drawn from the water up to the nothingness of space. It was something I did almost every full moon, just in case impurities, physical or psychic, had made their way into the water I valued so much.

Dropping my hands, I turned toward the house.

Where am I ever going to find a place with live water?

I pushed the thought from my mind and went inside. I had a date with a peanut butter swirl brownie.

The next morning I rose early and went for another run. I breathed easily as my feet pounded the pavement in an intoxicating rhythm that wiped away all thought. The air smelled green and floral. Dew sparkled beneath the light of the setting moon, and I saw the same raccoon family from the day before lounging along a different fence line.

After I showered and dressed in a purple skirt, a lavender T-shirt, and canvas sneakers, Mungo and I indulged in French toast with maple syrup and crispy bacon. Then I retrieved the potion, thanked the goddess energy of the moon, and poured a healthy swig into my travel mug. The rest I put into the refrigerator.

Lucy called me at six to let me know she was going to be late. I'd already made some headway into the day's baking, and was able to get most of the fresh goodies into the display case by the time Ben came in just before seven.

"Is everything all right with Lucy?" I asked as I finished arranging a tier of cherry chocolate cake slices. "She's not sick, is she?"

"Nah," he said. "She just had to wait for Bianca to pick up Colette this morning."

I paused and looked at him. His lips turned up, and his eyebrows went up and down.

"Bianca didn't come get her last night?" I asked.

"Nope. She called about nine and asked if Colette would mind staying the night."

"Huh," I said.

"That's what I thought," Ben said, and went to unlock the front door.

While my uncle handled the first customers, I set to work on the next baking project. When I'd arrived that morning, the first thing I'd done was remove two blocks of brown butter from the fridge. Iris had prepped them the day before, slowly heating the butter in a heavy pan until it turned golden and then gradually darkened to mahogany. The result was far different from regular melted butter, or even clarified butter. Brown butter was rich and savory, with a deep, nutty flavor. As I'd told Mrs. Standish, it was the secret ingredient in our increasingly popular chocolate chip cookies.

The brown butter had come to room temperature, so it was easy to mix up the batter with plenty of seventy percent cacao chocolate chips and toasted, sliced almonds, then drop the mounds of dough on baking sheets. Soon the distinct scent of brown butter, chocolate, and nuts joined the fragrance of fresh-baked sourdough bread, spicy muffins, and citrusy lemon bars. When they were done, I slid each one onto a rack to cool and added the final touch—a single grind of smoked Himalayan salt on top of each delectable cookie.

I was putting the salt grinder back in the cupboard when Lucy breezed in through the alley door, carrying Honeybee in a carrier.

"Sorry I'm a little late," she said, grabbing a blue-and-green-striped chef's apron from the hook on her way back to drop her purse and jacket in the office.

"We managed. I'll take Honeybee out to the reading area."

The captive feline gave my hand a head butt when I released her onto her window perch. I saw the question in her eyes, checked to see if anyone was near enough to hear, and said, "I'm fine today. You'd better get started on your day's lounging." She was purring when I walked away.

Lucy took the carrier. "You made more of Bianca's allergy potion last night?"

"Yep." I inhaled deeply. "Seems to be working great."

Arms behind her to tie the apron strings into a bow, she smiled. "Ben told you why I'm late, I suppose."

"He did. Bianca and Randy must have really hit it off," I said.

My aunt's eyes twinkled. "She didn't have time to tell me much when I saw her this morning."

My shoulders slumped. "Oh."

"But she promised to drop by later, so we can get the details at the same time."

I brightened.

Lucy laughed as she went out to see if Ben needed any help at the coffee counter.

Jaida came in around nine and set up her laptop at her usual corner table. I put a cardamom orange muffin on a plate and took it over to her. "Mocha?" I asked.

"Maybe two," she grumbled, then caught herself. "Sorry. I adore this place, but trying to get everything done here is difficult. Some of it is very private, and I don't feel comfortable working on client files where someone could possibly walk by and see. So last night I stayed up until after midnight finishing up some stuff, and of course, Anubis decided he needed a nice long walk at six this morning."

She waved her hand in the air. "So don't mind me. I'm just tired and cranky." Sitting down, she took a big bite of muffin. Her eyes widened as she chewed and swallowed. "This helps, though. What spice is that?"

"Cardamom." I patted her shoulder. "I'll be right back with a double mocha."

She gave me a grateful smile.

When I returned with the tall, steaming mug, she said, "Cookie called me last night."

I raised my eyebrows. "Oh?"

"She said she'd already told you. Or rather, that Lucy guessed she was expecting. Didn't want to wait until the next spellbook club meeting to tell everyone."

"Mrs. Standish was here when we found out," I said.

"Oh . . ." Jaida nodded her understanding. "So Cookie is calling everyone in order to outpace the gossip train. Good for her. I'm just so happy for her and Oscar. Who would have thought she'd be married and having kids before you?"

I gave her a look.

She ducked her head. "Sorry. Did I hit a sore point?"

"Not really," I said with a chuckle. "I'm content with moving slowly. Declan, on the other hand—"

"Not so much," Jaida said.

"He hasn't actually complained." *Yet.*

The bell jingled over the door, and Bianca came in.

"Speaking of the gossip train," I said. "Don't get too involved in your work yet." I gestured for our friend to join us.

Bianca practically wafted over to us, the gauzy material of her seafoam-colored dress floating behind her as if there were a wind machine hidden in the recesses of the bakery. I pulled out a chair and waved to Lucy behind the register. She nodded and poured out a two tumblers of hibiscus sweet tea, brought them over, and sat down.

Pushing an icy glass toward Bianca, my aunt asked, "So, how was your date?"

The puzzled expression cleared from Jaida's face. "Right! It was last night. Randy." The way she said his name emphasized the double entendre.

Bianca didn't notice. Her smile was dreamy. "It was wonderful."

We exchanged looks. "It must have been if you spent the night with him after the first date," I said.

She blinked, then laughed. "Oh, no. I didn't spend the night. Oh! Is that what Colette thinks?" She looked at Lucy. "I told you on the phone last night that we were having a nice conversation, and I didn't want to cut it short."

"You did, dear." Lucy patted her hand. "And Colette doesn't think a thing about it—only that she got to sleep in our guest room. Katie's just fishing."

"Well, maybe a little," I admitted.

Bianca shook her head. "That's okay. After all, you're the one who got us together."

"Nuh-uh," I said. "Randy got you together. I didn't have anything to do with it." And I wasn't going to take any blame if things went awry.

"Well, if I didn't know you, and you didn't know Declan—" she started.

Jaida broke in. "Oh, for heaven's sake. However it happened, you guys went on a date. Now, dish. How was the gallery opening?"

"Divine," Bianca breathed. "Honestly, I never expected it, but Randy knows a lot about art. Actually, he knows about a lot of things. Art, wine, books."

Randy? That goofball Declan hung around with? I was going to have to reassess my assumptions about him.

Bianca continued. "I ended up buying a piece from an up-and-coming visual artist who works in watercolors on rice paper. Simply stunning."

I refrained from asking what that had cost, and instead prompted her with, "And then you guys had coffee?"

"Actually, we grabbed a bite at a tapas bar, then walked along the river and back. Finally, ended up taking the ferry over to the Westin for a nightcap." She saw my expression. "And then we came *back*, and he took me home around midnight." Turning to my aunt, she said, "I hope it wasn't too much trouble keeping Colette overnight. I called from the Westin once I realized we'd never make it back before her bedtime—and on a school night."

"Of course not!" Lucy exclaimed. "I loved having

her. You let me know anytime you want to drop her overnight."

Bianca grinned. "Okay. I might take you up on that."

Jaida said wryly, "So I take it you and this Randy are going out again."

"Oh, yeah," Bianca said. "He's wonderful. Even though he's younger than me, he's a very old soul."

Lucy's eyes were dancing when she met my gaze. *Randy? An old soul? Who knew?*

"Now," Bianca said. "Enough about me. You all know about Cookie, I take it?"

We nodded. "But not when she's due," I said.

"October tenth," Jaida and Bianca said together.

"I'll mark the calendar," I said, and Lucy added, "We are going to have the best baby shower *ever* for that girl."

"And what about you, Katie?"

I blinked. "Me? I'm not pregnant."

Bianca laughed. "No, no, no. I was wondering if you'd learned anything useful from Ginnie Black last night. You two were thick as thieves over there in the corner with your organic egg dyes and whispers."

"I did learn a little," I admitted.

All three of them leaned forward.

"Ginnie met Finn in Florida when the family lived there and she was going to school. She was a street magician."

"Really? I had no idea," Bianca said, no doubt thinking back to the year her daughter had had Ginnie as a teacher.

"Does that have anything to do with Orla, though?" Lucy said.

"In a way. Orla defended Finn when he eloped with an outsider. See, John Black wanted to get the marriage annulled."

"The nerve!" Lucy exclaimed.

"And Ginnie also told me that John wanted to marry Orla," I said. "But she wasn't interested."

"He was in love with his brother's wife?" Bianca asked.

"I wonder if he fell for her before Mike died," my aunt said. "That was four years ago."

"I wonder if love had anything to do with it," I said. "Orla was thinking of moving to California, away from the family. Ginnie didn't know if John was aware of that, but my guess is that not much goes on in that family that he doesn't know about. If so, getting Orla to marry him would ensure she'd stay here."

"John sounds like a control freak," Lucy said.

"Or perhaps he's doing his best to maintain the integrity of his clan," I said. "One of the ways Irish travelers have maintained their identity among themselves is to, well, stay among themselves. It was all good for a while, but then his brother dies, and his nephew marries an outsider, and then Orla starts eyeing the West Coast."

"I wonder how far John would go to keep Orla from leaving," Lucy said thoughtfully.

Jaida had been listening with interest. "I don't suppose Ginnie let anything slip about Orla's life insurance."

Quickly, I explained to Bianca what she was talking about, then answered, "I wouldn't say she let anything slip, but I asked her outright about those five policies."

Lucy's eyes grew round. "You did?"

I made a face. "Yeah. That's why she decided to leave so suddenly."

Their faces fell.

"But not before she told me that taking out multiple life insurance policies on each other is standard operating procedure in some traveler families. She said it's perfectly legal, and extremely common." I grimaced. "Then she either decided that she'd said too much, or that I'd asked too much, because she grabbed Nuala and practically ran out the door."

"Left her eggs here and everything," Lucy said.

"I put them in the fridge," I told her. "I was planning to take them over to her this afternoon if I get the chance."

But Jaida wasn't done talking about insurance. Now she said in a speculative voice, "So she left before you could ask her about what would happen to someone who doesn't want someone in the Black family to have a life insurance policy on them anymore."

I sat back. "I wonder if that ever happened before. But you're right. The lawyer Orla was going to see . . . if she was going to California, maybe she wanted to cut ties with the family. And that meant canceling those policies."

Jaida shook her head. "I don't know. Even if she wanted to, I doubt she could cancel all five. In fact, maybe none of them. Once you've committed to someone else owning an insurance policy on your life, it's theirs as long as they keep paying the premium."

Lucy stood and began to gather dishes. "I can't believe Orla was trying to cut ties with her family, anyway. Or at least not all of them." She paused and looked around at us. "Do you seriously think she'd leave that granddaughter of hers behind? Of course not. Nor her two children. If Orla was going to California, she was taking her kids with her."

"Which would explain why Ginnie knew what she was planning," I said. "But would Fern go? And what about Taber? I can't imagine him agreeing to such a thing. He seems devoted to John."

Jaida opened her laptop and quickly typed. "Here it is again. The lawyer's name you found in the insurance file. Michael Barrion." She looked up. "Insurance cases—and *divorce*."

"Oh, dear," I said. "The only couples are Finn and Ginnie or Fern and Taber. Which?"

"Fern and Taber," everyone said in unison.

How would John Black deal with the threat of a divorce on top of all the other intrusions into his carefully protected world?

Chapter 16

I guided my Bug down Bull Street to Victory. Mungo sat on the passenger seat beside me, his ears flapping in the breeze that came through the open window. Soon we were turning into Ardsley Park, past Ben and Lucy's, and coming up on where the Black compound was located.

There were a lot of cars on the street, and I had to park nearly half a block away. I pulled to the curb and unbuckled my seat belt. "You hang out here and keep an eye on things," I said to my familiar. "I'll be right back."

He made a noise of agreement in the back of his throat as I retrieved the basket of decorated eggs from the backseat. I carried it to the orange door, juggling it with one arm so I could ring the doorbell.

A man I hadn't met before answered. I recognized him as the one who had driven away the flatbed truck the evening Cookie had shown Declan and me the place down the street from my aunt and uncle's. My guess was that this was Aiden Black, John's son.

"Hi," I said brightly, sticking out my hand.

"Mm." His eyes narrowed. They were pretty eyes, really. Not as appealing as Declan's, but blue under dark hair like his. The look in them wasn't particularly nice, however.

I felt the smile slide off my face like warm butter. Holding up the basket, I tried again. "Is Fern home? I brought these by for Nuala."

"Mm." This time it came out as more of a grunt. "Lemme see." And he shut the door in my face.

Disconcerted, I waited.

The door opened again. "Katie." Fern's smile was still sad, but today she'd upgraded her wardrobe to jeans, a plum-colored shirt, and boots. "It's so sweet of you to bring those by. I know Nuala had a great time last night."

"I'm so glad she came. Everyone loved having her—and she's quite the creative kid." I pointed to an egg Nuala had dyed in metallic stripes before adding a spray of feathers and an arrangement of weensy flower stickers. "Mixed media!"

Fern's smile grew wider. "She's an artist, that one." She held out her hands for the basket.

"Would it be all right if I gave them to her?" I asked.

She hesitated and looked over her shoulder. "Sure. Come on in."

I stepped inside and followed her down a short hallway to the kitchen. The man who had answered the door was nowhere in sight. The sound of a television program came from somewhere in the house. A large pot of soup simmered on the stove, the savory smell filling the air and making my mouth water. Rounds of fresh-baked bread sat on the counter, enough to feed everyone in the family.

"Do you all eat your meals together?" I asked, and set the basket on the big wooden table in the middle of the room.

Fern shrugged. "Sometimes."

Finn and Ginnie walked in the back door. They were deep in discussion and didn't see me standing at the end of the table.

"You or Fern should be the one to give the eulogy," Ginnie was saying to her husband. "Not John. He horns in on everything."

"We can all say something," Finn said easily. "Mother would have liked that."

"Well, okay. I guess. Now, what were her favorite flowers?" Ginnie looked up at Fern for an answer and finally saw me standing there. "Oh! Katie. Hello."

"Hi," I said. "Just bringing by the eggs Nuala did last night." I smiled. "Yours are in there, too."

"Thanks," she said flatly.

"Say, if you're looking for a florist, I know a really talented one," I said. "Mimsey Carmichael at Vase Value can provide anything you need for your mother's service. She was a friend of Orla's as well."

"We have a florist that we use," said a voice from behind me. I whirled to see Taber had joined us.

"Oh . . . um . . . okay," I stuttered. "I just thought . . ." I stopped, feeling oddly rattled.

Well, Mimsey warned me about Orla's family.

Squaring my shoulders, I asked, "Where is Orla's service going to be held? I'd like to attend, and I'm sure my aunt would, too."

"It will be a private ceremony," Taber said. "Just family."

I should have seen that coming, I thought.

Looking uncomfortable, Fern called, "Nuala! Can you come down here?"

The television chatter fell silent, and footsteps sounded on the stairs. "Yeah, Mom?" The girl came into the kitchen. Pausing, her eyes flitted from one adult to another, quickly reading the situation. They finally stopped on me, and I watched as she realized the source of the tension.

"Oh. Hi, Katie." Then she saw the eggs. "Oh! You brought them! The basket is so pretty, too. Is that real grass?" She crossed to the table and ran her fingertips over the stubby wheatgrass in the bottom of the basket. "It is!" Turning to Fern, she said, "Did you see?"

Fern smiled down at her daughter and nodded. "I sure did. They're beautiful."

The back door opened again, and this time John Black walked in.

Sheesh—doesn't anyone in this family knock?

He saw me and stopped dead. "You again?"

"Er," I managed, feeling myself wither beneath his gaze.

"And what is this big discussion about?" he asked, looking around at the others. "Is there something I should know?"

Everyone shook their heads.

"Of course not," Taber said. "She was just leaving."

John glared at me. "Why, exactly, are you here in the first place? Don't you have your own business to run without sticking your nose into ours?"

Nuala started to say something, but I stepped forward. "Hey, I came by to drop off some Easter eggs your grandniece decorated with a group of us last evening. I'm not trying to pry into your family secrets."

Never mind that that wasn't entirely true.

He didn't look particularly impressed with my denial, either. Gesturing with his chin, he said, "Ginn here told me you were asking her about life insurance policies on our Orla."

I turned to look at her, but she wouldn't meet my eyes.

"Now, we thank you for your attention to Nuala during a difficult time. We won't need your assistance in the future, however. Do you understand?"

I stared at him. "What is the matter with you?"

"Good-bye, Ms. Lightfoot."

Well, perhaps I should have chosen my words better, because the next thing I knew, I was back out by my car.

"That's a real friendly bunch in there, Mungo."

He looked up and grinned. I was pretty sure that after all this time with me, he had a fair handle on human sarcasm.

As I pulled away from the curb, my phone rang. I stopped at the end of the block to look at the screen. It wasn't a number I recognized. Shrugging, I accepted the call and put the phone to my ear.

A piercing whistle erupted from the speaker. I quickly hit the END button. "Jerk!" I looked over at Mungo. "As if getting telemarketing and political calls all the time wasn't enough."

Now thoroughly in a bad mood, I tossed the phone into my tote in the backseat.

Mungo whined. I looked over at him. "What's wrong, buddy? Did that hurt your ears?"

He wiggled out of his seat belt and stood with his feet on my leg.

"Now, you know you can't ride around in the car like that." I gently pushed him back over to the passenger seat. "You're supposed to be buckled in, but I'll let it slide this time. Stay over there, though."

Yip!

"Ow! Dang it, that was louder than that stupid prank call."

Yip!

"Mungo! Stop it!"

His eyes bored into me. I ignored him and kept driving.

Something's wrong. It was just a whisper, faint as gossamer. *Mungo knows, and he's trying to tell me.*

But I kept driving. I turned right, then left, then right again, and finally turned onto Old Louisville Road.

Colors on the other side of the window glass faded, washing everything to sepia as if someone had placed a photo filter over the world. Soon the Talmadge Bridge loomed ahead, spanning the Savannah River and taking cars to South Carolina.

Why am I here? I thought I was going back to the Honeybee.

Still, I kept driving.

Faster. Faster.

Too fast.

Katie . . . Katie, honey, stop. You have to stop now.

The smell of gardenias filled the car.

Mungo barked again, but I could hardly hear him. My ears felt muffled, insulated. Protected. Safe from his pesky, bothersome yapping.

My foot pressed down harder on the accelerator. The engine roared, and I shifted gears.

The Bug leaped forward. A horn honked, loud at first, and then fading as I sped onward.

Onward toward the bridge.

Katie! Stop! Fight it! You know how to fight! I'll help you. Katie, LISTEN TO ME.

Hmm. That's Nonna, I mused absently. *She wants me to stop.*

But I wanted to go. I just didn't know where. But it was vitally urgent that I get there.

The bridge was closer now. I could see the first supports towering over the street, holding up the bridge overpass. Solid, thick columns of concrete.

Mungo was barking nonstop now, bouncing around on the seat. The car vibrated with it. I sensed his lupine energy, his essential wolf nature, powerful and feral and protective.

And frightened.

In the edges of my awareness, I felt it meet my grandmother's energy, ghostly spirit and animal spirit coiling together, knitting into something more than the sum of the parts. It made me vaguely curious about why they'd do that, what could cause such a melding.

Need. They need to augment each other. I wonder why. . . .

The bridge support beckoned. I pushed the accelerator down a fraction more.

Mungo howled. I glanced over at him.

Look at how fast everything is going by outside.

He crouched, then, with a snarl, leaped at my arm.

And *bit* me.

A flash of light filled the car, and I came back into myself.

"What the . . . !"

I tromped down on the brake. The Bug skidded, the tires screeching on pavement. The little car slewed to the side, and Mungo tumbled into the passenger footwell. The car stalled and stopped dead.

The bumper was about six inches away from the bridge support.

Shaking, I jammed the transmission into park and reached for my dog.

He scrambled up to the seat, and I scooped him into my lap. He was whimpering and panting. Shaking like a leaf.

So was I.

I ran my hands over him, gently at first, then probing, checking. When I was done, I looked into his eyes. "Are you okay?"

Yip. A soft sound compared with his earlier bark.

He drew away then, staring down at the back of my wrist. I looked, too, and saw the two tiny drops of blood where he'd bitten me. Looking sorrowfully at me, he reached his tongue out to lick the wound.

"Oh, sweetie. Little sweet Mungo," I murmured, cupping his face so that he'd look up at me. "Please, please don't worry about that nip."

He whimpered again.

"No, no. It's okay. It's more than okay. *Thank you.*"

I licked my lips, quaking at my very core because of the truth of the words. "You saved my life."

He nuzzled my hand. I was glad to see his next look held a lot less guilt and a lot more curiosity. As if to say, *What were you thinking, witch o' mine?*

I cast a look upward, though I had no idea whether my grandmother's spirit existed in space at all. "And thank you, too."

The smell of gardenias grew stronger, and then suddenly disappeared. She was gone.

What had I been thinking? It had been as if I'd been taken over and didn't have any control over my actions. Except I had. I'd been the one driving the car. No one else. Except it hadn't felt like it had been all me. Had it felt like that for Declan when Connell had taken over his body?

I shuddered. No wonder he'd been so upset when it happened. It was a horrible feeling of being out of control.

A pickup truck pulled up behind me, and a woman got out. "You okay there?"

"Fine," I called, waving at her.

She looked puzzled, but I just smiled and started the car. As I put it in gear and pulled away, I realized my phone was ringing in the backseat.

Then I remembered the whistle. Both of them. The one on my phone right after I'd left the Black compound—and the one that I'd heard a split second before Orla had stepped in front of a moving car.

I began to shudder. Someone had just tried to kill me.

And I thought I knew how.

The same way that person had killed Orla Black.

The phone stopped, then began ringing again. Stopped and began again. Finally, I pulled into a parking space and reached for it. There was no way on the good green earth that I was going to answer a number I didn't know again, but I could at least see if it was the same one.

It was Declan. He'd called a dozen times. The first six I hadn't even heard. Quickly, I answered.

"Katie!" he shouted. "OhmygodKatieareyouokay?"

"I'm okay," I said.

"I've been trying to call you. Connell . . . Dang it, you scared the bejesus out of me!"

"Me or Connell?" I asked, achieving a wry tone despite the adrenaline hangover that was starting to set in. It felt like half my blood had been replaced with something thinner, and more caustic—like lighter fluid.

"Well, Connell to start with," Declan said. "Are you telling me nothing unusual has happened in the last half hour?"

"Oh, no. I wouldn't say that at all. Someone tried to kill me."

A beat, then: "Katie! Damn it!" I heard him take a deep breath, and when he spoke again, he was calmer. "You're all right?"

"I'm all right."

"Where are you?"

"I'm in my car, driving back to the Honeybee."

"But you're safe?"

"Yes," I assured him. "I'm pretty tough. Besides, no hypnotist can go up against me, Mungo, and Nonna and win." I didn't mention how close it had been, though.

Six inches.

"Nonna? Hypnotist?"

"Yeah—at least I think so. I almost drove into the Talmadge Bridge abutment, but Mungo stopped me." I smiled down at my familiar. He licked my hand.

"Almost . . . drove . . . into . . ." he spluttered.

"I think I was hypnotized," I said. "And I think Orla was, too. Only in her case, it worked."

"Who did it?" he demanded.

"I don't know," I admitted. "I'm kind of shaken up, but maybe I'll be able to put it together later." As I said it, I realized I was missing a chunk of time between when John had invited me to leave Fern's house and when I'd gotten into my car. That made me glance at my watch. Surprised, I said, "It's already four?"

"Just come home, Katie. Or I can come get you."

"Nah, I need to go back to work and help close up the bakery. Besides, Lucy and Ben will be wondering what happened to me."

That was going to be an interesting conversation.

Declan grumbled, but I told him I'd see him at the usual time and said good-bye.

Chapter 17

Lucy met me at the door of the Honeybee. "Declan called."

I groaned.

She shook her head. "I can't believe you drove here, but now that you have, I'm taking you home."

"But—"

"No argument. Cookie is here and can help Ben close. She remembers how."

Lucy took me by the arm and led me back to the office, where she sat me down in the computer chair. She said, "Jaida's coming back. She's going to drive my car, and we'll take yours. Ben will take Honeybee home."

"Now, come on," I protested. "I can drive myself home, for Pete's sake."

My aunt stood back and looked me up and down. "You are pale and sweating, and your hands are shaking. Declan said you might have been hypnotized?" She put her hands on her hips. "Now, how do you know the effect has worn off?"

The truth was, I didn't. The thought was less than comforting.

"I want to know exactly what happened, and then I'm going to make you a relaxing tea and put you to bed."

I had to admit that sounded like heaven.

"What's this?" she exclaimed, grabbing my hand. Mungo, who had followed us, ducked his head and looked up at her with apologetic brown eyes.

"It's nothing." I pulled my hand back. "Mungo had to do it, and he feels bad enough about it. Please, Lucy."

Her features softened, and she bent to give him a pat. "Good boy, Mungo." She straightened. "There have been a few times I've wanted to bite her, too." Amusement flickered behind her eyes. "Just a little."

My familiar and I both blinked, and then I laughed. It released a ton of tension and made me feel a lot better. Did I mention that my aunt possessed a toughness that not very many people got to see?

Ten minutes later, Lucy had loaded up ingredients for her magical tea—literally, I imagined—and Jaida was back. Lucy took over the wheel of the Bug, while Jaida handled my aunt's baby blue 1964 Thunderbird behind us.

Declan was waiting on the front porch when we got home, still in muddy gardening clothes and with a full day's worth of scruffy beard on his chin. I'd never been happier to see him.

Until he held out his cell. "It's your mother."

I could hear her voice through the speaker. "Katie? Katie, why didn't you answer your phone? Katie?"

Groaning, I took it from him and put it to my ear.

"Hello, Mama. I'm sorry I didn't answer. I didn't hear it ring."

Lucy made a sympathetic face before she and Jaida went inside. Declan leaned against the doorframe, unabashedly listening.

"Something happened," Mama stated without benefit of greeting. "What was it?"

I sighed and sank down on the top step. Mungo trotted over and leaned against my knee. "Nonna?" I asked.

"*What?* Are you asking if she told me . . . no. I just . . ." She trailed off. When she spoke again, her voice was calmer. "I had a feeling. It's a mother thing. You'll understand when you have kids. But you're obviously all right. You are, aren't you?"

"Yes."

"But it must have been bad if you think my mother would have contacted me from beyond the grave."

"Well, she kind of helped me out of a situation this afternoon. I thought she might have passed that on."

"Oh, my Lord," my mother muttered away from the phone. "I have to sit down, Skylar. I told you something was wrong. Mother was even involved."

"Katie?" My dad's voice was calm and reasonable. "I'm guessing that you're neck-deep in another one of your magical murder investigations."

"It sounds like something from a children's book when you put it that way," I said.

"I'll take that as a 'yes.' Do you want to tell us what happened? I'll put you on speaker."

So I repeated my story yet again, trying to smooth the edges of actual danger from my narrative. Then I had to give them at least a little context, so I had to explain what had happened to Orla.

When I was done, my dad said, "Hypnotized? I sure don't like the sound of that."

"Neither do I!" Mama said.

"I think you need to track down a real hypnotherapist and have them remove any posthypnotic suggestions that might be lingering in your psyche," my dad said.

Still standing in the doorway, Declan nodded his agreement.

"And I think you'd better call Detective Quinn and tell him what happened," my mother said. "Then he can march right over to those people and arrest someone."

"I don't think it works quite that way," I said. "For one thing, he's a homicide detective."

"Well, you think that woman who was hit by a car was murdered, so why isn't he investigating that?"

"Because he *doesn't* think she was murdered. It's complicated, Mama."

"It's not right—" she began, but my father broke in.

"Declan said that Lucy brought you home, Katie. Is she still there?"

"Yes, along with my friend Jaida."

"Mary Jane," he said to my mother, "how about if we let Katie recover from her ordeal this afternoon? She's in good hands."

"Oh, all right. Katie, will you call me if anything else happens?"

"Anything?" I asked in a teasing voice.

"Well, anything I should know about. And have you two set the date for the wedding yet?"

"Not yet, Mama."

"We have a lot of planning to do, and it's difficult to start when we don't even know what the weather might be like."

"Okay, Mama. We'll get right on that."

A pause, then: "I know you're teasing me. That's okay. I'm just worried about you."

"I know. But I'm okay. Really. I love you. Good-bye."

Lucy and Jaida were working in the kitchen. I saw the vapor curling from the spout of the kettle, then heard a muttered chant that included the words *heal*, *banish*, *calm*, and *mote*. They were making their own potion, it seemed.

Ambivalent about all the attention, I dutifully changed into a pair of soft cotton pajamas, though it seemed silly when it was still going to be light for a couple of hours. Jaida settled me on the couch with an afghan while Declan whipped up a cheese omelet. As soon as the smell hit my nose, I realized how famished I was. He brought it to me on a tray like I was some kind of queen, and I polished it off with very unregal fervor, along with two pieces of thick sourdough toast spread with spiced peach jam.

When I was finished, Lucy brought in a steaming cup of liquid and set it on the end table by the couch. "Drink this."

"Oh, gosh," I protested. "I'm not sick, you know. Just had a little scare. I'm fine." To prove my point, I threw off the afghan and stood.

"Sit down and drink that tea," Lucy said in a tone that brooked no argument.

I sat. "Tea? Or potion?"

"I know what an insomniac you are. That tea will

help you sleep. And when you sleep, you recover." She and Jaida exchanged a look. "We added a little something to it."

"Like what?" Declan asked, alarmed.

Jaida smiled and said, "Potions are spells in liquid form, you know. That's simply a tea made of angelica, caraway, passionflower, and agrimony. Those are all herbs to help Katie relax and sleep. We just added a little, you know, *oomph* to the mixture."

He frowned. "That's all well and good, I suppose. Katie probably does need to sleep, but not until later, okay? I agree with her dad. We need to find out whether she's still under some kind of hypnotic influence."

The two witches nodded. Lucy said, "What did you have in mind?"

"I don't know," he said. "Look in the phone book under hypnosis?"

I snorted. "That sounds like a good way to waste money. Isn't there some kind of professional organization or vetting board for hypnotists?"

Declan said, "Drink your tea—or potion or whatever it is. I'll do some research while you sleep."

I lifted the cup to my lips, but didn't drink. I set it back down. "I don't really feel like sleeping right now. It's not even seven o'clock."

Lucy sat down beside me. "Don't be afraid. Nothing bad will happen while you're asleep."

"Is that what you're worried about? That you'll wake up and try it again?" Declan asked.

A sudden shudder made the cup shake in my fingers. "Maybe. It felt kind of like I was sleepwalking."

He came and sat on my other side. "I'm not leaving

your side. And I promise I won't let anything happen to you."

I smiled up at him. "That's good enough for me." I was raising the cup to my lips when my phone buzzed on the coffee table. I put the cup down and reached for it.

"It can't be anything important," Lucy began to protest.

"Hello, Detective Quinn," I said.

Her eyes grew wide.

I stood and walked to the front window, feeling three pairs of eyes on my back. "What can I do for you?"

"For one thing, you can tell me why I received two phone calls about you in the last four hours, Lightfoot."

"Can't begin to guess," I said. "Perhaps if you told me who the calls were from."

"The first one was from John Black. He's— Well, you already know who he is, don't you?"

I didn't say anything.

"Of course you do, because that's why he called. Apparently, you've been sticking your nose into his sister-in-law's accident."

"It wasn't an accident," I said.

"Yes, it was!" he shouted.

I held the phone away from my ear and looked over my shoulder. Declan, Lucy, and Jaida were lined on the sofa like spectators on a bleacher seat, watching me with undisguised curiosity.

I heard him take a deep breath. "Ms. Black's death has been determined to be an accident," he said as if he hadn't just yelled at me. "And her brother-in-law doesn't want you harassing their family in their time of grief. I think you can sympathize with that, can't you?"

"Of course."

"They're making arrangements for a funeral, getting ready to say good-bye—you understand?"

"Isn't there a rule in sales that you should stop selling when you hear yes?"

"I do believe there is. But sometimes a salesman is trying to get through to someone who says yes just to stop the salesman from saying more. So I'm going to add one last thing—if you don't stop asking personal questions about the Black family, John Black is going to take out a restraining order on you."

"Great," I said. "You said you got two calls. Who else?"

"Your mother."

I winced.

"Mere minutes ago." He didn't sound very happy about it, either.

"Really? Whatever for?" As if I didn't know.

"Because she thinks I am neglecting my duty as an officer of the law. And she thinks that because I'm not investigating some murder that didn't even happen. She thinks *that* because her daughter told her there had been a murder, and that same daughter told her that she'd been investigating it without my help."

"I see." I turned and leaned my hip against the windowsill. "My mother can be quite, er, protective."

Lucy's eyes laughed as she realized her sister had called Quinn to complain. I, on the other hand, wanted to crawl under the carriage house and hide.

"Actually, I'd call it something else," Quinn said.

"Now, she said someone tried to kill you in the course of this so-called 'investigation' of yours. Is that true?"

"Yes."

There was a long moment of silence, then: "What happened?"

"I almost drove into a bridge support at full speed."

"You *what*?"

"That's right. I barely managed not to."

"Your brakes went out?"

"No, my brakes are fine. Thank God. Otherwise I wouldn't have been able to stop when I did. But I think that's what happened to Orla."

"Okay, hang on. Back up. First of all, are you feeling like you want to harm yourself right now?"

"No! I've never felt that way."

"Are you alone?"

"No, again. Declan, Lucy, and Jaida are sitting right here. Now listen to me, okay? Right before Orla Black stepped in front of that oncoming car on Broughton Street, I heard a sharp, loud whistle. Mungo heard it, too. He went crazy barking."

"A whistle," Quinn said, his voice dripping with skepticism.

"Yes, a whistle. Like some people can do with two fingers at the corners of their mouth? I've always wished I could do that. Anyway, before I almost drove into that hunk of concrete, I got a phone call from a number I didn't recognize. When I answered, the only sound was a loud whistle just like the one I heard before Orla died. After I heard it, it was like I was out of my mind. I mean, I was there, but not there. Driving way too fast, on a route that didn't take me to where I was supposed to be going, and if Mungo hadn't bitten me, I probably would have crashed my car." I took a deep breath. "Quinn, I think I was hypnotized, and so was Orla Black. Furthermore, I think perhaps John Black himself did it, to stop me from looking into their family secrets. If it wasn't him, I bet he knows which of them did it."

Another silence, then: "Mungo bit you?"

"Quinn!"

He sighed. "That's all well and good, and certainly along the lines of some of the other bizarre things you've thrown at me. But you can't just hypnotize someone to kill themselves."

"How would you know?" My tone was bitter.

"Katie, you actually didn't run into anything, did you?"

"No, but—"

"So you're fine."

"Yes, but—"

"Okay, then this is what we are going to do, understand? You're going to text me the phone number of this whistle call you claim to have received. God, I can't believe I'm investigating a prank call, but at least you can tell that 'protective' mother of yours that I'm helping you if she asks. And you are going to stop doing whatever you are doing to make people mad."

"So you think I brought this on myself?"

"I don't think there is a 'this.' I just know how you are."

This time my hand was shaking from anger rather than fear. "Thanks a lot." I gritted my teeth. "Can you tell me if there is a hypnotist that the police department uses?"

"Katie . . ."

"Is there?" I demanded.

"Yes, there's a woman who we use sometimes. But I don't think—"

"Just give me her name," I grated.

He sighed. "Dr. Alexandra Borlof."

"Alexandra Borlof. Thank you. Have a nice evening," I said, and hung up.

Declan came over and took the phone from my hand. "What did he say?"

"The short version? My mommy called to complain that the mean detective wasn't being nice to me, so I tried to explain, and now Quinn thinks I've gone completely nuts." I went over to the bookshelf and grabbed a piece of scratch paper. "However, I have the name of a hypnotist, and she's bound to be reliable if the police use her."

"Good idea," Lucy said.

I marched over and picked up the calming potion. "That man agitates the heck out of me. Even if I hadn't almost wrecked my car, I'd want this now." I downed the liquid in a few gulps.

It hit me like a sledgehammer. As I staggered into the bedroom, I heard Declan ask Lucy and Jaida what else they'd put in it.

"Nothing dear," my aunt said. "Hedgewitches are naturally more sensitive to the herbs they work with. Oh, and our incantation was a doozy, too. Now, I'm going to call that hypnotist and make an appointment for Katie tomorrow morning."

"That's a good idea, but what if she's booked?" Declan asked.

"Don't worry. I can be very convincing when I want to be," Lucy said.

Before my head hit the pillow and it was lights out, I did manage to text Quinn the number my phone had captured.

Prank call, indeed.

Chapter 18

Whatever Lucy had said, it worked, because when I awoke the next morning, I had an eleven forty-five appointment with Dr. Alexandra Borlof. I also had orders from Lucy not to come into work that morning, which was good because I slept in until the ungodly hour of eight o'clock. I didn't remember ever sleeping that long. The closest I'd come was when Lucy gave me some magical seven-layer bars, again containing agrimony, but even then, I'd slept only seven hours.

I took a leisurely shower. We ate a brunch of fruit salad and shrimp with grits on the back patio, and I read the *Savannah Morning News*. The whole thing. I didn't get to do that very often, either. Steve Dawes had written his Downtown Savannah column on the gallery opening Bianca and Randy had attended, and I got a hint of what she might have paid for her "piece," as she'd put it.

It was a lot.

"Cookie called after you went to sleep last night," Declan said, turning a page of the sports section. "She has a place she wants to show us tonight."

The familiar feeling of loss bloomed in my midsection. "Okay."

"Only if you're up for it. She didn't know about what happened, and was going to pick us up at the Honeybee. I said I'd call her back if you weren't feeling up to it, or if we wanted to go from here."

"Nah. We can meet her at the bakery," I said, reaching for the comics. As I did so, I saw Declan watching me.

"What?" I asked.

"You look nice," he said.

I glanced down. For once, I wasn't wearing my work uniform of simple skirt and T-shirt. Instead, I'd donned linen slacks the color of caramel and an ecru silk-blend blouse that draped off my shoulders like a dream. It would have been terrible for trying to knead dough or roll out pastry, but seemed just the ticket for wearing to a hypnotist's office. I wanted to look like someone she could take seriously, not some paranoid wacko who thought a mysterious hypnotist was out to get her.

"Thanks," I said.

"How do you feel?"

I thought about it. "Kind of fuzzy."

He frowned but didn't pursue it. We went back to reading the paper until it was time to leave for my appointment.

Declan insisted on driving. Sitting in his ginormous truck was like being on top of the world, looking down on the other cars around us. However, that was the only way in which I felt on top of anything. The episode the afternoon before had rattled me, and despite Lucy and Jaida's tea knocking me out for several hours, I'd had bad dreams. Twice I'd awoken to find Declan sitting beside me, watching me like a hawk.

No wonder he looked tired.

Now he was taking me to see a bona fide therapist, and in my discombobulated state I felt apprehensive at the prospect.

"Maybe we should just skip this," I said. "I mean, I feel fine. Muzzy from that tea, but fine otherwise."

"Katie, you need to do this."

"I'm not so sure—"

"Please. For me. I can't be wondering whether you're suddenly going to hear a whistle and drive off a cliff."

I was silent for a few seconds as that sank in. "Yeah. Okay."

Dr. Borlof's office was in a friendly professional complex with a large open lobby. No one else was there, and we settled in to wait. The retro blue chairs looked like they could have furnished the set on a sixties sitcom. The pale pink walls first struck me as kitschy; then after a few minutes I realized how calming the color was. My level of agitation had halved by the time a woman opened a nearby door and came out.

Her shoulder-length hair had been expertly colored and blown dry. Mascaraed lashes framed calm hazel eyes. She was dressed casually in jeans, a light mock-neck sweater, and desert boots. The smile that bloomed on her face when she saw us was warm and welcoming, and my anxiety ratcheted down another notch.

"Are you Kate?"

"Katie," I said. "Katie Lightfoot."

She smiled and nodded. "Right. Sorry. I'm Alex. Let's go into my office."

I took a deep breath and followed behind her.

When she saw Declan coming with me, she paused. "I think we'll be fine on our own."

"I want him there," I said.

She opened her mouth as if to say something, then closed it and nodded. "All right."

The office itself was small. The soft cream walls were covered with cheerful modernistic paintings in bright colors. There was a small desk in the corner, a sofa and an easy chair, and a table with a lamp, a clock, and a box of tissues.

Declan and I sat on the sofa, and Alex sat in the chair. She held a small hardback notebook, but hadn't opened it. A pair of half-glasses hung on a lanyard around her neck, and now she perched them on her nose and looked over the top of them at me.

"I understand you got my name from Detective Quinn."

"Yes. He said the department works with you sometimes."

She nodded. "Mostly I work with the victim advocate, but I've also helped a few people remember hazy details from events they've witnessed."

"With hypnosis?"

"Yes. Though mostly I use hypnosis in my practice in other ways. Habit reduction, stress management, improving focus—things like that." She settled back. "Now, tell me exactly why you're here. Your aunt said it was an emergency when she made the appointment."

I glanced at my fiancé. He gave me an encouraging nod, and I started with my story. I didn't tell all of it, of course. I knew that if I said I'd nearly rammed my car into a cement buttress, it would sound like I was potentially suicidal. Which, of course, I wasn't. And I couldn't really tell this woman who knew nothing about me that I was pretty sure someone had hypnotized me, but that I had no idea who it was. Or that I suspected that the same person might have used hypnotism to kill Orla Black. So I stuck to the fiction Declan and I had talked about on the way over.

"An acquaintance of mine was fooling around with hypnotizing a few of us. Like a parlor game, you know?"

She frowned but indicated I should continue.

"It was all very silly, and I didn't think it had worked. At least not on me. Then later that day, I found myself doing things that I don't normally do."

Alex raised an eyebrow. "Like what?"

"Like driving really fast. Reckless, really. I'm usually a very careful driver."

"She is," Declan said. "Buckles her dog into the seat, for heaven's sake."

"Anything else?" Alex asked.

"Well, I meant to drive to work, but I ended up in another part of town. And I could kind of, you know, *see* what I was doing while I was doing it, but I couldn't seem to stop myself."

The therapist looked skeptical. "You think you were operating under some kind of posthypnotic suggestion?"

"Exactly. So I thought I should come to an expert

and get things sussed out. In my brain, you know? I don't want that to happen again. It was scary."

A frown creased her brow. "I dislike it when people play around with hypnosis and don't know what they're doing. It can be such a useful tool. However, for the most part it's harmless. Despite what you might have seen on television, you can't hypnotize someone to do something they wouldn't do anyway." Her lips twitched. "It's sure interesting to see what people would do anyway, though."

"Guess you're a closet race car driver, hon," Declan joked.

I shot him a look. He offered an apologetic moue in return.

"Let's put you under and see if there's anything to worry about," Alex said in a brisk tone as she rose and dimmed the lights. She sat back down. "Close your eyes."

Panicked, I grabbed Declan's hand.

"It's all right," he said, and I heard a tiny lilt from Connell in his voice as well. For some reason, I found that comforting.

Letting go of his fingers, I placed my hands in my lap. "No swinging pendulum?"

She shook her head. "Afraid not."

I closed my eyes and waited.

Alex began to speak very slowly. "Breathe deeply. In. Out. In. Out. That's right." Her tone was smooth and calm. "Allow my voice to wash over you. Allow yourself to relax deeply into the sofa cushions. Be aware that you are safe and at peace. You can open your eyes if you want, or you can keep them closed.

You are in control over your own actions. You control what suggestions to take, and how they will benefit you."

Aware that Declan was sitting right there beside me, I let the tension flow out of my body. I felt myself drifting while at the same time anchored. A part of me acknowledged that this felt different from when I'd been driving the Bug like a madwoman. I knew I could stop whatever was happening to me at that moment if I wanted to.

"Are you relaxed now?"

I nodded.

"Good. Now we're going to look for any hidden suggestions that have been left behind. Are you okay with that?"

"Yes," I answered.

"All right. Do you sense anything? Can you see anything that might be a remnant of another time you were hypnotized?"

"I don't see anything." I felt myself frown.

"That's okay. It's possible there isn't anything. Don't force it. We're just checking."

"Okay." Then: "Wait. There is something."

Vaguely, I felt Declan shift beside me.

"What does it look like?" Alex asked, still slow and calm.

"It's . . . it's a box."

"Describe it."

"It's small." My hands came out in front of me, about six inches apart. "But it's heavy. I can barely lift it."

"That's fine. You don't have to lift it. Just look for the latch."

I felt my hands moving. "There's no latch."

"Is there a keyhole, maybe? Or another way to take off the lid of the box?"

I shook my head. "There's no lid. But there's something inside." I shuddered. "I can tell. It's . . . not nice."

There was silence for a few seconds. "You're sure there's no lid?"

"Yes."

"Okay, we're going to get rid of that box. Are you ready?"

"Yes."

"There's a garbage can by your right foot. I want you to lift that heavy box and drop it into the garbage."

I lifted the box. It took some effort, but I managed to hold it out and drop it.

"It's in the garbage can now?" Alex asked.

"Uh-huh."

"Nicely done. Now I'm going to take the garbage away and put it out on the curb. I'm taking it away now." A pause. "And now I've put it out on the curb. It was just in time, because the garbage truck is coming. Here it is. It's stopping." Another pause. "Okay, the men have loaded that heavy box into their truck, and they're taking it away. Can you hear them leaving?"

I nodded. The receding sound of the garbage truck was clear in my imagination, but I also knew there was, of course, no actual truck. That part of my mind completely understood what the doctor was doing, and I approved. Whatever that metaphorical box was, whatever it held, I was glad to be rid of it any way I could.

"Is there anything else like that box that you can see?" she asked.

"No."

"You're sure?"

I checked again. "Yes."

"Are you ready to wake up?"

"Yes."

"I'm going to count to five, and when I get to five, you will open your eyes and feel alive and refreshed and energized. One . . ."

When she reached five, my eyes popped open. Declan was watching me with frank curiosity.

"How was it?" he asked.

I blinked. "Good." I looked at the therapist. "I think it worked, too."

She smiled. "I think so, too." Then the smile dropped. "Tell your hypnotist friend to stop playing around. And if they try to put you under again, just walk away."

"Don't worry," I said, standing. "I will. Do I need to come back?"

"Not unless it happens again."

I thanked her profusely and promised to sing her praises to Detective Quinn the next time I got a chance. Once we were back in the truck, I asked Declan if we could pick up Mungo and then go to the Honeybee.

"Cookie's not going to meet us there until four," he said.

"I know. I just want to check in on things. Make sure Iris mixes the sourdough levain right."

He rolled his eyes but turned toward the carriage house. "She knows that stuff by now. Plus, Lucy is there. I think you're entitled to a day off once in a while."

"I'll take one soon," I promised. "Maybe we can go away for a few days."

His eyes cut sideways, then back to the road. "I'd like that, but I know better than to think that could happen while you're in the middle of one of your investigations."

I didn't say anything.

"Sorry. I guess that sounded like I'm complaining," he said. "I'm not. I get it."

I flashed him a grateful smile. "Thanks."

"So . . . what happened in there?"

"It was actually quite pleasant. Like being in a calm trance." I shuddered. "But that box was weird. I didn't expect that."

"Yeah, the therapist looked pretty puzzled when you said there was no way to get inside of it."

I turned in the seat. "Really?"

He nodded. "I think she made up the garbage thing on the spot."

I sat back. "Hm. I think it worked, though. I feel . . . lighter? Certainly like I got rid of something. But there are a couple of things that really disturb me."

"What she said about how hypnotism can't make people do something they don't want to do anyway?"

My chin dipped. "Yeah, that's kind of freaky. I mean, I'm glad. Otherwise you could have a bunch of hypnotists getting ahold of politicians or making people commit random acts of crime."

"Like in *The Manchurian Candidate*."

"Exactly."

"Do you think something happened to you—and Orla—besides hypnotism?" he asked.

My brow knit as I thought. "Actually, I think something happened *in addition* to hypnotism. Something that made it stronger or overcame that natural barrier people have against doing things they wouldn't normally do."

"Something magical?"

I shrugged. "The travelers, like other Gypsy clans, are said to have magical traditions. For all I know, they could augment a simple suggestion in a way that makes it an imperative."

"Like your Voice," he said.

I looked sideways at him. He didn't bring it up much, and I was very careful about using it ever since I'd accidentally stopped his heart and breathing with a single word.

"Yeah. Like my Voice." I moved on. "The other thing that bothers me is that I remember every second of what happened in Dr. Borlof's office, but I have no idea what happened at the Black compound. One minute I'd walked out of the O'Clearys' door, and the next I was in my car. Whatever happened in between is still a complete mystery to me."

"Maybe that's what was in that figurative sealed box you threw away."

"I imagine so. Now I kind of regret not trying harder to get inside. I'd have all the answers I need then. As it is, I can guess that one of the Black family tried to kill me with a posthypnotic suggestion, but I don't know which one."

"Or maybe which *ones*."

I sighed. "Right. Heck, it could be all of them."

Declan put his hand on my leg. "Well, even if you

don't remember, I'm glad this trip to Dr. Borlof was successful. I couldn't go through too many more nights like last one."

Weaving my fingers into his, I leaned against his shoulder. "Thanks for taking care of me."

He kissed my hair. "Only for the rest of our lives."

Chapter 19

Declan was right, of course. Iris had the sourdough well in hand, and everything was operating smoothly. So at the bakery, I made a couple of sandwiches and poured sweet tea and grabbed Mungo's leash. Then my fiancé and I spent the next three hours strolling through the historic squares and eating a picnic in Forsyth Park. It was a rare treat, especially after sleeping in, and when we went back to meet Cookie, I felt rejuvenated. Even Declan looked bright-eyed and bushy-tailed.

"I just know you're going to love this one!" Cookie said, ushering us out to her car.

I exchanged grins with Declan. "I'm sure we will."

She stopped and put her hands on her hips. "Really, you two. I'm not kidding. This. Is. The. One."

"Bring it on, darlin'!" he said with a laugh.

She drove us to Paradise Park, wending down streets lined with live oak trees that dripped with Spanish moss. However, a few lots sprawled bare and treeless from the street. She stopped in front of one of these. The only tree on the property was a lone magnolia by the front corner of the house.

Just like at my house.

It was a brick two-story on an oversized lot, also very similar in appearance to the carriage house. The driveway led up the right side of the home, and ended at a two-car garage.

As Declan had requested.

We got out, and Mungo immediately ran to the middle of the front yard.

Yip!

"Okay, little guy." I laughed. "Let's not jump the gun." But I could see why Cookie was beaming from ear to ear.

"It only has two bedrooms," she said. "So it's not too big. But there are also one and three-quarters baths, so you wouldn't have to share—or one could be a guest bath. And there's a den, which you could use to watch television like you have in your loft right now. Come on!"

She hurried to the front door, retrieved the key from the lockbox, and led us inside.

The windows had shutters, and the floors were the same color of wood. The planks weren't as old as the ones in the carriage house, but very similar. Declan grinned as he pointed to a built-in bookcase. It was even in the same part of the living room. We went upstairs to the bedrooms, examining light fixtures, paint condition, and how nicely the closet doors slid open. Real closet doors, not freestanding armoires. We checked out the bright and cheery bathrooms, both of which had been recently updated, and the den, which could just as easily have been called a third bedroom except that it opened off the living room.

"It doesn't have French doors, but you could install them," Cookie said, gesturing us out to the backyard. "And the yard needs to be fenced. It's a clear palette for whatever gardens you want to put in, though. You could even move your gazebo over here. And look!" She pointed to a tower of stones about six feet tall. "It's a fountain. Not the same as your stream, but it's still a water feature."

I smiled. "You are a gem, Cookie. How long did it take you to find this?" Never mind that it didn't feel exactly right. If we bought it, it would become a real home soon enough, right?

"Forever, it seems like. Come see the kitchen."

We trailed back inside. "It's the only downfall," she said. "I mean, it's bigger, but not *too* big. It needs to be updated, for sure. The owners know that, though, and might be willing to come down on the price."

Turning in a circle, I took in the older appliances, the deep windowsill suitable for a row of potted plants, a work surface three times bigger than the small spot on the counter I currently had. She was right that the space could use some updates, but that was doable.

I didn't hate it. I didn't love it as much as I did my carriage house, but it was definitely the best thing we'd seen so far.

It's not going to get any better than this. Stop procrastinating and bite the bullet. Make a decision.

Make the sacrifice—and move on.

"What do you think, Deck?" I asked.

"Do you like it?" he countered.

Cookie looked hopeful.

I smiled. "It has definite possibilities."

My fiancé let out a breath and gave me a small smile. "I think so, too."

"Do you want to make an offer?" Cookie asked.

"Um, can we think about it?" I asked.

"Not for very long," she said. "We need to jump on it as soon as you know you want it."

"Noted," Declan said. "We just need to chat about a few things."

The front door opened, and a very pregnant woman walked in. She was about my age, and she looked surprised to see us. "Oh! I'm sorry. I didn't mean to interrupt. I was just seeing if we'd left a certain teddy bear here that last time we came over. It was never her favorite before, but my daughter has decided that she will simply perish if she can't have it. Excuse me."

She went upstairs, and we heard the closet doors slide. Seconds later, she'd returned. "Nope. It's probably still in one of the boxes I haven't gotten to unpacking yet." She smiled and stuck out her hand. "Laura Brand."

I shook it. "Katie Lightfoot—and this is Declan McCarthy."

She eyed the sapphire engagement ring on my finger. "Ah. What do you think of the place? My husband and I loved it, but the family is getting too big for this space." She patted her ample baby bump.

Before either of us could answer, Cookie stepped forward. "They might be interested. I mentioned the kitchen, however. It's in desperate need of updating."

"True enough," Laura said easily. "We had to choose between that or fixing our badly cracked driveway. We chose the concrete work." A dragonfly buzzed behind her head. She laughed. "It's one of the best driveways in the neighborhood now, though."

Concrete. Could it be?

We went outside to take a look. Leaving Declan to inspect the particulars of the driveway, I asked, "Who did the work?"

"Black and Sons," she said.

Bingo.

Declan heard and came back to stand by me. "It looks like they did a good job," he said.

"Absolutely."

"Did it take very long?" he asked.

"Only a few days," Laura said. "They sent a crew over, and they worked like crazy jackhammering the old cement out and pouring the new drive. And John Black was great to work with. Called every day to update us on where they were in the project. Plus, they came in right on budget."

"So you'd recommend them?"

"Sure." She got a funny look on her face. "But you know, we needed a new driveway. Our old one was in terrible shape. But the Atencios over in that yellow house?" Laura pointed. "They had the same company replace their driveway, even though it was in perfect shape." She shrugged. "Maybe there was something structurally wrong with it, water damage or tree roots or something. Or maybe we're trendsetters! Ha. Anyway, if you need some work done and are looking for more feedback on the company, you might check with them."

We thanked her, and she left to try to unearth her daughter's toy in their new home. As she drove away, Declan and I looked at each other.

"It can't hurt to talk to them," I said.

"Let's go," he said.

"Wait! What about this house?" Cookie demanded.

Yip!

"Well, Mungo's voted," I said.

"We've seen all we need to, and we'll talk it over tonight," Declan said, taking her by the arm and steering her toward the Atencios' yellow house. "Right now, we need to talk to a man about some concrete work."

It wasn't a man who answered the door, though. It was a woman—tall and bony, with vertical creases around her mouth, wearing white polyester pants and a floral print top. She peered at us through thick glasses, saying, "Can I help you?"

Declan smiled at her. "Hello, ma'am. My name is Declan McCarthy. We were just looking at the house down the street there that's for sale?"

She looked between us, then out at Cookie, who had veered over to look at the driveway. "And you were wondering about the neighborhood."

"Well, um, yes," I said.

"Most of the people here are good folks," she said. "There's a bit of riffraff, though. Gonna find that anywhere, I guess. Still, the place has run down a bit, if you ask me. Now, you two look like you'd be a good addition. Hate it that the Brands are selling, but they've got that new one on the way, so it's understandable." She shook her head. "Can't tell you about the schools, though. You'll have to ask some of the people with kids about that. Or you might be able to get some information about that on that Internet. I don't hold with all those fancy computers much, myself. I think you all spend too much time looking at screens nowadays. Itty-bitty screens and middle-sized screens and big ol' TV screens. Lordy, some of those things should be in a theater. You have little ones?"

"Er, not yet," I said.

"Well, when you do, you be sure to have them run around outside in the sunshine, not camp in front of the boob tube like my son lets my grandkids do. Isn't good for them." She suddenly stopped talking, taking us by surprise.

"Um, we were just admiring your driveway. We might need some concrete work done, and Laura Brand said you both had Black and Sons do yours?"

Mrs. Atencio's face clouded. "Oh, we sure did. *We.* Ha. That husband of mine did. Now, the Brands needed a new driveway, absolutely they did. But we absolutely did not. For some dad-blamed reason, my husband got it into his head that he wanted a fancy stamped-concrete thing out there. We have the one car, a Buick we've owned for nearly fifteen years now, and all of a sudden he thinks it deserves some kind of red carpet to drive on from the street into the garage. For Pete's sake. I don't know how that man from Black's convinced him to do such a thing. By the time I found out about it, they had half the old driveway torn out, or believe you me, I would have put a stop to that nonsense faster than you can say 'Jack Robinson.' Yes, I would have. But once they tore it up, they had to finish it, didn't they? At least I told them to just pour a regular old strip of concrete in there." She made a rude noise. "Stamped concrete, supposed to look like steppingstones or something. Ridiculous." She wagged her head back and forth again. "My husband is not usually one to make snap decisions, but it was as if that salesman from Black and Sons hypnotized the foolish man."

I felt the blood drain from my face. "Is that so?" I managed.

"I can't think of another reason he'd tear up a perfectly good driveway just to put in another one."

"Who was the salesman?" I asked.

"I don't know. Had dark hair."

That covered most of the males in the Black family that I'd met, other than Finn. However, Laura had said she'd worked with John Black, so that was probably who had talked to the Atencios.

Heaven knew John had made it fairly clear he didn't like yours truly, first with his antisocial behavior and then by actually threatening to take out a restraining order. He'd been at the top of my suspect list ever since I realized I'd been hypnotized.

Declan looked a question at me. I gave an infinitesimal shake of my head. I couldn't think of anything else to ask her.

"Thank you very much, ma'am," he said.

"You're very welcome. You stop on by if you decide to buy the house. I'll introduce you around to the other neighbors."

We turned to go.

Behind us, she called, "And if you decide to get any concrete work done, stay away from Black and Sons."

Cookie started extolling the virtues of the house we'd just looked at as soon as we got in her car. Declan and I waited for her to wind down, but it didn't happen before we'd reached the bakery. It was after five by then, and the Honeybee was closed. Declan and I told Cookie that we'd call her first thing in the morning with our decision and waved as she drove away.

Once we got in Declan's pickup, I brought up what Mrs. Atencio had said about her husband seeming to be under some kind of thrall when he'd ordered their driveway work. "Do you think John Black uses hypnotism to get work for their company?"

He grimaced. "Maybe. And Mrs. Atencio, as relentlessly opinionated as she is, seemed almost sure there was some unusual influence on her husband."

I gave a kind of facial shrug. "That's more than we've heard about either John Black or Ginnie. I don't even know if Ginnie is really a hypnotist. I just remember her listing it as one of many talents in the Black family." I snapped my fingers. "She did say the skills from her magic act are still useful in the classroom. I'm going to call Colette when we get home and see if she can tell me anything."

He reached over and massaged the back of my neck. "Careful. She's only eight."

"Mmm. That feels great. And of course I'll be careful."

After our brunch and then the late picnic in Forsyth Park, we weren't very hungry for supper. So Declan started on a salad, and I called Bianca. She was happy to let me talk with her daughter, but Colette only said that Mrs. Black had sometimes done card tricks when the class got rowdy. It had grabbed their attention, and all year they'd tried to figure out how she did it. As a kind of going-away present, on the last day of school, she'd shown them how she could always guess the cards they picked.

"It was something about how she handed them to us. I don't remember now," she said.

I thanked her and rang off. So much for Ginnie killing off Orla. Honestly, I'd never thought of her as much of a suspect anyway.

Neither of us ate much salad. Mungo, on the other hand, had made short work of his supper of canned salmon, green peas, and wild rice. He eyed my movements as I packed the rest of the salad and his leftovers into refrigerator dishes. Other than one more sliver of salmon, I ignored his silent pleas. Declan rinsed plates and put them in the dishwasher, and I got out the leftover Pinot Grigio from the fridge.

Neither of us had wanted a drink with dinner, and now we looked at each other. The plan had been to spend the evening after supper curled together on the futon up in the loft, watching a movie. Normally, that would have involved wine.

"None for me," Declan said when he saw the bottle in my hand.

"Yeah, me, too." Returning the bottle, I said, "Tonight I feel—I don't know . . . itchy."

He nodded. "Like on the inside of your brain."

I pointed at him. "Exactly! I take it you feel the same."

"Me and Connell both."

"Uh-oh. That can't be good. I figured my problem is that we're fairly sure who killed Orla, but we can't do anything about it." Furiously, I gave the sink a quick scrub.

"That's bothering me, too," Declan said. "Maybe we need to figure out an action plan."

"Like what?" I said, dropping the sponge in its holder. "Quinn would die laughing if I added a supernatural 'Voice' to my hypnosis theory."

"But Finn and Fern might not. They might know exactly what John is." He held his arms out to me.

I folded into his embrace. "You know, they just might. But John is the head of the family."

Declan stepped back and held me by the shoulders. "You think she'd be okay with him killing her mother?"

"Of course not. But she might not believe he did it. Sometimes it's hard to convince someone they've been duped, you know? They'll keep making excuses rather than admit they were wrong in the first place, especially if they have a vested interest in not accepting the truth."

"A vested interest like a ten-year-old daughter?"

"Or a way of life."

"But Finn doesn't have that investment. Neither does his wife."

I nodded and took his hand. Leading him out to the living room, I said, "You're right. Maybe they will help. Will you go with me tomorrow to talk with them?"

"Of course, my sweet. Now, can we go watch our movie?"

I nodded. "Yeah. I do feel better having a game plan."

Chapter 20

We went upstairs. I got out the comfy blanket to snuggle under, while Declan fed the DVD into the player. I opened the window to let in fresh air, then went down and changed into yoga pants, a sweatshirt, and a pair of Declan's thick cotton socks.

Back in the loft, I rolled my eyes when I saw he'd selected *Jaws* for our viewing pleasure. "I don't know why we don't just stream something."

"Because then you'd be able to veto this movie," he said. "This way, you have to watch it with me because I rented the DVD."

Shaking my head, I settled down with him on the futon. The opening credits started to roll, and I stood back up. "How about some popcorn?"

"Yeah, okay," he said, standing as well. "I'll help."

Ten minutes later we were back upstairs, popcorn in hand, movie rolling again. Five minutes later, I was back on my feet. "How about hot chocolate?"

"Sounds great," he said, and came down to the kitchen to help make it.

"Now, listen," I said when we were both back upstairs with our steaming mugs and popcorn-greased fingers. "We are going to settle down and watch a movie. There's nothing we can do about John Black tonight."

"Right," he said decisively.

And we did manage to watch some of the movie. Once in a while one of us would get up and look out the window or gaze down into the darkened living room, but for the most part we stuck with the plan. Until the scene where the giant shark tried to chomp the boat in half. Right then was when Declan paused the movie.

"Thank heavens," I said, heaving a sigh. "This is nerve-racking."

"Did you hear something?" he asked, going to look down toward the front door again.

"Over that *dun dun dun dun* on the TV? No."

"I thought I did. Probably just the wind."

I frowned. If we were in the movie we'd just been watching, *probably just the wind* would have meant anything but.

Mungo sprang to the floor and stopped still, his feet foursquare. He cocked his head one way, then the other, then suddenly let out a long series of sharp barks. He was headed for the stairs when the sound of glass breaking echoed from down below. He yelped and scampered back as I bolted to my feet.

"It's the front window!" Declan said. "Someone threw something—" He was cut off by a loud whooshing sound accompanied by the smell of gasoline.

"Molotov cocktail," he yelled. "Katie, get outside!"

I ran for the stairs, one part of my brain in complete panic and the other part cataloging what I was seeing: flames erupting from the middle of the living room, licking along the wooden floor, already creeping up the legs of the wingback chairs and reaching for the purple couch. The firelight was reflected in glittering glass shards from the front window, which I hadn't yet shuttered against the night. Thick smoke began to rise toward the ceiling.

"No! No, Katie, over here!"

Following the sound of his voice, I saw Declan had opened the window at the back of the loft all the way. He punched out the screen with a single blow of his fist and hooked a rope ladder over the edge of the sill. I vaguely remembered the ladder as part of a fire kit he'd insisted I keep in one of the cupboards. I'd scoffed at the time, calling it overkill.

I'll never scoff again at anything he does, ever, if we get out of this alive.

"Come on!" he yelled.

"You go first," I said, grabbing up Mungo.

"No. You go. I'll hand you Mungo."

There wasn't time to argue. I ran to the window, handed Declan my familiar, and swung my leg outside. I found the first rung with my foot and brought the other one out. Holding on to the windowsill with one hand, I bundled Mungo against my chest with the other. He tucked his head and held still, never letting out so much as a whimper or a wiggle.

"Good boy," I whispered. "I've got you."

"Go on down," Declan called in a loud voice. "I'll be right behind you."

I stepped down to the next rung. I would have given nearly anything to have a sling or my tote bag, or any safe way to carry Mungo, but I didn't. I also didn't want to let go with the one hand I could really use to hang on to the unsteady ladder. So I ended up running my hand from the sill to the rope at the side of the ladder, inching it down to the next rung, where I could take purchase, and taking another step down.

Then I did it all over again.

It seemed to take an eternity to get from one step to the next. About halfway down, my fingers cramped, and I nearly lost my grip. Hooking my arm around a rung, I hung there for a moment, catching my breath and trying to convince myself that I didn't have to hang on *quite* so hard.

With a pang, I realized I was making Declan wait. He couldn't get onto a flimsy ladder like this if I was still on it. Heck, I wasn't sure it would hold him once I was on the ground. But right now he was up there in the loft where all the toxic smoke was rising from the burning furniture below him.

Hurry.

I took the next step and looked up to tell him I was almost down, but he wasn't watching out the window. Panic rose in my chest. Why wasn't he there?

Mungo nosed my neck, reminding me that we were still stuck twelve feet above the ground.

"Okay, okay," I muttered, and began inching my way down again.

Finally, I stepped on solid ground. I quickly put Mungo down. "I need to check inside. You stay safe."

Yip!

I knew I could trust him. As I turned to run to the back patio, I felt in my pocket. My phone! I took a couple of steps and realized a shadowy figure was standing between me and the back door to the carriage house. My heart bucked, and adrenaline flooded my veins. Then I saw who it was.

"Margie? Oh, thank God. Where are the kids? They need to stay inside."

"They're with Redding at his mother's."

"Whew!" I held up my phone. "Have you already called 911?"

"No."

"Oh." I frowned. Why did she sound so funny? "I'll do it." I began to dial.

She stepped forward and knocked the phone out of my hand.

I stared at her, stunned. "What . . . Why did you do that?" I spluttered.

As she moved her left arm, I realized she'd been holding something behind her back. Now she brought it up, and I saw what it was.

A butcher knife. It looked brand-new. Very shiny—and sharp.

"What is wrong with you?" I screamed, utterly terrified to see my friend like this—not to mention that I had a particular phobia about knives anywhere but in the kitchen. And yet, as the question came out of my mouth, I already knew the answer.

The sharp whistle that came from the back corner of the yard confirmed my worst fear.

Margie took a step toward me. I backed away, toward the direction the whistle had come from.

Where is Declan?

Slowly, I continued backward, Margie keeping pace, her eyes not seeming to recognize me, her hand surer on that knife blade than it would ever have been in her kitchen.

"John!" I called. "I know it's you behind this. I know what you did to me. And I know what you did to Orla."

A low laugh sounded behind me. It gave me the chills. I glanced over my shoulder, but saw only the moonlit garden beds. It wasn't like I could turn my back on Margie for a proper look, either.

"The police know about Orla, too. And they know about how you manipulate people into getting concrete work they don't need."

This time there was no laugh, only silence. Did he believe me? Or was he up to something else? Could he have left now that he had Margie hypnotized to do his dirty work?

Movement in the shadows of the gazebo made my heart leap. Had John moved?

Hoping against hope that it was Declan hiding by the gazebo, and not John Black, I narrowed my eyes in an attempt to see better.

Margie took advantage of my attention wandering from her to take two quick steps toward me, and I stumbled backward.

The figure behind her stepped into the moonlight. It wasn't Declan. It was the head of the Black clan.

Quietly, he padded toward Margie.

"Watch out!" I screamed. "Margie, turn around!"

It was as if she hadn't heard me at all. She didn't even blink.

He came up behind her and met my eyes for a split second before he wrapped his arms around hers, pinning them to her sides. She bent and twisted, trying to throw him off. She was a big girl, and he wasn't terribly tall or young, but he was muscular nonetheless. He managed to hang on.

"Leave her alone!" I yelled.

"I'm trying to keep her from killing you, you nitwit. I've been trying to keep you safe from that boy ever since I found out he killed Orla." Pain shone in his eyes. *"Go."* He grunted with the effort of holding Margie. "Run."

He's trying to save me . . . ? From whom?

My mind flicked through the possibilities in a flash as I turned to run.

Finn?

No. He didn't kill his mother.

Aiden?

What possible motive?

Taber?

The ventriloquist who could throw his voice. The one who had been right there when Orla had had trouble with a client on the riverfront, and the one who had helped threaten Spud the juggler. The man who benefited from his mother-in-law's life insurance through both his wife and his daughter, a payout that wouldn't occur if his wife divorced him or if Orla somehow managed to cancel the insurance on her own life.

Yes. Taber.

Declan came around the corner of the house. His face was smudged with soot, and one side of his hair was matted to his head. Water dripped from his T-shirt. He grabbed the hem of the wet fabric as he walked, and pulled it up to wipe his face and red-rimmed eyes.

"Aargh!" Margie cried out as John wrestled her to the ground. I stopped in my tracks. She still had the knife, and I was afraid for him.

Still, what I called out was, "Don't hurt her. She doesn't know what she's doing."

"I know that!" he gritted out, finally getting a hold on her wrist and pressing until she opened her hand.

The butcher knife fell to the ground. Silently, she reached for it with her other hand. I rushed forward and kicked it away.

"What the hell is going on?" Declan demanded.

"Nice," Taber said, stepping out from behind the witch hazel bush. He was carrying Cobby, the creepy wooden dummy. "We'll just have to try again." But the next words came from Cobby, the voice high and thready, like that of a querulous old woman. "John, get up."

Hearing that voice brought it all flooding back. Everything that had been in the heavy seamless box that Dr. Borlof had helped me get rid of that morning. I began shaking all over as I remembered.

The afternoon before, after I'd left Fern's town house and was walking down the block to my car, Taber had stepped out from the end unit, the second one with a red door, and invited me in. I'd hesitated, and then he'd held up Cobby, and Cobby had invited me in. And I'd gone.

He'd told me what route to take home. He'd told me when I got to Louisville Road to speed up and head for the bridge support as fast as my car would take me. And he'd told me to forget that he'd talked to me, and that all I'd need was to hear the whistle.

It hadn't been regular hypnosis, not the kind Dr. Borlof had used that morning to clear away Taber's ugly suggestions. It had been something *like* hypnosis—plus exactly what Declan and I had suspected. His Voice.

Taber O'Cleary had a very powerful Voice indeed, but he seemed to need the dummy to make it work.

Well, two could play at that game.

Then I remembered the last thing he'd done right before he'd sent me off to my car—and my death.

He'd kissed me on the cheek. His lips had felt moist, like two worms against my skin. The memory made me ill, and instinctively I wiped at my face with the back of my hand as if I could erase the violation.

Then I got angry.

I picked up the knife. Not because I had any intention of using it, but because I didn't want anyone else to use it at Taber's—or Cobby's—behest. But Taber didn't know that.

"John, take that knife away from her," the dummy shrieked. "Hurry!"

The older man shook his head, as if trying to throw off Cobby's suggestion. Then he took a step toward me.

"John, go wait out front," I said, layering my own considerable Voice between the words. It felt rusty. I'd been too frightened to use it.

Now I didn't have a choice.

John hesitated.

"Go on," I said to him. "It's okay." I added a little more Voice.

"Get the knife!" Cobby demanded.

John stayed where he was.

Margie got to her feet, though. She seemed confused. Declan was striding toward me.

Too much was going on at once, and every time I used my Voice, I felt like I was betraying myself—and Declan. I'd almost killed him with it once, and though I'd slipped a couple of times since then and used it in its mildest form possible, I'd sworn I'd never use it full force again.

Now I *wanted* to use it. I needed to. But what if it was wrong? What if I hurt someone again?

As if he sensed my hesitation, Taber lunged forward. Holding the dummy high, he turned toward Declan, who was now ten feet away from me, blinking in a red-eyed daze.

Oh. Hell no.

Without thinking, I leaped in front of Declan, reaching out to everything I knew. To the thrumming energy of the earth below, to the spirits of the water in the stream, to the elements of air all around us, and to the fire of the flames that had flown through my window and the cold fire of Luna shining down on us from above. I invoked the archangels Michael, Gabriel, Raphael, and Uriel, and grabbed the tendrils of power extended to me by Mungo nearby and Connell deep inside Declan. Nonna was there, too, and someone new.

Orla?

In less than an instant, I wove the energies together into a shield in front of Declan and myself, spreading my arms wide and finalizing it with one Voice-laden word.

No.

A streak of moonlight sparked on the tip of the knife I still held in my right hand and shot down my arm. My skin erupted with light.

Taber's eyes grew wide. For a few seconds, he stood rooted to the spot, his mouth open, his dummy silent. Then he turned and ran.

"Oh, no, you don't!" I ran after him.

He was laughing as he clambered over the back fence. He moved like a monkey, and it was true that there was no way I could catch him.

But I didn't want Taber.

A split second before Orla's murderer was over it, I reached the fence. Dropping the knife, I grabbed Cobby by the shoulders and pulled. Hard.

"No, no, let go, let *go*," Taber protested. Only it was the dummy's voice. Or, rather, the dummy's Voice.

"Doesn't work on me anymore," I said, and gave another yank.

The wooden doll came flying out of his grasp. Taber howled, standing on the other side of the fence. Holding the awful thing as far away from me as I could, I ran over to the stream. Declan caught up with me there.

"What are you going to do?" he asked.

"Drown it."

Did it just twitch in my hand? *Yes.*

I shuddered and almost dropped it. Then I gritted my teeth and tightened my grip.

"What are you talking about?" he asked. "It's made of wood."

I held it above the water. "I've neutralized other things in this stream. Maybe it will work on this." I plunged the dummy into the recently moon-blessed, spring-fed, live water.

A cloud of steam rose, as if the dummy had been molten steel. The stream boiled and hissed. Stunned and frightened, I leaped away.

Declan caught me, and we stood like that for what seemed like a long time, watching the steam dissipate, the water settle. A cloudiness marred the sparkling surface for a few minutes; then that washed away, too. Hesitantly, I dipped my fingers into the cool, clear water, touching a submersed wooden leg.

It just felt like wood. It didn't seem creepy at all.

Cobby was dead.

A soft sob came from the direction of the fence, then a rustling. We ran over, and I pulled myself up in time to see Taber running away through the field on the other side.

Declan started to climb over, but I put my hand on his arm. "Let him go. He can't do any harm now. We'll tell the police about . . . Well, we'll think of something."

I looked back and saw John Black still stood in the

middle of the yard. His eyes were clear now, though full of a deep, incomprehensible sorrow.

"Taber killed Orla, didn't he?" I asked.

He nodded. "Yes."

"Why didn't you turn him in?" I asked.

"No one would have believed me," he said. "And even if they had, it would have destroyed the family." His jaw set. "I would have punished him in time, though."

I believed him.

Turning, John Black walked out toward the street. Perhaps he knew where Taber had gone. Perhaps he wanted only to return to his family. A sharp arrow of gratitude caught me by surprise. The man had tried to warn me away numerous times—not to threaten me, but to protect me from Taber's nasty manipulations.

"Katie? I seem to . . . I think I might have had a little too much wine."

Margie was swaying on her feet beside the gazebo. Mungo hovered protectively by her foot.

I hurried over, pulling Declan with me. "Oh, honey, that's okay. I think we've all had a bit too much wine. Don't you, Deck?"

He stared at me, then blinked. "Right," he said, then turned a high-wattage smile on Margie. "Let me walk you home. Where's Redding again?"

"He took the kids over to his mother's for the night. It's funny—I don't feel like I had too much wine, but how did . . . ?"

"We had some excitement," Declan said, meeting

my eyes before turning away. "It's all kind of a blur for me, too."

"Why is your shirt wet?" Margie asked as she and Declan went through the gate to the front yard.

"Oh no! The fire!" I gasped, and ran to the patio, Mungo close at my heel.

Chapter 21

I rushed to the French doors, pulled them open, and went inside. The smell was horrific, a mean chemical scent of burned upholstery and varnish, and fire extinguisher chemicals. My throat tightened against it, and for a moment, it felt like I was choking.

Fire extinguisher. It's out. Declan put the fire out. He saved the carriage house.

Hoping against hope, I reached into the kitchen and flipped the switch by the door. Yellow light flooded through the opening, illuminating enough of the living room to reveal the extent of the damage. Breathing into the crook of my elbow, I surveyed the ruin one flaming bottle of gasoline had wrought.

The floor was streaked with black, and in places it was burned through to leave only striated swaths of charcoal. The chairs and couch were utter trash, singed and soggy, slumped in permanent defeat. The trunk had survived the Civil War, but not the Molotov cocktail. The metal might be able to be saved, but the wood along the sides was as black as the middle of the floor. The bookcase looked relatively unscathed, though the protective basil wreath above it had burned to delicate white ash. That smell would permeate everything I owned. I wouldn't be able to keep much of anything.

I didn't care. The house was okay.

The front door was open. The garden hose still lay across the threshold where Declan had left it after using it to help put out the fire. That was why he hadn't come down the rope ladder behind me. A firefighter through and through, he'd saved me, then come back to fight the flames.

Having delivered my neighbor back home, he was suddenly there, filling the doorway with his broad-shouldered, narrow-hipped silhouette.

"Katie?"

"Oh, Declan."

In a few long strides, he was gathering me into his arms.

"You saved my house," I sobbed into his shirt. "You came back and saved it." I seemed to be repeating myself, but I couldn't help it.

He held me close and murmured into my hair. "You really love this place, don't you?"

"Yes! I love it. And I love you."

And then came the ugly cry.

Not the gentle tear wending its way down a genteel cheek. Not the eyes welling and gracefully spilling over. Not even the tear-streaked face of sadness or melancholy.

No, the ugly cry is the one where you can't talk, can barely choke breath in and out of your lungs. Can't form words, can't even *think* words, only animal grunts and wails and groans. The cry that takes over your whole body, tightens every muscle, makes you consider the possibility that you might be, just might be, completely losing your mind. And there are so many tears coursing out of your tear ducts that they splash on your shirt and his shirt and the dog, and you come out of it dehydrated and weak and shaking, your eyes and face so puffy and swollen that you look like an alien from another planet, and you can barely see, and you feel like you could sleep for days once you're through.

That kind of ugly cry.

And Declan just stood there and held me, saying, "I didn't know. It's okay. It's going to be okay."

It might have gone on for even longer if the flashing lights and sirens hadn't pulled up in front.

"I called them," Declan said, almost apologetically.

"Right. Of course," I managed, pushing back from his now double-soaked shirt and wiping furiously at my streaming eyes.

I ran into the kitchen and blew my nose on a paper towel, then went to the freezer for ice to shock myself into normalcy. Instead, I found myself reaching into the fridge and pulling out my jar of moon potion. I slopped out a handful and rubbed the chilled liquid on my face.

It helped. I stopped crying in record time. I blew my nose again. I breathed deep.

And with a hiccup, I went out to greet the firemen.

The front yard was lit up like a stadium, and Declan had gone out to talk to the responders. Someone was standing in the living room, but with the bright light behind him, I couldn't make out who it was until he turned.

Detective Peter Quinn.

Great.

Eyes smarting from smoke and tears and xenon lights, I turned and went out to the backyard.

Quinn trailed behind me all the way out to the gazebo.

I climbed the steps and pulled over a thrift-store chair. He grabbed another one and sat down across the small table. Mungo put his paws on my thigh, and I reached down and scooped him up. His warm, furry form gave me some comfort as I tried to figure out what to tell Quinn.

Wait a minute. . . .

"Why are you here?" I asked. "No one's dead."

"Orla Black is dead. And from what you told me yesterday, you came close."

"You believe me now?"

"I got another call from John Black a few minutes ago. Since I'd talked to him before, they forwarded it to my cell. He told me his nephew-in-law tried to kill you tonight."

"The Molotov cocktail through my front window." Of course, technically I didn't know if Taber had done that or forced Margie to.

"Anything else?"

"Isn't that enough?"

"No more hypnotism?" Quinn asked.

With great control, I set Mungo on the floor and then stood. "Listen, I've had a really difficult day, so

I don't need your condescending, holier-than-thou attitude, Detective Quinn. I don't care whether you believe me or not. Taber O'Cleary hypnotized me yesterday and nearly made me run my car head-on into a chunk of cement. In fact, I went to your very capable Dr. Borlof this morning, and she removed the posthypnotic suggestion he left."

His eyes widened. "Really?"

"Yes. You can ask her. I'll sign whatever she wants so she can answer your questions. And as a result of that single session with her and then seeing the jerk tonight, I remember exactly what he did when he hypnotized me. I'll testify to it in court. Furthermore, I'm positive that he did the same thing to Orla." I shoved the chair under the table, hitting the leg and making it rock back and forth. "But don't believe me. Oh, no, don't even bother. Ask John Black himself. If he's willing to tell you that Taber tried to kill us here tonight, then I hope he'll be willing to tell you all about his nephew-in-law's abilities with ventriloquism and hypnosis.

"Now, if you'll excuse me, I'm going to go see if I can salvage any of my clothes to take to Declan's for the night, because we obviously can't sleep here after the fire. Good night, Detective."

And with that, I exited the gazebo and walked back to the house with as much dignity as I could muster. When I looked outside later, he was gone.

It was nearly midnight when we got to Declan's apartment. I'd salvaged some clothes from the armoire, the doors of which luckily had a very tight seal. Now I threw them in his washer and plopped down on his sofa. He poured two glasses of wine, which we both were quite ready for by then, and joined me.

Handing me a glass, he said, "Are you going to tell Cookie, or am I?"

"Tell her what?" I asked.

He rolled his eyes. "That we're not going to make an offer on the house she showed us today." He looked at his watch. "Make that yesterday."

I was silent for almost a minute. "You're sure you don't want to make an offer? It's what you want, isn't it?"

He laughed. "I thought it was what you wanted."

"But what do *you* want?" I insisted.

"First off, I want you to be happy." When I opened my mouth to speak, he held up his hand. "Let me finish. Having said that, there are a few things I wouldn't mind having that we don't currently have at the carriage house."

"Like a lot more space." I sipped my wine.

"No, not a lot. A little more, yes. And I would like a garage. Not just for the truck, but for some of my hobbies."

My forehead creased. "Like what?"

"Like woodworking." He took a swallow and replaced his glass on his beat-up bachelor coffee table.

"Since when do you like woodworking?" I asked.

"I've always liked it, but I've never had a place where I could do it. Heck, I don't even know if I'm any good at it. I just enjoyed it in school, and I'd like to take it up."

"I had no idea. Why didn't you say something?"

He shrugged. "I said I wanted a garage."

"And more living space."

"We need a little more room in the kitchen," he said. "Again, not a lot more than we have now in the carriage house. Say, another ten square feet. Maybe fifteen. And a full bath with a tub. A separate room for the washer and dryer. And honestly, I think we need another bedroom. At least I hope we'll need one at some point. We can always have guests stay in the loft like they do now, but someday we might need another bedroom for, you know . . ."

I raised my eyebrows.

"More family."

"Is your mother going to come live with us?" I teased.

"You know what I mean. I'm just thinking ahead. I mean . . . you do want children, don't you?"

"At least one," I said. "After that, we'll see."

He grinned. "It's a start."

"So you just gave a long list of all the things we need, and all those things are in the house we looked at today. But you also said something about putting guests in the loft. There wasn't a loft in that house."

He stared at me.

"What?"

"You don't know what I'm talking about, do you?" he asked. "You love that carriage house. I mean, it's like a part of you or something. Taking you away from it would be like taking away a family member."

I shuddered, thinking of Orla.

"Sorry. You know what I mean. That was you crying in my arms a few hours ago when you realized your home hadn't burned to the ground, wasn't it?"

"It was a very long day, and someone had just tried to kill me, and you, and the Molotov—"

"Katie!" he interrupted. "That fire was an opportunity."

"You mean . . . ?" I was afraid to hope.

"We're going to have to make repairs anyway. Why don't we add in a few renovations as well?"

"To the carriage house?" I asked in a small voice.

"Yes! Katie, we're living together there now. Have been for months. When was the last time I stayed here? We've been doing okay with the space we have at your place, really. But there have been times when it's too crowded, and a little more room might be nice for the long haul. We can build an addition off the back hallway and the current bedroom, in order to add another, smaller bedroom and increase the size of the bathroom. Plus, there would be space for a little laundry room. Then we extend the kitchen a few feet on the other side. That will actually make the patio deeper, which will make it more of an outdoor room."

"And the garage?"

"A freestanding one at the end of the existing driveway. How does all that sound?"

I get to keep my carriage house. Our *carriage house. All the gardens. The stream. The rowan tree.*

Tears welled in my eyes. "It sounds perfect," I said in a warbling voice.

Declan looked alarmed.

I laughed and wiped my eyes. This was not the occasion for another ugly cry. This was an occasion for happy tears.

Yip!

Mungo apparently agreed.

Chapter 22

Cookie didn't take the news too badly. In fact, she didn't take it badly at all. When we told her we'd decided to renovate the carriage house and continue to live there, I might even have detected a flicker of relief that she wouldn't have to deal with our fussy real estate demands anymore. Plus, she'd managed to sell the town house down the street from Lucy and Ben, and was getting her full commission from that sale rather than the half that she'd offered to take from Declan and me.

She was also distracted as anything, reading parenting books and augmenting her maternity wardrobe with only slightly more conservative styles than usual. Then she brought in the ultrasound, and I knew the shopping was about to increase tenfold.

"Can you tell if it's a girl or a boy?" Lucy asked, leaning closer. The spellbook club was gathered in the reading area of the Honeybee, with a new pile of books to supply the bookshelves. I'd brought back *Telling Fortunes for Fun and Profit* in case someone else needed it and thrown in a copy of Julie Andrews' classic orphan tale, *Mandy*.

"Nope," Bianca said. "At three months, it's still a little bean of a thing. Maybe the next time."

Mimsey, today dressed head to toe in fuchsia, looked over at Cookie. "Do you want to know?"

The mother-to-be shrugged. "I don't know. Oscar kind of wants it to be a surprise. I can work with that. I'm already starting to decorate the nursery in gender-neutral colors. Actually, all colors." She whipped out a catalog. "Look at this adorable little mobile for over the crib!"

Jaida, who was finally back to working in her newly decorated office, leaned closer. "Is that a constellation night-light?"

And so began the shopping. . . .

Steve walked in, and I reached for a cappuccino mug. He laid a copy of the *Savannah Morning News* on the counter. "Have you seen this?"

I peered at the article he was pointing at, and Ben took over making his drink. When he was done, he set it down in front of Steve and asked me, "What is it?"

"Taber O'Cleary has been arrested for Orla Black's murder." I looked up, unable to keep the surprise off my face. "He confessed."

Steve nodded. "From what I hear from my former sources on the crime beat, John Black encouraged him to cooperate with the police."

I raised an eyebrow. "I wonder what form that encouragement took."

He shook his head. "Apparently, Taber was a kind of enforcer for his uncle. But then Orla began lobbying her son and daughter to move to California with her. Fern was open to the idea, but Taber didn't want to go. So to prevent the breakup of the family—his own small one and the Black clan as a whole—Taber killed his mother-in-law—who happened to also be the woman John wanted to marry. That was bound to end poorly."

"But Orla didn't want to marry John."

Steve smiled. "Rejection doesn't make the heart grow less fond."

A less-than-oblique reference to our history? "How's Angie?"

His face softened, as did his smile. That was enough to put my mind at rest. "She's opening her own nursery," he said. "It's hard work."

"Her own business? That's great." And I had no doubt that Dawes Corp. was bankrolling it.

Good for them.

A smiling Vera Smythe came into the Honeybee. Her hair was back in a precise French twist, her eye makeup was flawlessly applied, and her pale pink lipstick immaculate. She wore a beige twinset with white slacks and beige heels that would have killed me in less than ten minutes.

Her arm was looped through that of a handsome man. He was a bit older than her, with a salt-and-pepper brush cut and soulful brown eyes. I noticed she was still wearing her wedding ring, then saw that he was wearing one, too. Then I saw that both rings had the Greek letter omega in the setting.

Matching wedding rings. This was Vera's husband, not a date.

"You came back," I said. "I'm so glad. What would you like to try today? We have caramel-dipped vanilla whoopie pies for our daily special. Or if you like a little tartness, the lemon bars turned out especially good."

"A lemon bar sounds great," he said. "And a cup of black pekoe tea, if you have it."

"Coming right up," I said.

"Katie, this is my husband, Robert," she said. "This is Katie Lightfoot. I met her at Vase Value, and now I'm addicted to the baked goods here."

He reddened a bit when she mentioned Mimsey's flower shop.

"Welcome to the Honeybee Bakery, Robert. We hope you'll come back again and again."

"I'll try the rosemary Parmesan muffin," Vera said. "And lemon water."

Rosemary for fidelity.

"Good choice." I put their selections onto a tray, and Vera handed it to Robert. He carried it over to a table, while Vera lingered by the register.

"Are the flowers arriving again?" I asked with a smile.

"We're not including flowers in our budget anymore," Vera said.

When I looked surprised, she added, "I wanted to bring these books back. They were very helpful, but I don't need them anymore."

She placed the books she'd borrowed from the Honeybee library on the coffee counter. I recognized the one on divorce, but hadn't seen the title of the other one: *Mindful Loving.*

"I'm glad," I said. Vera could easily have returned the books to the shelves with no one the wiser. She wanted to talk.

"Well, one was helpful. The other one, it turns out, I didn't need at all." She sighed and looked at Robert over her shoulder. "See, that fortune-teller told me my husband was distracted from our marriage. Naturally, I immediately assumed that to mean he was having an affair. Then the carnations he'd sent every week for years stopped coming, and I was sure of it. I was devastated, but I wasn't going to let him take advantage of me. Then I read that book." She pointed to the second one. "And I decided to simply ask him why he wasn't sending the flowers anymore. No accusations, no blame or defensiveness. And do you know what he said?"

I shook my head.

"That he was having financial problems in his business, and had to cut back." She sounded almost delighted. Then she sobered. "It's only temporary, but he was too ashamed to tell me. Poor man. And here I was, all ready to find a lawyer and start divorce proceedings." She wagged a finger. "So whatever the fortune-teller told you, be careful about how you interpret it."

Thinking of my worries about having to give up the carriage house in order to be with Declan, I had to agree. Maybe not all sacrifices felt like sacrifices in the end.

* * *

"I like deviled eggs. I could eat them every day," Iris said.

"They're okay," I said. "But I think I like egg salad better. With lots of sour pickles, dill, and a little mustard. Some chopped capers, maybe. Scooped onto a soda cracker, or open-faced on a toasted English muffin."

Iris slowly worked cold cubes of butter into a bowl of flour with her fingertips. I was cleaning while she practiced her scone-making technique, and we were passing the time by discussing options for using up leftover Easter eggs after the holiday.

"My stepmom soaks the peeled eggs in red wine before making them into deviled eggs," Iris said. "They're really pretty on a plate."

I made a note to try that.

"You know the best recipe I've found for hard-boiled eggs is in chocolate chip cookies," I said.

"Very funny."

"No, I'm serious."

Iris' fingers stilled in the bowl as she peered at me. "Seriously?"

"Yup. You cut them up really small, and add them to the batter instead of raw eggs. The batter is a little drier, and the end result is a little more dense, but they're really good."

"Trust a baker to do something like that," she muttered.

"Keep working that butter," I said with a grin.

She went back to her scones, and I went back to scrubbing.

I heard Detective Quinn's voice before I saw him. A part of me wanted to scurry into the office, shut the door, and pretend I didn't know he was in the bakery. While I was debating whether to follow that instinct, Lucy called me out to the register.

Squaring my shoulders, I took a deep breath and came out from behind the rack of shelves I'd been wiping down. Quinn stood by the display case, waiting. Briskly, I joined my aunt.

"Detective," I said, "what can we get for you today? The croissants are especially good."

"Can we talk?" he asked.

Ah, those words almost no one wants to hear.

Lucy's eyes darted between us.

Ben had been watching from the coffee counter, and walked over. "Hello, Peter." He had his best poker face on, but I knew he was being protective.

Quinn inclined his head. "Ben. Good to see you. How have things been?"

"Fine."

A silence stretched out for several seconds, long enough to hear a laughing couple pass by on the sidewalk outside the door.

"Oh, for heaven's sake," I said. "Come back to the office. We can talk there."

The detective gave a quick nod and followed me through the kitchen. My aunt and uncle watched him every step of the way.

"We can talk in here, Detective," I said, repeating myself but hoping to give Mungo a heads-up.

It worked. When I opened the door and walked in, he was nowhere to be seen. Quickly, I moved the afghan he slept on from the club chair and gestured to Quinn.

"Please, have a seat."

He remained standing, looking all around the room. "Where's the dog?"

I raised my eyebrows in question and blinked as innocently as I knew how.

Quinn's lips turned up in a wry quirk. "He's not in the reading area, so he must be back here. Did you really think I didn't know?"

"Um . . ."

"I'm a homicide detective. Why do you think I'd care about your dog sleeping in the office?"

Mungo wiggled out from behind the file cabinet, and Quinn reached down to pet him. A slight smile still hovered on his face as he straightened; then it was gone.

"Is that what you wanted to talk to me about? My dog?"

Quinn looked away. He started to rub his hands together, then caught himself and abruptly stopped. "Not exactly."

I folded my arms, ready for a lecture.

"I came to tell you that you were right, and I was wrong."

My jaw slackened. "What?" I asked stupidly.

"You were right. I was wrong." He sighed, and sat down in Mungo's chair. "I should have listened to you."

Slowly, I sank into the desk chair and swiveled to face him. "Um . . . thanks?"

He leaned back and regarded me. "So how did you know?"

"You mean about Orla?"

He looked briefly at the ceiling, then back at me. "Yes, about Orla. How did you know from the very beginning that her death was suspicious?"

"Oh." I tried to think of an answer that wouldn't involve familiars, my dead grandmother, or Connell. "You know that conversation we had after the murder on the movie set? About intuition and gut feelings?"

"It was more than that," he said flatly.

I held his gaze. "Yeah. Maybe it was."

"What?"

"I can't tell you."

"Because I won't believe you?"

I didn't say anything. But I didn't look away, either.

Finally, he looked down at his hands. Nodded to himself. Looked back up. "I saw you glow that night. In the back of the Fox and Hound."

"Glow?"

"Stop it. This is the seventh time you've been responsible for bringing a murderer to justice in two years. That's my job—"

"I didn't mean to step on your toes."

He held up his hand. "Wait. Let me finish. I was going to say, that's my job—solving murders. It can be stressful, and difficult, but I love it, and I believe it's important."

"It is!" I said.

"And even though you make me crazy, getting in trouble and asking questions all over the place and making people mad, and . . ." He trailed off. Took a deep breath. ". . . and making me listen to your weird theories, you've helped me do my job."

I blinked. Unsure of what to say, I didn't say anything at all.

Quinn leaned forward. "So I think I'm not only stuck with you, but that there might be a reason I'm stuck with you."

"Like fate?"

One shoulder rose and dropped. "Maybe something like that. Or maybe something else."

My breath caught in my throat. "Like what?"

"I don't know. I've thought a lot about how you seem to know things I don't, or find out things I can't. Part of it is because you're a civilian, of course, and a woman. But there's something else. And there are other things, too. That crazy scene in the graveyard, the strange connection between you and my old partner, the cases that ended up involving voodoo, and that thing in the swamp. Not to mention this last time. You glowed, Katie. *Glowed.* I saw it. And I saw you do something else that didn't seem human."

I laughed a shaky laugh. "Maybe you think I'm from outer space?"

He didn't crack a smile. "Katie. Seriously. What *are* you?"

All my senses felt like they were in overdrive, almost like when I found myself in danger. But I didn't feel any danger coming from Quinn. Only curiosity—and quite a bit of nervousness.

Well, he'd asked.

"I'm a witch."

He barked a laugh, then covered his mouth with his hand. When he saw I was serious, he dropped it. "A witch."

I nodded. "A hedgewitch, actually. Runs in the family." *Sorry, Lucy. Didn't mean to out you without your permission.* "Kitchen magic. Garden magic. Like the women healers of days gone by."

"Okay." He drew out the words. "So you're into that kind of thing."

I bristled.

"But that does not explain this—this *attraction* you have to murder. To finding criminals."

"Apparently, I'm also what they call a catalyst," I said reluctantly. Wasn't it enough that I'd revealed I was a witch? Did I have to tell him the rest? "So things kind of happen around me."

"Uh-huh. They sure do."

"And, uh, Franklin Taite is the one who told me I'm also a lightwitch. That's what I think you're really asking. It's kind of like a calling to seek out justice when needed."

His eyes had widened more than I'd ever seen them. Had I told him too much? It didn't matter. I plunged on.

"And other than Mavis Templeton, all of your cases that I've been involved in have had some kind of magical element to them. For all I know, hers did, too. In retrospect, I think she might have been a witch who practiced dark magic. *Unlike* me."

He opened his mouth. Closed it. Finally, he spluttered, "Franklin Taite! He was in on this whole thing!"

"He was a hunter," I said.

"A—" He clamped his mouth shut.

"A witch hunter. All evil really." I shrugged. "But I don't practice dark magic. I mean, there is a lot of gray magic, and it gets complicated, but yeah. He thought I was bad news at first—then there was that whole lightwitch thing." I took a breath and looked at Mungo. My poor familiar looked stunned that I was telling Quinn all of this. "See, he saw me glow, too." I held up my hand. "I only do it under duress, see. But he saw it, and that was when he told me I was a lightwitch. Of course he also lied about what that meant, and—"

Quinn held up both hands to stop me. "Okay, okay. That's all I can absorb for the moment."

I stopped talking. It had been like a flood I couldn't hold back, such a relief to be able to tell him. But as soon as silence descended between us, I wanted to pull back the words, swallow them whole, make him forget that he'd heard them. Sitting there under his gaze, I felt raw and vulnerable, unsure and frightened.

For a nanosecond, I thought of using my Voice the same way that Taber O'Cleary had, to try to wipe Quinn's memory clean of all that I'd just revealed.

No. No, no, no. I will not do that.

I raised my chin and waited.

"Well," he said finally. "That certainly explains a lot. And it gives me a lot to think about." He stood, and as he looked down at me, his gaze softened. "Don't look like that, Katie. I know you think I'm an ogre sometimes, probably because sometimes I am. But I believe you. You know, as best I can. I know one thing for sure, though—you're a good person, and you've helped me immeasurably."

I stood. "I, uh, don't go spreading what I told you around, you know?"

He looked insulted. "Of course not." Then he gave

me a little grin. "As if anyone would believe me. And you know, I'm glad we had this little talk."

"Me, too," I said, and opened the office door.

Lucy and Ben were still watching as we came back out front. Ben glowered, but Lucy was asking me a dozen questions with her eyes.

"I'll take one of those croissants," Quinn said, pulling out his wallet.

Quickly, I wrapped one up to go. He noticed and smiled when I handed it to him. "I've missed your pastries." He walked to the door. Before exiting, he turned and grinned. "See you tomorrow for another one."

Ben and Lucy were instantly at my side. "What did he say?"

"I told him I'm a hedgewitch. And a lightwitch."

Lucy gasped, then recovered. "Being a hedgewitch is one thing. What did he think about the other?"

My eyes followed Detective Quinn through the window as he crossed the street to his car. "I'm not sure. But I think if there's another magic-related crime in Savannah, we'll be able to work together on it."

Then I caught myself. Another magic-related crime in Savannah? Nah. After so many in the last two years, I was ready for a break.

That night, Declan and I were lying side by side in the bed in his apartment. His breathing had slowed, and I knew the next sound he'd make would be a little snort, then more deep breathing, as he drifted into a deep sleep. The moon shone through his bedroom window, illuminating the stack of boxes he'd already packed in anticipation of moving into our new home. I hadn't realized how ready he'd been. Now it was going to be a while longer. Tomorrow we were meeting with an architect and contractors to talk about our plans to expand the carriage house. He thought it would probably take about four months for the project to be completed.

Four months for Carriage House 2.0, as I'd already begun to think of it, to be ready for occupancy by the Lightfoot-McCarthys. In the meantime, we'd stay at his place. Everything about it felt right, though. And there had been sacrifice—of the first version of the carriage house for the new one. Maybe that had been what Orla meant. Or perhaps she'd seen that I'd make the split-second decision to put myself between Taber and Declan. Had that been a sacrifice, though? Some would think so. To me, it had simply been the only thing I could do.

I suddenly remembered the future card I'd seen in my tarot spread. The Tower. The destruction of the old to bring in the new. But I hadn't realized until that moment how the card had literally played out that night in the loft. The image of two people jumping out of a tower and falling to the ground below. The flames licking from the windows of the tower.

The loft had been the tower, my descent to the ground precarious on the ladder but ultimately successful. But the flames had been far more real than the stylized depictions on the Rider-Waite card, the destruction inside the tower more literal than metaphorical. I wondered what Jaida would say when I told her about it.

Declan gave the little snort. On my other side, Mungo echoed it.

Before my fiancé fell completely asleep, I reached over and took his hand.

"Mm."

"You awake?" I asked.

"Mmph."

"Declan, let's get married on August fifteenth."

The deep breathing stopped, and he propped himself up on one elbow to look at me. "Really?"

"Really."

"Why August fifteenth?"

"Because the house should be ready by then, and it gives us plenty of time to plan the wedding. And it was Nonna's birthday."

"The house might not be done," he said. "And do you really want to plan a wedding while your house is under construction?"

"*Our* house. And we'll manage."

"Our house. And okay." He leaned over and kissed me.

Recipes

Brown Butter Chocolate Chip Cookies

1½ cups (3 sticks) butter
1 cup slivered almonds
2¼ cups all-purpose flour
1 tsp. baking soda
1 tsp. salt
¾ cup granulated sugar
¾ cup packed dark brown sugar
1 tsp. vanilla
2 large eggs
1 10 oz. package 70% cacao chocolate chips
smoked salt (optional)

Place butter in a heavy saucepan, preferably with a light-colored bottom so you can judge the color of the butter as it browns. Place over medium heat. Stir now and then to make sure the butter is cooking evenly. It will start to foam, then turn tan, then a darker brown. The foam will brown and crisp and fall to the bottom of the pan. When the butter has browned—about the color of light maple syrup—remove from heat and transfer all but 2 tablespoons into another container to cool. You should have at least 1 cup, as the butter decreases in volume when the liquid cooks out. If you have a bit more, set the extra aside to add to pasta, steamed vegetables, or even oatmeal. It's delicious and will keep in the refrigerator for months.

Add the slivered almonds to the butter left in the pan and cook over medium heat until crisp and lightly browned. Set aside.

Preheat oven to 375° F. Cover a baking sheet with parchment paper or a silicone mat. Combine flour, baking soda, and salt. Set aside. Using a mixer, beat together 1 cup of the brown butter, sugars, and vanilla. Add the eggs, one at a time. Beat in the flour mixture. Stir in the chocolate chips and almonds. Drop by rounded tablespoon onto the baking sheet about two inches apart. Bake for 9 to 11 minutes until golden brown. Immediately sprinkle/grind a little smoked salt on top if you wish. Move to wire racks to cool.

Makes about 4 dozen cookies.

Rhubarb and Ricotta Crostini

2½ cups rhubarb, trimmed and sliced ¼ inch thick
⅔ cup sugar, plus more to taste
Zest of one orange plus 4 tbsp. of juice
1 baguette, sliced ¼ inch thick
1 cup ricotta cheese
¼ cup honey

Place the rhubarb, sugar, orange zest, and orange juice in a heavy saucepan. Bring to a boil, then turn to low and simmer until the rhubarb is cooked through but still pink and holds its shape—about five minutes. Add a tablespoon of water if it starts to stick, but avoid making the mixture runny. Set aside to cool. When still slightly warm, add any additional sugar to taste.

Toast the baguette slices under a broiler. When golden brown on one side, flip and brown the other side. The toast should be crisp, but still slightly tender on the inside.

When ready to serve, spread a bit of stewed rhubarb on each slice of toasted bread, followed by a dollop of ricotta and a drizzle of honey.

This makes a great appetizer, a nice addition to brunch, or a light breakfast.

If you love Bailey Cates's *New York Times* bestselling Magical Bakery Mysteries, read on for an excerpt from the first book in Bailey Cattrell's Enchanted Garden Mystery series,

Daisies for Innocence

Available now wherever books are sold

The sweet, slightly astringent aroma of *Lavandula stoechas* teased my nose. I couldn't help closing my eyes for a moment to appreciate its layered fragrance drifting on the light morning breeze. Spanish lavender, or "topped" lavender—according to my gamma, it had been one of my mother's favorites. It was a flower that had instilled calm and soothed the skin for time eternal, a humble herb still used to ease headache and heartache alike. I remembered Gamma murmuring to me in her garden when I was five years old:

Breathe deeply, Elliana. Notice how you can actually taste the scent when you inhale it? Pliny the Elder brewed this into his spiced wine, and Romans used it to flavor their ancient sauces. In the language of flowers, it signifies the acknowledgment of love.

Not that I'd be using it in that capacity anytime soon.

But Gamma had been gone for over twenty years, and my mother had died when I was only four. Shaking my head, I returned my attention to the tiny mosaic pathway next to where I knelt. Carefully, I added a piece of foggy sea glass to the design. The path was three feet long and four inches wide, and led from beneath a tumble of forget-me-nots to a violet-colored fairy door set into the base of the east fence. Some people referred to them as "gnome doors," but whatever you called them, the decorative miniature garden phenomena were gaining popularity with adults and children alike. The soft green and blue of the water-polished, glass-nugget path seemed to morph directly from the clusters of azure flowers, curving around a lichen-covered rock to the ten-inch round door. I wondered how long it would take one of my customers to notice this new addition to the verdant garden behind my perfume and aromatherapy shop, Scents & Nonsense.

The rattle of the latch on the gate to my left interrupted my thoughts. Surprised, I looked up and saw Dash trotting toward me on his short corgi legs. His lips pulled back in a grin as he reached my side, and I smoothed the thick ruff of fur around his foxy face. Astrid Moneypenny—my best friend in Poppyville, or anywhere else, for that matter—strode behind him at a more sedate pace. Her latest foster dog, Tally, a Newfoundland mix with a graying muzzle, lumbered beside her.

"Hey, Ellie! There was a customer waiting on the boardwalk out front," Astrid said. "I let her in to look around. Tally, sit."

I bolted to my feet, the fairy path forgotten. "Oh, no. I totally lost track of time. Is it already ten o'clock?"

The skin around Astrid's willow-green eyes crinkled in a smile. They were a startling contrast to her auburn hair and freckled nose. "Relax. I'll watch the shop while you get cleaned up." She jammed her hand into the pocket of her hemp dress and pulled out a cookie wrapped in a napkin. "Snickerdoodles today."

I took it and inhaled the buttery cinnamon goodness. "You're the best."

Astrid grinned. "I have a couple of hours before my next gig. Tally can hang out here with Dash." She was a part-time technician at the veterinary clinic and a self-proclaimed petrepreneur—dog walker and pet sitter specializing in animals with medical needs. "But isn't Josie supposed to be working today?"

"She should be here soon," I said. "She called last night and left a message that she might be late. Something about a morning hike to take pictures of the wildflowers." I began gathering pruners and trowel, kneeling pad and weed digger into a handled basket. "They say things are blooming like crazy in the foothills right now."

Astrid turned to go, then stopped. Her eyes caught mine. "Ellie . . ."

"What?"

She shook her head. "It's just that you look so happy working out here."

I took in the leafy greenery, the scarlet roses climbing the north fence, tiered beds that overflowed with herbs and scented blooms, and the miniature gardens and doors tucked into surprising nooks and alcoves. A downy woodpecker rapped against the trunk of the oak at the rear of the lot, and two hummingbirds whizzed by on their way to drink from the handblown glass feeder near the back patio of Scents & Nonsense. An asymmetrical boulder hunkered in the middle of the yard, the words ENCHANTED GARDEN etched into it by a local stone carver. He'd also carved words into river rocks I'd placed in snug crannies throughout the half-acre space. The one next to where Dash had flopped down read BELIEVE. Mismatched rocking chairs on the patio, along with the porch swing hanging from the pergola, offered opportunities for customers to sit back, relax, sip a cup of tea or coffee, and nibble on the cookies Astrid baked up each morning.

"I am happy," I said quietly. More than that. *Grateful.* A sense of contentment settled deep into my bones, and my smile broadened.

"I'm glad things have worked out so well for you." Her smile held affection that warmed me in spite of the cool morning.

"It hasn't been easy, but it's true that time smooths a lot of rough edges." I rolled my eyes. "Of course, it's taken me nearly a year."

A year of letting my heart heal from the bruises of infidelity, of divorce, of everyone in town knowing my—and my ex's—business. In fact, perfect cliché that it was, everyone except me seemed to know Harris had been having an affair with Wanda Simmons, the owner of one of Poppyville's ubiquitous souvenir shops. Once I was out of the picture, though, he'd turned the full spectrum of his demanding personality on her. She'd bolted within weeks, going so far as to move back to her hometown in Texas. I still couldn't decide whether that was funny or sad.

I'd held my ground, however. Poppyville, California, nestled near the foothills of the Sierra Nevada Mountains, was *my* hometown, and I wasn't about to leave. The town's history reached back to the gold rush, and tourists flocked to its Old West style; its easy access to outdoor activities like hiking, biking, and fly fishing; and to the small hot spring a few miles to the south.

After the divorce, I'd purchased a storefront with the money Harris paid to buy me out of our restaurant, the Roux Grill. The property was perfect for what I wanted: a retail store to cater to townspeople and tourists alike and a business that would allow me to pursue my passion for all things scentual. Add in the unexpected—and largely free—living space included in the deal, and I couldn't turn it down.

Sense & Nonsense was in a much sought after location at the end of Corona Street's parade of bric-a-brac dens. The kite shop was next door to the north, but to the south, Raven Creek Park marked the edge of town with a rambling green space punctuated with playground equipment, picnic tables, and a fitness trail. The facade of my store had an inviting, cottagelike feel, with painted shutters above bright window boxes and a rooster weathervane twirling on the peaked roof. The acre lot extended in a rectangle behind the business to the front door of my small-scale home, which snugged up against the back property line.

With a lot of work and plenty of advice from local nurserywoman Thea Nelson, I'd transformed what had started as a barren, empty lot between the two structures into an elaborate garden open to my customers, friends, and the occasional catered event. As I'd added more and more whimsical details, word of the Enchanted Garden had spread. I loved sharing it with others, and it was good for business, too.

"Well, it's nice to have you back, sweetie. Now we just have to find a man for you." Astrid reached down to stroke Tally's neck. The big dog gazed up at her with adoration, while I struggled to keep a look of horror off my face.

"Man?" I heard myself squeak. That was the last thing on my mind. Well, almost. I cleared my throat. "What about your love life?" I managed in a more normal tone.

She snorted. "I have plenty of men, Ellie. Don't you worry about me."

It was true. Astrid attracted men like milkweed attracted monarch butterflies. At thirty-seven, she'd never been married, and seemed determined to keep it that way.

"Astrid," I began, but she'd already turned on her heel so fast that her copper-colored locks whirled like tassels on a lampshade. Her hips swung ever so slightly beneath the skirt of her dress, the hem of which skimmed her bicycle-strong calves as she returned to the back door of Scents & Nonsense to look after things. Tally followed her and settled down on the patio flagstones as my friend went inside. I saw Nabokov, the Russian blue shorthair who made it his business to guard the store day and night, watching the big dog through the window with undisguised feline disdain.

Basket in hand, I hurried down the winding stone pathway to my living quarters. "God, I hope she doesn't get it into her head to set me up with someone," I muttered around a bite of still-warm snickerdoodle.

Dash, trotting by my left heel, glanced up at me with skeptical brown eyes. He'd been one of Astrid's foster dogs about six months earlier. She'd told me he was probably purebred, but there was no way of knowing, as he'd been found at a highway rest stop and brought, a bit dehydrated but otherwise fine, to the vet's office where she worked. Of course, Astrid agreed to take care of him until a home could be found—which was about ten seconds after she brought him into Scents & Nonsense. I'd fallen hard for him, and he'd been my near constant companion ever since.

"Okay. It's possible, just possible, that it would be nice to finally go on an actual date," I said to him now. Leery of my bad judgment in the past, I'd sworn off the opposite sex since my marriage ended. But now that Scents & Nonsense wasn't demanding all my energy and time, I had to admit that a sense of loneliness had begun to seep into my evenings.

"But you know what they say about the men in Poppyville, Dash. The odds here are good, but the goods are pretty odd."

A hawk screeched from the heights of a pine in the open meadow behind my house. Ignoring it, Dash darted away to nose the diminutive gazebo and ferns beneath the ancient gnarled trunk of the apple tree. He made a small noise in the back of his throat and sat back on his haunches beside the little door I'd made from a weathered cedar shake and set into a notch in the bark. Absently, I called him back, distracted by how sun-warmed mint combined so nicely with the musk of incense cedar, a bright but earthy fragrance that followed us to my front door.

Granted, my home had started as a glorified shed, but it worked for a Pembroke Welsh corgi and a woman who sometimes had to shop in the boys' section to find jeans that fit. The "tiny house" movement was about living simply in small spaces. I hadn't known anything about it until my half brother, Colby, mentioned it in one of his phone calls from wherever he'd stopped his Westfalia van for the week. The idea had immediately appealed to my inner child, who had always wanted a playhouse of her very own, while my environmental side appreciated the smaller, greener footprint. I'd hired a contractor from a nearby town who specialized in tiny-house renovations. He'd made a ramshackle three-hundred-twenty-square-foot shed into a super-efficient living space.

There were loads of built-in niches, an alcove in the main living area for a television and stereo, extra fold-out seating, a drop-down dining table, and even a desk that tucked away into the wall until needed. A circular staircase led to the sleeping loft above, which boasted a queen bed surrounded by cupboards for linens and clothing and a skylight set into the angled roof. The staircase partially separated the living area from the galley kitchen, and the practical placement of shelves under the spiraling steps made it not only visually stunning, but a terrific place to house my considerable library of horticulture and aromatherapy books.

Most of the year, the back porch, which ran the seventeen-foot width of the house, was my favorite place to hang out when not in the garden or Scents & Nonsense. It looked out on an expanse of meadow running up to the craggy foothills of Kestrel Peak. Our resident mule deer herd often congregated there near sunset.

After a quick sluice in the shower, I slipped into a blue cotton sundress that matched my eyes, ran fingers through my dark shoulder-length curls in a feeble attempt to tame them, skipped the makeup, and slid my feet into soft leather sandals. Dash at my heel, I hurried down the path to the shop. I inhaled bee balm, a hint of basil, lemon verbena, and . . . what was *that*?

My steps paused, and I felt my forehead wrinkle. I knew every flower, every leaf in this garden, and every scent they gave off. I again thought of my gamma, who had taught me about plants and aromatherapy—though she never would have used that word. She would have known immediately what created this intoxicating fragrance.

Check her garden journal. Though without more information it would be difficult to search the tattered, dog-eared volume in which she'd recorded her botanical observations, sketches, flower recipes, and lore.

A flutter in my peripheral vision made me turn my head, but where I'd expected to see a bird winging into one of the many feeders, there was nothing. At the same time, a sudden breeze grabbed away the mysterious fragrance and tickled the wind chimes.

Glancing down, I noticed the engraved river rock by the fairy path I'd been forming earlier appeared to have shifted.

For a second, I thought it read BEWARE.

My head whipped up as I wildly searched the garden. When I looked down again, the word BELIEVE cheerfully beckoned again.

Just a trick of the light, Ellie.

Still, I stared at the smooth stone for what felt like a long time. Then I shook my head and continued to the patio. After giving Tally a quick pat on the head, I wended my way between two rocking chairs and opened the sliding door to Scents & Nonsense.

Nabby slipped outside, rubbing his gray velvety self against my bare leg before he touched noses with Dash, threw Tally a warning look, and padded out to bask in the sunshine. A brilliant blue butterfly settled near the cat and opened its iridescent wings to the warming day. As I turned away, two more floated in to join the first. As the cat moved toward his preferred perch on the retaining wall, the butterflies wafted behind him like balloons on a string. It was funny—they seemed to seek him out, and once I'd seen two or three find him in the garden, I knew more blue wings would soon follow.

ABOUT THE AUTHOR

Bailey Cates believes magic is all around us if we only look for it. She is the *New York Times* bestselling author of the Magical Bakery Mysteries, including *Spells and Scones*, *Magic and Macaroons*, and *Some Enchanted Éclair*. Writing as Bailey Cattrell, she is also the author of the Enchanted Garden Mysteries, which began with *Daisies for Innocence*. Visit her online at baileycates.com.